ABANDON ALL LOGIC, YE WHO ENTER HERE!

Dispense with reason, suspend your disbelief! Get ready to confront the anti-rational, the supra-real!

D. R. Bensen, editor of the unique magazine of fantasy, THE UNKNOWN, has selected brilliant fiction by the masters designed to chill, charm, tantalize, and enchant you!

So abandon all logic and prepare to experience the trip into

THE UNKNOWN

Also Published by Jove/HBJ

THE UNKNOWN FIVE!

ISAAC ASIMOV
INTRODUCES THE BEST STORIES EVER PUBLISHED IN THE GREAT FANTASY MAGAZINE.
EDITED BY D.R. BENSEN
ILLUSTRATED BY EDD CARTIER

The Unknown

A JOVE/HBJ BOOK

FOR ANNE
who didn't like the stuff until she read it.

Copyright © 1963 by Jove Publications, Inc.

All rights reserved. No part of this publication may be reproduced or transmitted in any form or by any means, electronic or mechanical, including photocopy, recording, or any information storage and retrieval system, without permission in writing from the publisher.

Two Previous Printings
First Jove/HBJ edition published August 1978

ACKNOWLEDGMENTS

All these stories first appeared in the magazine UNKNOWN (later known as UNKNOWN WORLDS), published by Street & Smith, Inc. The assistance of The Conde Nast Publications, Inc., successors to Street & Smith, is gratefully acknowledged.

"The Misguided Halo," by Henry Kuttner (August 1939); copyright 1939 by Street & Smith; reprinted by permission of Harold Matson Co.

"Prescience," by Nelson S. Bond (October 1941); copyright 1941 by Street & Smith; reprinted by permission of the author.

"Yesterday Was Monday," by Theodore Sturgeon (June 1941); copyright 1941 by Street & Smith; reprinted by permission of the author.

"The Gnarly Man," by L. Sprague de Camp (June 1939); copyright 1939 by Street & Smith; reprinted by permission of the author.

"The Bleak Shore," by Fritz Leiber (November 1940); copyright 1940 by Street & Smith; reprinted by permission of the author and the author's agent, General Artists Corp.

"Trouble With Water," by H. L. Gold (March 1939); copyright 1939 by Street & Smith; reprinted by permission of the author.

"Doubled and Redoubled," by Malcolm Jameson (February 1941); copyright 1941 by Street & Smith; reprinted by permission of the author's agent, Otis Kline Associates, Inc.

"When It Was Moonlight," by Manly Wade Wellman (February 1940); copyright 1940 by Street & Smith; reprinted by permission of the author and the author's agent, Otis Kline Associates, Inc.

"Mr. Jinx," by Robert Arthur, and "Armageddon," by Fredric Brown (August 1941); copyright 1941 by Street & Smith; reprinted by permission of the authors and the authors' agent, Scott Meredith Literary Agency, Inc.

"Snulbug," by Anthony Boucher (December 1941); copyright 1941 by Street & Smith; reprinted by permission of the author and the author's agent, Willis Kingsley Wing.

Printed in the United States of America

Jove/HBJ books are published by Jove Publications, Inc.
(Harcourt Brace Jovanovich) 757 Third Avenue,
New York, N.Y. 10017

Contents

7 FOREWORD
Isaac Asimov

11 INTRODUCTION

13 THE MISGUIDED HALO
Henry Kuttner

31 PRESCIENCE
Nelson S. Bond

43 YESTERDAY WAS MONDAY
Theodore Sturgeon

63 THE GNARLY MAN
L. Sprague de Camp

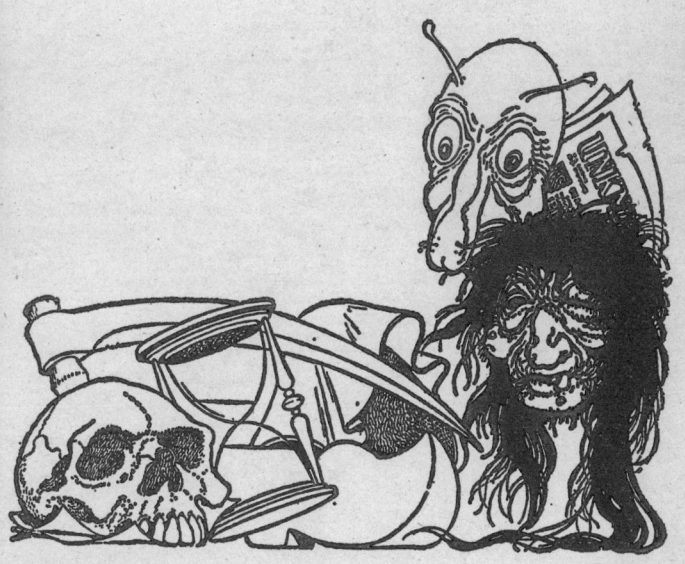

Contents

85 THE BLEAK SHORE
   Fritz Leiber

97 TROUBLE WITH WATER
   H. L. Gold

119 DOUBLE AND REDOUBLED
    Malcolm Jameson

137 WHEN IT WAS MOONLIGHT
    Manly Wade Wellman

153 MR. JINX
    Robert Arthur

171 SNULBUG
    Anthony Boucher

187 ARMAGEDDON
    Fredric Brown

Foreword

It is now just twenty years since *Unknown* died, but for us who knew it in its glory, it can never really die. We who knew it then are in early middle age now and some of us sag a bit and have a touch of gray here and there, but while the memory of *Unknown* is bright, we have our youth yet.

Unknown lasted for three and one-half years, for thirty-nine issues, and there was never anything like it before and never anything like it since.

Mind you, I don't say that there was never fantasy before *Unknown;* or that there has been no fantasy since *Unknown*. There was and there has been—even fantasy of renown. But not fantasy like *Unknown*.

Before *Unknown*, there was *Weird Tales*, and after *Unknown* there was (and is) *The Magazine of Fantasy and Science Fiction*. If there is a word to associate with *Weird Tales*, it is "grim." And if there is a word to associate with *F & SF* it is "literate."

It is unfair to try to characterize anything with one word; I know that. Nor do I advance the words as descriptive. They are mere associations.

But what associations would I have for *Unknown?* Grim? Oh, it had its grim tales. Some of them are included in this volume. Wellman's *When it was Moonlight* is certainly unrelievedly grim, as is Leiber's *The Bleak Shore*. Literate? It had its literate tales, too. De Camp's *The Gnarly Man* is as literate as you can possibly want.

But though *Unknown* had its grim stories and its literate stories, neither was characteristic. Neither gave it its peculiar flavor which is and was (and perhaps will be) found nowhere else and which made us of 1939-1943 blessed above all mortals for we could every so often go to a news-stand and buy a copy of *Unknown*, fresh and unwrinkled, intact and new—for a quarter.

The word I associate with *Unknown* is "impudent" with

the accent on the imp. It dealt with the supernatural in cavalier fashion. It educated its demons and made them human.

Consider the non-human characters in Sturgeon's *Yesterday Was Monday*. You recognize them, don't you. Quite human. No arcane grimness at all. In fact, it's funny, outrageously funny, unreasonably funny. —But are you sure there's just humor in it? Are you quite certain you won't someday wake up in the wrong scene? And after you think about it a while, will you ever be able, quite, to relax again?

True horror is not in the ghastly and gory. It can be in odd places. In Kuttner's *The Misguided Halo* it can be in an angel's gift, surely a wonderful one. Surely? In Jameson's *Doubled and Redoubled* it is the reliving of a wonderful day. Wonderful?

Where but in *Unknown* is the attempt to manipulate the future pictured not in terms of the tragic, but merely as frustration?—and, heaven help us, even amid the laughter, it begins to seem to us that frustration is the worse of the two. See Boucher's *Snulbug*. And where did insolence to the little people draw a funnier curse than the one on Greenberg in Gold's *Trouble with Water?*—a curse so funny that the horror of it only slowly seeps through the cackling.

But if we're going to discuss horror and frustration let me give you two personal examples that are almost *Unknown*ish in their intensity.

I was a charter reader of *Unknown*; of course I was. I picked up the March 1939 issue, the very first one and bought every succeeding issue, too. And I was smart; I kept them all. Every one.

Do you know what a complete intact collection of *Unknown* is worth? Every page present? Every cover uncreased and unmarred? Not in money, for I would never sell it. Rather, in the personal satisfaction of owning it? Of having it to show people? Of seeing it lined up on the shelves? Of reading any story in any of the thirty-nine issues at any time I wished?

Well, toward the end of *Unknown's* reign, I married and, for a while I lived in a succession of cramped quarters and there was no room for my collection. I put it in a safe place.

Only I don't know where.

And I don't know what has happened to it.

Mind you, I have a perfect memory; it is the marvel of all

who know me; I wonder at it myself sometimes. But I don't know where my *Unknown* collection is or what happened to it. Is it possible that someone took possession with magical rites and once a year renews the spell that keeps me from remembering?

And here is a second frustration. I have written for just about every American science fiction and/or fantasy magazine of consequence—except *Unknown*. It is the one magazine I would be most proud to have written for, but I didn't. Nowhere on the honored and holy list of *Unknown* authors is my name to be found.

Why not? Well, to begin with, precious years slipped by while I dared not even submit a manuscript. I felt I couldn't; I wasn't capable enough; I wasn't—well—worthy.

Then, in 1943, I decided to try. With a great effort I wrote a story called *Author! Author!* and sent it to *Unknown*. It was my first attempt to breach its bastions, my very first, and, by heaven, the manuscript was accepted!

I was an *Unknown* author!

Only— Before it could be published, *Unknown* ceased publication, and I was not an *Unknown* author after all.

You can see, then, that when given the chance to write a Foreword to this volume, the well-feigned reluctance with which I usually approach such tasks (designed to increase the offered fee) was absent.

"Yes," I burbled. "Yes, yes, yes, yes—"

For now, in a very indirect and tangential fashion, I am an *Unknown* author at last.

At least, something I have written is included within the covers of a book that is entirely filled with *Unknown* authors, and surely that makes me one, too, doesn't it?

Please say it does!
Please!

ISAAC ASIMOV
West Newton, Mass.
January 1963

Preface to the 1978 Edition

To paraphrase Dr. Asimov's opening to the Introduction which follows this note, it is just fifteen years since *The Unknown* was published . . . and Things Have Happened since then.

One was a direct result of this anthology's publication. Dr. Asimov's story, "Author! Author!", of which he writes so wistfully, actually made it into print—in *The Unknown Five*, which Jove/HBJ is shrewdly making available once again. Thus his statement is —to use a term related to a political phenomenon unthinkable in 1963 and only scar tissue now—no longer operative.

So are some—surprisingly few—of the prefatory notes to the stories. For instance, the description of Eighth Avenue in New York that goes with "Mr. Jinx" is likely to read like fantasy in itself now. I mean, Madison Square Garden *uptown!* Everybody knows it's part of the Penn Station complex. (Readers who remember the Garden when it was down on Madison Square, with a statue of Diana on top, will please refrain from confusing the issue.) I urge you to accept these anachronisms as relics of the past, not mistakes—flies of history embedded in the amber of time.

Another effect of the passage of years has been the identification of the book with its editor. Look, in the past fifteen years, I've worked for a number of publishing houses, freelanced at all sorts of things, written a dozen books, even illustrated an Asimov story for a magazine . . . but at any science fiction convention I go to, it's a nearly sure thing that some beardless (or bearded) youth will squint at my name tag and say, "Oh . . . yeah, *The Unknown*. Wow. I remember, when I was eight, it really *got* to me."

Now that is a considerable compliment, if a little two-edged. I accept it, not so much for myself, but on behalf of the authors herein, who, writing at the peak of their powers, produced a body of truly memorable stories for their time—stories which, from the evidence, aren't nearly ready to lie down and die just yet.

Many of them have since appeared in other anthologies or collections, but I like to think that they are most at home here—in the company of their peers, and adorned with illustrations by an artist who was as much a part of the magic atmosphere of the magazine as any of the writers.

It's almost like having *Unknown* back again. And how I wish we could.

D. R. Bensen
Croton-on-Hudson, NY
March, 1978

Introduction

Strictly speaking, Dr. Asimov *is* accurate in saying that he was not an *Unknown* author—but he was, very definitely, an *Unknown* writer. Or possibly, *Unknown*-writer, in the sense of one who wrote to, or about, *Unknown*. His ratings of stories in his letters to editor John Campbell (published in the readers' column, "—And Having Writ—"), were rigorous, just, and . . . quotable. Anyhow, I've quoted one of them in the prefatory note to Sprague de Camp's *The Gnarly Man*, being always willing to use Authority as a backstop. Like all true fans, Asimov the Younger (that is, the same Asimov, only twenty-some years ago), took a passionate interest in the physical details of his obsession, writing at one point: "The copy that reached my candy store had ragged edges. How come?"

Ray Bradbury was another *Unknown*-writer (long before he got to Mars), though never an *Unknown* author, alas. A couple of months after the first issue, he wrote Campbell: "What many of us . . . have wanted in the way of fantasy has come true. AND CAMPBELL DID IT FOR US. . . . No more houses of dripping blood, grinning harridans with butcher knives, bodies dangling from razor-bladed rafters."[*]

All right . . . what was it that Campbell had done? The magazine was a good one, in the ordinary sense (ha!) of using good writers, well-constructed stories, properly balanced issues; but there was clearly an extra, some special quality or notion the editor contributed. It seems to me that this extra was the sense—paradoxically enough—of *logic* in these tales of the fantastic.

Look carefully, and in almost every *Unknown* story—the ones in this book, and those that have filled the anthologies over the years—you will find that there is one circumstance and one circumstance only that is "supernatural." Everything else—setting, characters, motivation—is perfectly "natural"

---

[*] What on earth do you suppose he'd been reading?

and logical, once allowance is made for the "magic factor." This is the most satisfying kind of fantasy, because the most believable—once you've accepted, say, that someone *can* learn to conjure up a demon, the rest follows as rationally as any detective story, and more than some. The kind of fantasy that keeps ringing in extra impossibilities, just to keep the action going, gets to bore the reader pretty fast, since he knows the author doesn't have to use much ingenuity to work things out. At any rate, it clearly bored Campbell—for which I, as another charter reader, four of whose formative years were gloriously gilded by *Unknown,* and as editor of this collection, am enormously and forever grateful. I am very glad to have the chance here to acknowledge this debt.

I also owe thanks to The Condé Nast Publications, Inc., for permission to use the illustrations by Edd Cartier, all of which originally appeared in *Unknown* and the collection *From Unknown Worlds;* and to the omniscient Sam Moskowitz, whose help in locating some of the authors speeded the preparation of this book.

D. R. BENSEN
New York City
February 1963

The many memorable stories Henry Kuttner wrote for Unknown *established him as a master of grim or humorous irony. Compliments of the Author, Design for Dreaming, and The Devil We Know are probably the most famous of them, and have showed up in far too many anthologies for me to be happy about including them in this one.*

Kuttner's first Unknown *story has not, so far as I know, been anthologized, at least not lately. It's also the first Kuttner I ever read (and an editor has his privileges, including sentiment) and probably the funniest. It cracked me up over twenty years ago, and it still does. One reader complained of another Kuttner story that it was a steal from Thorne Smith, to which Editor Campbell replied that Kuttner was an admirer of Smith (who wrote the* Topper *stories and many other great ribald fantasies, as younger readers may not know), and was "trying to write stories Smith might have written if he'd lived longer." In* The Misguided Halo, *I think he's succeeded brilliantly in doing just that, which I consider very high praise.*

The Misguided Halo

Henry Kuttner

The youngest angel could scarcely be blamed for the error. They had given him a brand-new, shining halo and pointed down to the particular planet they meant. He had followed directions implicitly, feeling quite proud of the responsibility. This was the first time the youngest angel had ever been commissioned to bestow sainthood on a human.

So he swooped down to the earth, located Asia, and came to rest at the mouth of a cavern that gaped halfway up a Himalayan peak. He entered the cave, his heart beating wildly with excitement, preparing to materialize and give the holy lama his richly earned reward. For ten years the ascetic Tibetan Kai Yung had sat motionless, thinking holy thoughts. For ten more years he had dwelt on top of a pillar, acquiring additional merit. And for the last decade he had lived in this cave, a hermit, forsaking fleshly things.

The youngest angel crossed the threshold and stopped with a gasp of amazement. Obviously he was in the wrong place. An overpowering odor of fragrant *sake* assailed his nostrils, and he stared aghast at the wizened, drunken little man who squatted happily beside a fire, roasting a bit of goat flesh. A den of iniquity!

Naturally, the youngest angel, knowing little of the ways of the world, could not understand what had led to the lama's fall from grace. The great pot of *sake* that some misguidedly pious one had left at the cave mouth was an offering, and the lama had tasted, and tasted again. And by this time he was clearly not a suitable candidate for sainthood.

The youngest angel hesitated. The directions had been explicit. But surely this tippling reprobate could not be intended to wear a halo. The lama hiccuped loudly and reached for another cup of *sake* and thereby decided the angel, who unfurled his wings and departed with an air of outraged dignity.

Now, in a Midwestern State of North America there is a town called Tibbett. Who can blame the angel if he alighted there, and, after a brief search, discovered a man apparently ripe for sainthood, whose name, as stated on the door of his small suburban home, was K. Young?

"I may have got it wrong," the youngest angel thought. "They said it was Kai Yung. But this is Tibbett, all right. He must be the man. Looks holy enough, anyway.

"Well," said the youngest angel, "here goes. Now, where's that halo?"

Mr. Young sat on the edge of his bed, with head lowered, brooding. A depressing spectacle. At length he arose and donned various garments. This done, and shaved and washed and combed, he descended the stairway to breakfast.

Jill Young, his wife, sat examining the paper and sipping orange juice. She was a small, scarcely middle-aged, and quite pretty woman who had long ago given up trying to understand life. It was, she decided, much too complicated. Strange things were continually happening. Much better to remain a bystander and simply let them happen. As a result of this attitude, she kept her charming face unwrinkled and added numerous gray hairs to her husband's head.

More will be said presently of Mr. Young's head. It had, of course, been transfigured during the night. But as yet he was unaware of this, and Jill drank orange juice and placidly approved a silly-looking hat in an advertisement.

"Hello, Filthy," said Young. "Morning."

He was not addressing his wife. A small and raffish Scotty had made its appearance, capering hysterically about its master's feet, and going into a fit of sheer madness when the man pulled its hairy ears. The raffish Scotty flung its head sidewise upon the carpet and skated about the room on its muzzle, uttering strangled squeaks of delight. Growing tired of this at last, the Scotty, whose name was Filthy McNasty, began thumping its head on the floor with the apparent intention of dashing out its brains, if any.

Young ignored the familiar sight. He sat down, unfolded his napkin, and examined his food. With a slight grunt of appreciation he began to eat.

He became aware that his wife was eying him with an odd and distrait expression. Hastily he dabbed at his lips with the napkin. But Jill still stared.

Young scrutinized his shirt front. It was, if not immaculate, at least free from stray shreds of bacon or egg. He looked at his wife, and realized that she was staring at a point slightly above his head. He looked up.

Jill started slightly. She whispered, "Kenneth, what *is* that?"

Young smoothed his hair. "Er . . . what, dear?"

"That thing on your head."

The man ran exploring fingers across his scalp. "My head? How do you mean?"

"It's shining," Jill explained. "What on earth have you been doing to yourself?"

Mr. Young felt slightly irritated. "I have been doing nothing to myself. A man grows bald eventually."

Jill frowned and drank orange juice. Her fascinated gaze crept up again. Finally she said, "Kenneth, I wish you'd—"

"What?"

She pointed to a mirror on the wall.

With a disgusted grunt Young arose and faced the image in the glass. At first he saw nothing unusual. It was the same face he had been seeing in mirrors for years. Not an extraordinary face—not one at which a man could point with pride and say: "Look. *My face*." But, on the other hand, certainly not a countenance which would cause consternation. All in all, an ordinary, clean, well-shaved, and rosy face. Long association with it had given Mr. Young a feeling of tolerance, if not of actual admiration.

But topped by a halo it acquired a certain eerieness.

The halo hung unsuspended about five inches from the scalp. It measured perhaps seven inches in diameter, and seemed like a glowing, luminous ring of white light. It was impalpable, and Young passed his hand through it several times in a dazed manner.

"It's a . . . halo," he said at last, and turned to stare at Jill.

The Scotty, Filthy McNasty, noticed the luminous adornment for the first time. He was greatly interested. He did not, of course, know what it was, but there was always a chance that it might be edible. He was not a very bright dog.

Filthy sat up and whined. He was ignored. Barking loudly, he sprang forward and attempted to climb up his master's body in a mad attempt to reach and rend the halo. Since it had made no hostile move, it was evidently fair prey.

Young defended himself, clutched the Scotty by the nape of its neck, and carried the yelping dog into another room, where he left it. Then he returned and once more looked at Jill.

At length she observed, "Angels wear halos."

"Do I look like an angel?" Young asked. "It's a . . . a scientific manifestation. Like . . . like that girl whose bed kept bouncing around. You read about that."

Jill had. "She did it with her muscles."

"Well, I'm not," Young said definitely. "How could I? It's scientific. Lots of things shine by themselves."

"Oh, yes. Toadstools."

The man winced and rubbed his head. "Thank you, my dear. I suppose you know you're being no help at all."

"Angels have halos," Jill said with a sort of dreadful insistence.

Young was at the mirror again. "Darling, would you mind keeping your trap shut for a while? I'm scared as hell, and you're far from encouraging."

Jill burst into tears, left the room, and was presently heard talking in a low voice to Filthy.

Young finished his coffee, but it was tasteless. He was not as frightened as he had indicated. The manifestation was strange, weird, but in no way terrible. Horns, perhaps, would have caused horror and consternation. But a halo— Mr.

Young read the Sunday newspaper supplements, and had learned that everything odd could be attributed to the bizarre workings of science. Somewhere he had heard that all mythology had a basis in scientific fact. This comforted him, until he was ready to leave for the office.

He donned a derby. Unfortunately the halo was too large. The hat seemed to have two brims, the upper one whitely luminous.

"Damn!" said Young in a heartfelt manner. He searched the closet and tried on one hat after another. None would hide the halo. Certainly he could not enter a crowded bus in such a state.

A large furry object in a corner caught his gaze. He dragged it out and eyed the thing with loathing. It was a deformed, gigantic woolly headpiece, resembling a shako, which had once formed a part of a masquerade costume. The suit itself had long since vanished, but the hat remained to the comfort of Filthy, who sometimes slept on it.

Yet it would hide the halo. Gingerly Young drew the monstrosity on his head and crept toward the mirror. One glance was enough. Mouthing a brief prayer, he opened the door and fled.

Choosing between two evils is often difficult. More than once during that nightmare ride downtown Young decided he had made the wrong choice. Yet, somehow, he could not bring himself to tear off the hat and stamp it underfoot, though he was longing to do so. Huddled in a corner of the bus, he steadily contemplated his fingernails and wished he was dead. He heard titters and muffled laughter, and was conscious of probing glances riveted on his shrinking head.

A small child tore open the scar tissue on Young's heart and scrabbled about in the open wound with rosy, ruthless fingers.

"Mamma," said the small child piercingly, "look at the funny man."

"Yes, honey," came a woman's voice. "Be quiet."

"What's that on his head?" the brat demanded.

There was a significant pause. Finally the woman said, "Well, I don't really know," in a baffled manner.

"What's he got it on for?"

No answer.

"Mamma!"

"Yes, honey."

"Is he crazy?"

"Be quiet," said the woman, dodging the issue.

"But what *is* it?"

Young could stand it no longer. He arose and made his way with dignity through the bus, his glazed eyes seeing nothing. Standing on the outer platform, he kept his face averted from the fascinated gaze of the conductor.

As the vehicle slowed down Young felt a hand laid on his arm. He turned. The small child's mother was standing there, frowning.

"Well?" Young inquired snappishly.

"It's Billy," the woman said. "I try to keep nothing from him. Would you mind telling me just what that is on your head?"

"It's Rasputin's beard," Young grated. "He willed it to me." The man leaped from the bus and, ignoring a half-heard question from the still-puzzled woman, tried to lose himself in the crowd.

This was difficult. Many were intrigued by the remarkable hat. But, luckily, Young was only a few blocks from his office, and at last, breathing hoarsely, he stepped into the elevator, glared murderously at the operator, and said, "Ninth floor."

"Excuse me, Mr. Young," the boy said mildly. "There's something on your head."

"I know," Young replied. "I put it there."

This seemed to settle the question. But after the passenger had left the elevator, the boy grinned widely. When he saw the janitor a few minutes later he said:

"You know Mr. Young? The guy—"

"I know him. So what?"

"Drunk as a lord."

"Him? You're screwy."

"Tighter'n a drum," declared the youth, "swelp me Gawd."

Meanwhile, the sainted Mr. Young made his way to the office of Dr. French, a physician whom he knew slightly, and who was conveniently located in the same building. He had not long to wait. The nurse, after one startled glance at the remarkable hat, vanished, and almost immediately reappeared to usher the patient into the inner sanctum.

Dr. French, a large, bland man with a waxed, yellow mustache, greeted Young almost effusively.

"Come in, come in. How are you today? Nothing wrong, I hope. Let me take your hat."

"Wait," Young said, fending off the physician. "First let me explain. There's something on my head."

"Cut, bruise or fracture?" the literal-minded doctor inquired. "I'll fix you up in a jiffy."

"I'm not *sick*," said Young. "At least, I hope not. I've got a . . . um . . . a halo."

"Ha, ha," Dr. French applauded. "A halo, eh? Surely you're not that good."

"Oh, the hell with it!" Young snapped, and snatched off his hat. The doctor retreated a step. Then, interested, he approached and tried to finger the halo. He failed.

"I'll be— This is odd," he said at last. "Does look rather like one, doesn't it?"

"What is it? That's what I want to know."

French hesitated. He plucked at his mustache. "Well, it's rather out of my line. A physicist might— No. Perhaps Mayo's. Does it come off?"

"Of course not. You can't even touch the thing."

"Ah. I see. Well, I should like some specialists' opinions. In the meantime, let me see—" There was orderly tumult. Young's heart, temperature, blood, saliva and epidermis were tested and approved.

At length French said: "You're fit as a fiddle. Come in tomorrow, at ten. I'll have some other specialists here then."

"You . . . uh . . . you can't get rid of this?"

"I'd rather not try just yet. It's obviously some form of radioactivity. A radium treatment may be necessary—"

Young left the man mumbling about alpha and gamma rays. Discouraged, he donned his strange hat and went down the hall to his own office.

The Atlas Advertising Agency was the most conservative of all advertising agencies. Two brothers with white whiskers had started the firm in 1820, and the company still seemed to wear dignified mental whiskers. Changes were frowned upon by the board of directors, who, in 1938, were finally convinced that radio had come to stay, and had accepted contracts for advertising broadcasts.

Once a junior vice president had been discharged for wearing a red necktie.

Young slunk into his office. It was vacant. He slid into his chair behind the desk, removed his hat, and gazed at it with loathing. The headpiece seemed to have grown even more horrid than it had appeared at first. It was shedding, and, moreover, gave off a faint but unmistakable aroma of unbathed Scotties.

After investigating the halo, and realizing that it was still firmly fixed in its place, Young turned to his work. But the Norns were casting baleful glances in his direction, for presently the door opened and Edwin G. Kipp, president of Atlas, entered. Young barely had time to duck his head beneath the desk and hide the halo.

Kipp was a small, dapper, and dignified man who wore pince-nez and Vandyke with the air of a reserved fish. His blood had long since been metamorphosed into ammonia. He moved, if not in beauty, at least in an almost visible aura of grim conservatism.

"Good morning, Mr. Young," he said. "Er . . . is that you?"

"Yes," said the invisible Young. "Good morning. I'm tying my shoelace."

To this Kipp made no reply save for an almost inaudible cough. Time passed. The desk was silent.

"Er . . . Mr. Young?"

"I'm . . . still here," said the wretched Young. "It's knotted. The shoelace, I mean. Did you want me?"

"Yes."

Kipp waited with gradually increasing impatience. There were no signs of a forthcoming emergence. The president considered the advisability of his advancing to the desk and peering under it. But the mental picture of a conversation conducted in so grotesque a manner was harrowing. He simply gave up and told Young what he wanted.

"Mr. Devlin has just telephoned," Kipp observed. "He will arrive shortly. He wishes to . . . er . . . to be shown the town, as he put it."

The invisible Young nodded. Devlin was one of their best clients. Or, rather, he had been until last year, when he suddenly began to do business with another firm, to the discomfiture of Kipp and the board of directors.

The president went on. "He told me he is hesitating about his new contract. He had planned to give it to World, but I had some correspondence with him on the matter, and suggested that a personal discussion might be of value. So he is visiting our city, and wishes to go . . . er . . . sightseeing."

Kipp grew confidential. "I may say that Mr. Devlin told

me rather definitely that he prefers a less conservative firm. 'Stodgy,' his term was. He will dine with me tonight, and I shall endeavor to convince him that our service will be of value. Yet"—Kipp coughed again—"yet dipolmacy is, of course, important. I should appreciate your entertaining Mr. Devlin today."

The desk had remained silent during this oration. Now it said convulsively: "I'm sick. I can't—"

"You are ill? Shall I summon a physician?"

Young hastily refused the offer, but remained in hiding. "No, I . . . but I mean—"

"You are behaving most strangely," Kipp said with commendable restraint. "There is something you should know, Mr. Young. I had not intended to tell you as yet, but . . . at any rate, the board has taken notice of you. There was a discussion at the last meeting. We have planned to offer you a vice presidency in the firm."

The desk was stricken dumb.

"You have upheld our standards for fifteen years," said Kipp. "There has been no hint of scandal attached to your name. I congratulate you, Mr. Young."

The president stepped forward, extending his hand. An arm emerged from beneath the desk, shook Kipp's, and quickly vanished.

Nothing further happened. Young tenaciously remained in his sanctuary. Kipp realized that, short of dragging the man out bodily, he could not hope to view an entire Kenneth Young for the present. With an admonitory cough he withdrew.

The miserable Young emerged, wincing as his cramped muscles relaxed. A pretty kettle of fish. How could he entertain Devlin while he wore a halo? And it was vitally necessary that Devlin be entertained, else the elusive vice presidency would be immediately withdrawn. Young knew only too well that employees of Atlas Advertising Agency trod a perilous pathway.

His reverie was interrupted by the sudden appearance of an angel atop the bookcase.

It was not a high bookcase, and the supernatural visitor sat there calmly enough, heels dangling and wings furled. A scanty robe of white samite made up the angel's wardrobe— that and a shining halo, at sight of which Young felt a wave of nausea sweep him.

"This," he said with rigid restraint, "is the end. A halo may be due to mass hypnotism. But when I start seeing angels—"

"Don't be afraid," said the other. "I'm real enough."

Young's eyes were wild. "How do I know? I'm obviously talking to empty air. It's schizo-something. Go away."

The angel wriggled his toes and looked embarrassed. "I can't, just yet. The fact is, I made a bad mistake. You may have noticed that you've a slight halo—"

Young gave a short, bitter laugh. "Oh, yes. I've *noticed* it."

Before the angel could reply the door opened. Kipp looked in, saw that Young was engaged, and murmured, "Excuse me," as he withdrew.

The angel scratched his golden curls. "Well, your halo was intended for somebody else—a Tibetan lama, in fact. But through a certain chain of circumstances I was led to believe that you were the candidate for sainthood. So—" The visitor made a comprehensive gesture.

Young was baffled. "I don't quite—"

"The lama . . . well, sinned. No sinner may wear a halo. And, as I say, I gave it to you through error."

"Then you can take it away again?" Amazed delight suffused Young's face. But the angel raised a benevolent hand.

"Fear not. I have checked with the recording angel. You have led a blameless life. As a reward, you will be permitted to keep the halo of sainthood."

The horrified man sprang to his feet, making feeble swimming motions with his arms. "But . . . but . . . but—"

"Peace and blessings be upon you," said the angel, and vanished.

Young fell back into his chair and massaged his aching brow. Simultaneously the door opened and Kipp stood on the threshold. Luckily Young's hands temporarily hid the halo.

"Mr. Devlin is here," the president said. "Er . . . who was that on the bookcase?"

Young was too crushed to lie plausibly. He muttered, "An angel."

Kipp nodded in satisfaction. "Yes, of course. . . . *What?* You say an angel . . . an angel? Oh, my gosh!" The man turned quite white and hastily took his departure.

Young contemplated his hat. The thing still lay on the desk, wincing slightly under the baleful stare directed at it. To go through life wearing a halo was only less endurable than the thought of continually wearing the loathsome hat. Young brought his fist down viciously on the desk.

"I won't stand it! I . . . I don't have to—" He stopped abruptly. A dazed look grew in his eyes.

"I'll be . . . that's right! I don't *have* to stand it. If that lama got out of it . . . of course. 'No sinner may wear a halo.'" Young's round face twisted into a mask of sheer evil. "I'll be a sinner, then! I'll break all the Commandments—"

He pondered. At the moment he couldn't remember what they were. "Thou shalt not covet thy neighbor's wife." That was one.

Young thought of his neighbor's wife—a certain Mrs. Clay, a behemothic damsel of some fifty summers, with a face like a desiccated pudding. That was one Commandment he had no intention of breaking.

But probably one good, healthy sin would bring back the angel in a hurry to remove the halo. What crimes would result in the least inconvenience? Young furrowed his brow.

Nothing occurred to him. He decided to go for a walk. No doubt some sinful opportunity would present itself.

He forced himself to don the shako and had reached the elevator when a hoarse voice was heard hallooing after him. Racing along the hall was a fat man.

Young knew instinctively that this was Mr. Devlin.

The adjective "fat," as applied to Devlin, was a considerable understatement. The man bulged. His feet, strangled in biliously yellow shoes, burst out at the ankles like blossoming flowers. They merged into calves that seemed to gather momentum as they spread and mounted, flung themselves up with mad abandon, and revealed themselves in their complete, unrestrained glory at Devlin's middle. The man resembled, in silhouette, a pineapple with elephantiasis. A great mass of flesh poured out of his collar, forming a pale, sagging lump in which Young discerned some vague resemblance to a face.

Such was Devlin, and he charged along the hall, as mammoths thunder by, with earth-shaking tramplings of his crashing hoofs.

"You're Young!" he wheezed. "Almost missed me, eh? I was waiting in the office—" Devlin paused, his fascinated gaze upon the hat. Then, with an effort at politeness, he laughed falsely and glanced away. "Well, I'm all ready and r'aring to go."

Young felt himself impaled painfully on the horns of a dilemma. Failure to entertain Devlin would mean the loss of that vice presidency. But the halo weighed like a flatiron on Young's throbbing head. One thought was foremost in his mind: he *had* to get rid of the blessed thing.

Once he had done that, he would trust to luck and diplomacy. Obviously, to take out his guest now would be fatal, insanity. The hat alone would be fatal.

"Sorry," Young grunted. "Got an important engagement. I'll be back for you as soon as I can."

Wheezing laughter, Devlin attached himself firmly to the other's arm. "No, you don't. You're showing me the town! Right now!" An unmistakable alcoholic odor was wafted to Young's nostrils. He thought quickly.

"All right," he said at last. "Come along. There's a bar downstairs. We'll have a drink, eh?"

"Now you're talking," said the jovial Devlin, almost incapacitating Young with a comradely slap on the back. "Here's the elevator."

They crowded into the cage. Young shut his eyes and suffered as interested stares were directed upon the hat. He fell into a state of coma, arousing only at the ground floor, where Devlin dragged him out and into the adjacent bar.

Now Young's plan was this: he would pour drink after drink down his companion's capacious gullet, and await his chance to slip away unobserved. It was a shrewd scheme, but it had one flaw—Devlin refused to drink alone.

"One for you and one for me," he said. "That's fair. Have another."

Young could not refuse, under the circumstances. The worst of it was that Devlin's liquor seemed to seep into every cell of his huge body, leaving him, finally, in the same state of glowing happiness which had been his originally. But poor Young was, to put it as charitably as possible, tight.

He sat quietly in a booth, glaring across at Devlin. Each time the waiter arrived, Young knew that the man's eyes were riveted upon the hat. And each round made the thought of that more irritating.

Also, Young worried about his halo. He brooded over sins. Arson, burglary, sabotage, and murder passed in quick review through his befuddled mind. Once he attempted to snatch the waiter's change, but the man was too alert. He laughed pleasantly and placed a fresh glass before Young.

The latter eyed it with distaste. Suddenly coming to a decision, he arose and wavered toward the door. Devlin overtook him on the sidewalk.

"What's the matter? Let's have another—"

"I have work to do," said Young with painful distinctness. He snatched a walking cane from a passing pedestrian and made threatening gestures with it until the remonstrating victim fled hurriedly. Hefting the stick in his hand, he brooded blackly.

"But why work?" Devlin inquired largely. "Show me the town."

"I have important matters to attend to." Young scrutinized a small child who had halted by the curb and was returning the stare with interest. The tot looked remarkably like the brat who had been so insulting on the bus.

"What's important?" Devlin demanded. "Important matters, eh? Such as what?"

"Beating small children," said Young, and rushed upon the startled child, brandishing his cane. The youngster uttered a shrill scream and fled. Young pursued for a few feet and then became entangled with a lamp-post. The lamp-post was impolite and dictatorial. It refused to allow Young to pass. The man remonstrated and, finally, argued, but to no avail.

The child had long since disappeared. Administering a brusque and snappy rebuke to the lamp-post, Young turned away.

"What in Pete's name are you trying to do?" Devlin inquired. "That cop's looking at us. Come along." He took the other's arm and led him along the crowded sidewalk.

"What am I trying to do?" Young sneered. "It's obvious, isn't it? I wish to sin."

"Er . . . sin?"

"Sin."

"Why?"

Young tapped his hat meaningly, but Devlin put an altogether wrong interpretation on the gesture. "You're nuts?"

"Oh, shut up," Young snapped in a sudden burst of rage, and thrust his cane between the legs of a passing bank president whom he knew slightly. The unfortunate man fell heavily to the cement, but arose without injury save to his dignity.

"I beg your pardon!" he barked.

Young was going through a strange series of gestures. He had fled to a show-window mirror and was doing fantastic things to his hat, apparently trying to lift it in order to catch a glimpse of the top of his head—a sight, it seemed, to be shielded jealously from profane eyes. At length he cursed loudly, turned, gave the bank president a contemptuous stare, and hurried away, trailing the puzzled Devlin like a captive balloon.

Young was muttering thickly to himself.

"Got to sin—really sin. Something big. Burn down an orphan asylum. Kill m' mother-in-law. Kill . . . anybody!" He looked quickly at Devlin, and the latter shrank back in sudden fear. But finally Young gave a disgusted grunt.

"Nrgh. Too much blubber. Couldn't use a gun or a knife. Have to blast— Look!" Young said, clutching Devlin's arm. "Stealing's a sin, isn't it?"

"Sure is," the diplomatic Devlin agreed. "But you're not—"

Young shook his head. "No. Too crowded here. No use going to jail. Come on!"

He plunged forward. Devlin followed. And Young fulfilled his promise to show his guest the town, though afterward neither of them could remember exactly what had happened. Presently Devlin paused in a liquor store for refueling, and emerged with bottles protruding here and there from his clothing.

Hours merged into an alcoholic haze. Life began to assume an air of foggy unreality to the unfortunate Devlin. He sank presently into a coma, dimly conscious of various events which marched with celerity through the afternoon and long into the night. Finally he roused himself sufficiently to realize that he was standing with Young confronting a wooden Indian which stood quietly outside a cigar store. It was, perhaps, the last of the wooden Indians. The outworn relic of a bygone day, it seemed to stare with faded glass eyes at the bundle of wooden cigars it held in an extended hand.

Young was no longer wearing a hat. And Devlin suddenly noticed something decidedly peculiar about his companion.

He said softly, "You've got a halo."

Young started slightly. "Yes," he replied, "I've got a halo. This Indian—" He paused.

Devlin eyed the image with disfavor. To his somewhat fuzzy brain the wooden Indian appeared even more horrid than the surprising halo. He shuddered and hastily averted his gaze.

"Stealing's a sin," Young said under his breath, and then, with an elated cry, stooped to lift the Indian. He fell immediately under its weight, emitting a string of smoking oaths as he attempted to dislodge the incubus.

"Heavy," he said, rising at last. "Give me a hand."

Devlin had long since given up any hope of finding sanity in this madman's actions. Young was obviously determined to sin, and the fact that he possessed a halo was somewhat disquieting, even to the drunken Devlin. As a result, the two men proceeded down the street, bearing with them the rigid body of a wooden Indian.

The proprietor of the cigar shop came out and looked after them, rubbing his hands. His eyes followed the departing statue with unmitigated joy.

"For ten years I've tried to get rid of that thing," he whispered gleefully. "And now . . . aha!"

He re-entered the store and lit a Corona to celebrate his emancipation.

Meanwhile, Young and Devlin found a taxi stand. One cab stood there; the driver sat puffing a cigarette and listening to his radio. Young hailed the man.

"Cab, sir?" The driver sprang to life, bounced out of the car, and flung open the door. Then he remained frozen in a half-crouching position, his eyes revolving wildly in their sockets.

He had never believed in ghosts. He was, in fact, somewhat of a cynic. But in the face of a bulbous ghoul and a decadent angel bearing the stiff corpse of an Indian, he felt with a sudden, blinding shock of realization that beyond life lies a black abyss teeming with horror unimaginable. Whining shrilly, the terrified man leaped back into his cab, got the thing into motion, and vanished as smoke before the gale.

Young and Devlin looked at one another ruefully.

"What now?" the latter asked.

"Well," said Young, "I don't live far from here. Only ten blocks or so. Come on!"

It was very late, and few pedestrians were abroad. These few, for the sake of their sanity, were quite willing to ignore the wanderers and go their separate ways. So eventually Young, Devlin, and the wooden Indian arrived at their destination.

The door of Young's home was locked, and he could not locate the key. He was curiously averse to arousing Jill. But, for some strange reason, he felt it vitally necessary that the wooden Indian be concealed. The cellar was the logical place. He dragged his two companions to a basement window, smashed it as quietly as possible, and slid the image through the gap.

"Do you really live here?" asked Devlin, who had his doubts.

"Hush!" Young said warningly. "Come on!"

He followed the wooden Indian, landing with a crash in a heap of coal. Devlin joined him after much wheezing and grunting. It was not dark. The halo provided about as much illumination as a twenty-five-watt globe.

Young left Devlin to nurse his bruises and began searching for the wooden Indian. It had unaccountably vanished. But he found it at last cowering beneath a washtub, dragged the object out, and set it up in a corner. Then he stepped back and faced it, swaying a little.

"That's a sin, all right," he chuckled. "Theft. It isn't the amount that matters. It's the principle of the thing. A wooden Indian is just as important as a million dollars, eh, Devlin?"

"I'd like to chop that Indian into fragments," said Devlin with passion. "You made me carry it for three miles." He paused, listening. "What in heaven's name is that?"

A small tumult was approaching. Filthy, having been instructed often in his duties as a watchdog, now faced opportunity. Noises were proceeding from the cellar. Burglars, no doubt. The raffish Scotty cascaded down the stairs in a babel of frightful threats and oaths. Loudly declaring his intention of eviscerating the intruders, he flung himself upon Young, who made hasty clucking sounds intended to soothe the Scotty's aroused passions.

Filthy had other ideas. He spun like a dervish, yelling bloody murder. Young wavered, made a vain snatch at the air, and fell prostrate to the ground. He remained face down, while Filthy, seeing the halo, rushed at it and trampled upon his master's head.

The wretched Young felt the ghosts of a dozen and more drinks rising to confront him. He clutched at the dog, missed, and gripped instead the feet of the wooden Indian. The image swayed perilously. Filthy cocked up an apprehensive eye and fled down the length of his master's body, pausing halfway as he remembered his duty. With a muffled curse he sank his teeth into the nearest portion of Young and attempted to yank off the miserable man's pants.

Meanwhile, Young remained face down, clutching the feet of the wooden Indian in a despairing grip.

There was a resounding clap of thunder. White light blazed through the cellar. The angel appeared.

Devlin's legs gave way. He sat down in a plump heap, shut his eyes, and began chattering quietly to himself. Filthy swore at the intruder, made an unsuccessful attempt to attain a firm grasp on one of the gently fanning wings, and went back to think it over, arguing throatily. The wing had an unsatisfying lack of substantiality.

The angel stood over Young with golden fires glowing in his eyes, and a benign look of pleasure molding his noble features. "This," he said quietly, "shall be taken as a symbol of your first successful good deed since your enhalment." A wingtip brushed the dark and grimy visage of the Indian. Forthwith, there was no Indian. "You have lightened the heart of a fellow man—little, to be sure, but some, and at a cost of much labor on your part.

"For a day you have struggled with this sort to redeem him, but for this no success has rewarded you, albeit the morrow's pains will afflict you.

"Go forth, K. Young, rewarded and protected from all sin alike by your halo." The youngest angel faded quietly, for which alone Young was grateful. His head was beginning to ache and he'd feared a possible thunderous vanishment.

Filthy laughed nastily, and renewed his attack on the halo. Young found the unpleasant act of standing upright necessary. While it made the walls and tubs spin round like all the hosts of heaven, it made impossible Filthy's dervish dance on his face.

Some time later he awoke, cold sober and regretful of the fact. He lay between cool sheets, watching morning sunlight lance through the windows, his eyes, and feeling it splinter in jagged bits in his brain. His stomach was making spasmodic attempts to leap up and squeeze itself out through his burning throat.

Simultaneous with awakening came realization of three things: the pains of the morrow had indeed afflicted him; the halo mirrored still in the glass above the dressing table—and the parting words of the angel.

30 | *The Unknown*

He groaned a heartfelt triple groan. The headache would pass, but the halo, he knew, would not. Only by sinning could one become unworthy of it, and—shining protector!—it made him unlike other men. His deeds must all be good, his works a help to men. He could not sin!

I expect a lot of derelict Unknown *readers felt a familiar thrill when* The Search for Bridey Murphy *came out, with its sure-fire combination of modern scientific technique ("age-regression" under hypnosis) and the supernatural (recall of former lives)—the* Unknown *"mixture as before." And more's the pity that it seems to have turned out to be All Wrong. However, as long as the fictional treatments of whatever goes on Beyond the Veil hold up, there's no reason to complain if the cold facts aren't as entertaining. And Nelson Bond's* Prescience *is guaranteed to hold up; at least it's done so through many years and many forms, including radio and television adaptations. This version is a touch different from the one that first appeared in* Unknown, *the author having worked it over and improved it from time to time—a rarely granted second chance. Readers who happen to have a copy of the October 1941 issue of the magazine in their files are invited to check the two versions against each other.*

Prescience

Nelson S. Bond

His visitor said fearfully, "It's that way whenever I find myself in a crowded room, doctor. Or if I walk down a busy street during the rush hour. I get so nervous and upset . . . terribly afraid. I want to scream and kick and claw my way out of the crowd that stifles me . . ."

Dr. Barton said, "Yes, yes, I understand." But his tone was not entirely sympathetic. It was brusque, hurried, impatient. He said, "Mr. Peters, I'm going to give you these tablets. Keep them on your person. Whenever you feel one of these . . . uh . . . nervous attacks coming on, take one tablet. And get plenty of rest."

"But, Doctor, you don't understand. I don't need sedatives. There's nothing wrong with me physically. I've been to a dozen expert diagnosticians, and they all tell me—"

"Mr. Peters—" Dr. Barton rose. "I'm not interested in

the conclusions of other doctors. I believe I understand your case perfectly. If you will be so kind as to follow my suggestions—?"

He let his words dwindle off. The patient colored, impressed. He scraped his chair backward, picked up the tablets and moved hesitantly toward the door.

"Of course, doctor. I didn't mean to offend you. It's simply that . . . Well, if you're sure I'm going to be all right—?"

"Positive, Mr. Peters. Now if you'll come in again next Tuesday? At three-thirty?"

"At three-thirty."

"Very well. Good day, sir."

The patient left. For a lingering moment Dr. Barton continued to stare at the door panel. Then he dropped into his chair, his eyes mirroring the distaste he felt.

Dr. Barton was utterly fed up with neurotics. And that was particularly awkward because he—Dr. Homer Barton— was numbered among the town's most eminent and accomplished psychiatrists.

Into his soothing, apple-green walled office during the past twelve years had crept a steady stream of patients suffering an infinitude of mental ailments. He had seen, and spoken with, and treated all kinds from cringing claustrophobiacs to wild-eyed schizophrenics.

Ofttimes his quiet, competent manner had brought about cures. At other times he had succeeded in arresting partly developed cases. He had known failure, too. The big, white hospital on the Hill held some of them; held them in thickly padded rooms behind doors barred with steel.

But Dr. Barton was utterly fed up with neurotic people. He voiced his grievance now to the nurse who had opened the door and was silently waiting his attention.

"Fools, Miss Allen!" he snapped. "Cowards and fools, the lot of them! Neuroses . . . phobias . . . complexes . . . poppycock! Basically there's only one cause for their mental ailments. Fear!"

Miss Allen said, "Fear?"

"Exactly!" repeated Dr. Barton bitterly. "And do you know *what* they fear, Miss Allen? Not open or closed spaces, animals or sharp points or height, heat or cold or any of those multitudinous things they whine and complain to me about. Those are but substitutes; manifestations of the one basic fear that possesses all of them.

"They fear, Miss Allen—death! Twelve years in this miserable profession has convinced me there is but one factor underlying all the complexes and phobias of my patients. They are afraid to die. And since their puny minds refuse to acknowledge the cause of their fear, their subconscious gives them a palliative. A secondary fear to supplant the real one they dare not name, even to themselves!"

Miss Allen nodded understandingly. She said, "Then that should make their cure even more simple, doctor. Or am I too optimistic?"

"Barring physiological defects," continued Barton, musing, "little children are completely sane. Why? Because they do not fear death. There is relatively little insanity among aborigines, the so-called 'backward' or 'pagan' people. Nor among the laboring classes of our race.

"*I* would never become a mental case, Miss Allen, because I am a realist. I do not needlessly torture myself with vain ponderings on my after life. I accept, calmly and as a matter of fact, the credo that the real 'I' is everlasting, imperishable.

"With this comfort, with the assurance that death holds no horrors for me, my mind is balanced."

He looked at her as if seeing her for the first time.

"I'm sorry," he said. "I did not mean to bother you with my annoyance. But I am so everlastingly weary of soothing frightened people—"

Nurse Allen knew her employer's moods perfectly.

"Yes, doctor," she said. "There is a Mrs. Williams waiting. Shall I show her in?"

"Not today," said Barton. "Ask her to come back tomorrow. I'm tired."

"But if you'll excuse me, doctor, she's been waiting more than an hour—"

Barton shrugged. After all, this *was* the business. A business which paid him handsomely.

"Oh, very well!" he said resignedly. "Show her in."

"Yes, sir." The nurse vanished. When the door opened softly a few seconds later, Dr. Barton's ire had completely disappeared. He was a living model of complacency; a twentieth century soothsayer sitting behind a soft, rubbed walnut desk, hands folded before him with the smooth quietude of a reflecting Buddha. He rose as his patient entered.

"Mrs. Williams? Please be seated."

She was a drab little woman. For a moment he could not

help wondering where she had heard of him, or even if he had been wise in admitting her. Her clothes were definitely not Fifth Avenue. Her hands were work-coarsened and red. A shopgirl, possibly, or someone's cook. She could never afford to pay Dr. Barton's prices if this were so—

"I came to see you, doctor," she said, "because I could not stay away any longer. And my employer, Mrs. Rand, said you were wonderful at solving troubles of the—mind?"

"Mrs. Rand?" Dr. Barton remembered her dimly. An elderly woman with nervous indigestion. Her trouble was late hours and overrich food. Dr. Barton had given it a fancy name—he had long since learned the layman's love for polysyllables—and suggested a course in Yoga. The Yoga concept had given Mrs. Rand something to think about. The enforced rigidity of diet had effected a cure.

"Yes, Mrs. Williams. And your trouble—?"

The little woman twisted a handkerchief nervously.

"I . . . I see things, doctor. I see them before they actually happen."

Dr. Barton's face remained placid, but he yawned mentally. There were no variations in this job. Only the same recurrent themes, over and over again. But he said politely, "Yes? Go on, please."

"It is something with which I have been gifted—or cursed —ever since I was a little girl. But lately it has happened with such frequency, almost every time I go to bed, as a matter of fact, that it . . . it frightens me.

"I have dreams—but they are not just dreams. For within a few weeks, or a few days, that scene which was so clear to me in my dream actually *happens*!"

She looked at him hopefully. "Did you ever hear of anything like that before?"

Dr. Barton avoided answering. Of course he had. Everyone had. But he said, noncommittally, "Please go on."

"Three nights ago, for instance, I dreamed I was in a strange room. A room I had never seen before in my life. It was the drawing room of a large home, and somehow I was aware that I had come after something.

"As I was wondering what this thing was, a strange lady appeared in the doorway. She held out to me an oblong box.

" 'Can you identify these?' she asked.

" 'I'll try, ma'am,' I said. I opened the box. In it lay a pair of white evening gloves which belonged to my employer.

" 'Yes, ma'am,' I said in my dream. 'These belong to Mrs. Rand.' "

" 'Then you may take them to her,' said the strange lady. 'And here's a little gift for your trouble.' And she gave me a dollar bill. I remember it particularly because it had— Here, I'll show you!"

Mrs. Williams fumbled in a worn handbag, brought out a dollar bill which she passed across the desk to the doctor. Barton looked at it.

"See that red ink blot?" said Mrs. Williams. "That was the identifying mark on the dollar bill the lady gave me in my dream."

Barton handed back the bill. He said, "You got this bill *where*, Mrs. Williams?"

"This morning," said the little woman, "Mrs. Rand was very excited. Last night at the opera she mislaid her evening gloves. She telephoned an advertisement to the newspapers at once.

"Early this afternoon she received a call from a lady in Westchester. A perfect stranger. And since Thomas, the chauffeur, had driven Mr. Rand downtown, Mrs. Rand asked *me* to go out after the gloves."

"And then—?"

"When I got there," said Mrs. Williams, "into that house, I knew *instantly* it was the one I had visited in my dream two nights before. I even knew what was going to happen. But I couldn't do anything about it.

"It was a dreadful feeling. I felt captive; bound by a chain too strong for breaking. I saw the lady, strange no longer, appear in the doorway. I watched her lips open as if fascinated. I knew she was going to say, 'Can you identify these?'—and she did. I knew what *I* was going to say. And I tried to stop myself; to say something different. Somehow I had an idea if I could only change the words, something important would come about—"

"Well?" said Barton.

Mrs. Williams shook her head miserably. "It was no use. The words came from my lips and I couldn't stop them. I said, 'Yes, Ma'am. These belong to Mrs. Rand—' "

Dr. Barton tried hard not to frown. He was more than ever disgusted with his occupation. The same old groove, over and over again. Escape mechanism! A drab little woman, dissatisfied with her lot, knowing she would soon leave this earth, who subconsciously projected her servile present into the past, attributing to herself strange powers—

"Is it . . . does it mean anything, doctor?" asked the little woman fearfully.

Dr. Barton's impatience surged suddenly. After all, this was no wealthy patient who must be cajoled, deferred to, handled with kid gloves. He said:

"Mrs. Williams, yours is by no means an unusual case. The phenomenon which troubles you is as old as the history of mankind, has been studied and discussed since the days of the first doctors.

"I think I should tell you that despite what you may think you did *not* dream this first, then have the event happen to you. Actually you experienced what one philosopher has called 'the memory of the present.'

"*This* is what really happened. You entered a strange house. You were a trifle tired, or hungry, or affected by a touch of the sun. Possibly excited by an unaccustomed responsibility. However that may be, your nervous system suffered a momentary synapse—a breaking of the nervous current as an electrical current may be disturbed by a bolt of lightning.

"That brief fraction of a second sufficed to erase from your mind, completely, all which had gone before. Thus when you snapped out of your mental hiatus it seemed to you that you had been through the scene before. Actually, it was the *first* time you had ever witnessed it."

The little woman wrung her handkerchief annoyingly.

"But, doctor," she cried. "The dollar bill? I remembered it from the dream."

Dr. Barton said, "Nonsense! The human mind remembers, consciously, that which it wishes to remember. You say you have such experiences often. Has it ever occurred to you to rise from your sleep and write down one of these episodes? So that later you might check the dream against a happening?"

"No, sir. I never remember the dream until the scene is re-enacted—"

"Exactly! In other words, it is just what I told you it was." Dr. Barton rose. "If you wish to be cured, Mrs. Williams, all you need do is stop worrying."

"Worrying, doctor?" Mrs. Williams rose uncertainly. "But I'm not worrying about anything. I have sufficient money for my needs. I have no children. I—"

"I strongly suspect, madam," said Barton caustically, "you are worrying about the salvation of your soul. You fear the afterworld. Therein lies your reason for dreaming these strange daydreams. Good day, Mrs. Williams."

The little woman flushed. She scrabbled in her old handbag. There were tears in her eyes; Dr. Barton saw them not with compassion, but with annoyance.

"There is no charge, Mrs. Williams," he said gruffly. "It has been a pleasure to be able to tell someone the cold truth for a change. The truth that most people are cowards."

"Yes, doctor," said the little woman humbly. Then, halfway to the door, "But if I have one of these experiences again—? Is there anything I should do?"

"There is nothing. You must not—"

Dr. Barton stopped suddenly. Never had his exasperation been so great. Now a great thought came to him. He had no wealthy client in this patient. Why not use her as a guinea pig? At one time allay her fears forevermore—and prove his own theory. His brow cleared. He smiled.

"Mrs. Williams?" he said.

The woman turned hopefully. "Yes, doctor?"

"You say you have these dreams frequently?"

"Yes, sir."

"Good. Then come with me. I think I can cure your case."

It was to his inner office he led her. There he had a small cot for invalid patients; a number of impressive machines used in treating those whose cases demanded imposing paraphernalia.

"Lie down, Mrs. Williams," he said. Gone was Dr. Barton's impatience now. He was once again the suave psychiatrist, handling with smooth deftness a nerve-wracked victim of strain. "Right there. That's right.

"Now—relax. Stretch if you want to. Ease all your muscles. There—that's right. Look up, now, please—"

He snapped a switch. In the quiet gloom of the room one tiny light began to flicker. A many-faceted globe in the machine suspended just over the patient's head swirled into motion. The facets caught the light and shifted into dancing colors.

"Don't look away, Mrs. Williams. Look at the light. There —that's it. See how soothing it is? So pleasant. So relaxing. And you are tired . . . tired . . . terribly tired—"

There was no sound save the somewhat heavier breath-

ing of the patient. The distant hum of the machine. Dr. Barton spoke again in a whisper.

"Now you are sleeping . . . sleeping. Aren't you, Mrs. Williams?"

The little woman's voice was like a wisp from far away.

"I . . . am sleeping—"

Dr. Barton smiled sardonically. There was no problem here. She was more susceptible than most to hypnosis. That indicated a receptive will. No wonder she had been prey to these repetitive dreams.

He said, "Are you dreaming now, Mrs. Williams? Tell me your dream."

"I am . . . dreaming . . . doctor."

"Tell me."

The woman's voice was slow, faltering, unaccented.

"I am . . . in my room. It is night . . . I think . . . because the lights are on. But not . . . for long. I am . . . getting ready for bed. Now I am turning off the lights—"

There was a long silence. Dr. Barton said, "And now, Mrs. Williams?"

"It is dark . . . but there is a light from the street lamp outside. I am . . . shifting . . . turning. I am restless. It seems there is something . . . I am trying to remember . . . something important. But I cannot quite . . . remember what it is—"

Again silence. Barton smiled. He persisted, "Yes?"

"I do not know. I am asleep now—"

Barton almost laughed aloud. Asleep! That should amuse his fellow psychiatrists. He had hypnotized a woman into believing she was asleep! Sleep within sleep—

Despite himself, he started. For suddenly from Mrs. Williams' throat had burst a gasp; a startled cry. Swiftly he touched her pulse. It was strong; almost too strong. It was pounding as though from panic.

"Yes, Mrs. Williams?" he purred excitedly. "A dream has come to you?"

"No! No! I am awake again! There is redness . . . in my room. It is . . . fire! I can . . . feel the heat!" Her voice rose. "I am . . . climbing out of my bed. I . . . run to the door . . . but the panels are . . . too hot. I dare not . . . open it—

"Now I am . . . running to the window. I . . . throw it open. I climb out. The fire escape . . . is cold against my bare feet—"

Dr. Barton nodded silently. Strange how detailed these fear dreams were. Fire, now. That was a convincing proof of his theory. Had not mankind, from time immemorable, conjoined thoughts of heat and flame with their dread of the afterworld? Like the others, this little woman feared death. And with that fear in her subconscious, she dreamed such dreams as this—

Her voice went on, harsh with horror.

"I hear . . . the wailing of sirens . . . and the cries . . . of people in the streets . . . below. I am . . . climbing down the . . . fire escape now. A burst of flame . . . licks from one of the windows . . . and scorches my hands.

"But I am nearing . . . safety . . . The crackling of fire . . . sounds in my ears . . . and I am panting. Just a few more steps—"

Dr. Barton frowned. He saw, now, what he must do. He must teach this woman, once and for all, that dreams are not harmful things. That this fire, this flame, this awful heat and the fear of impending death lived only in her mind. He spoke sharply.

"Do you hear me, Mrs. Williams?"

"The house is crumbling . . . into ruin—" A pause; a shifting of the head as though hearing a far-away sound. "Yes, I hear you . . . doctor—"

"You must not avoid this fire," said Barton crisply. "It cannot hurt you. It is but a dream; a hallucination. You are lying in your bed, asleep. This is only a dream."

"A . . . dream?"

"Yes. Only a dream, Mrs. Williams. Now you must go back into the house. Is there a window near you?"

"There is . . . a window . . . But from it leap . . . red tongues of flame. The heat burns me . . even as I wait—"

"You must go in the window!" said Barton firmly "I *command* you to go into the window. The fire will turn cool before you. You will not be harmed! Go in!"

Before him, the little woman's body twisted as in an agony of indecision.

"I . . . cannot . . . doctor."

"You *must!* Enter the window!"

"Yes . . . doctor." A brief silence. Then, "I am . . . entering . . . the window. But it is hot . . . Now the fire . . . the great flames—*Ooooh!*"

Her scream tore the throbbing silence of the room into tattered fragments of sound. Barton felt a shudder course coldly through him. There was stark agony in that scream. Torment and fear and anguish. But he steeled himself to speak.

"You see, Mrs. Williams? There was nothing to fear. You are safe. You are all right now?"

Only the faint humming of the machine. The distant sound of the woman's labored breathing. Dr. Barton spoke again, sharply.

"You are all right now?"

And then the answer. In a dreary voice. A toneless voice. "I am . . . all right . . . now."

"Good. There is no heat?"

"There is . . . no heat."

"Now you will return to your room. Find your bed, lie down in it. Sleep peacefully. And dream no more."

Brief silence. Then, "I cannot find . . . my room. I cannot find . . . my bed—"

"Then you are still dreaming, Mrs. Williams. What is your dream *now?* What do you see?"

"There is . . . no heat. I cannot find . . . my room. It is dark. I am still dreaming. I see nothing . . . in my dream . . . but writhing darkness. I stand alone . . . on a vast, empty plain. But I am not alone. Mists surround me. And out of the mists—"

Dr. Barton was startled at what happened then, so unexpected was it. The woman's voice changed suddenly; her throat was torn with a wild and terrifying scream. Then came laughter. A wild cacophony of sound like that which sometimes echoed from the cells of the big white building on the Hill.

Words began tumbling from her lips, madly, wildly, gloatingly, as she told what she saw; told it in its every revolting detail, every intricate little movement and meaning. Words, thoughts, ideas of evil older than Earth itself poured from her in a furious flood.

For stark seconds Barton listened, horrified. It was incredible that the mind of a demure little woman like this should be host to such thoughts; that from her lips could spill such a repugnant stream. The things she told were such that even Dr. Barton, experienced psychiatrist as he was, tasted the weak bile of disgust on his lips.

The creatures she envisioned in her dreaming were the embodiment of sheer horror; her hateful words swept all the cleanliness and good from the thing called Man, made him a loathsome creature asquat in a mire of abomination!

With a swift motion Dr. Barton touched the ray switch, flicked it off. The humming ceased. The light ended its flickering. Dr. Barton called, "Mrs. Williams—waken! I command you to wake!"

The body on the cot stirred, opened its eyes. Mrs. Williams, meek and humble again, rose to a sitting posture.

"Yes, doctor? What is it you want me to do?"

"It is already done, Mrs. Williams." Dr. Barton could scarcely realize that from this quiet creature's lips a moment ago had flooded words and thoughts unspeakable in their vileness. "Our experiment is finished."

"And did you . . . I mean, is everything—?"

"You will be all right now," promised Barton. "You can go home now and dream no more, I believe."

He did not tell her about the final stage of her dreaming.

It was enough that he had allayed her fears. He felt certain, did Dr. Barton, that there would be in the future no more prescient dreams—

Dr. Barton saw no more patients that afternoon. He found time for a round of golf before sundown. After that he had dinner at the club and enjoyed a movie in the evening. He went home and slept soundly. His mind was untroubled, for Dr. Barton was prey to no personal neuroses, phobias, or complexes. His code of living was simple. His philosophy of life admitted no hindering fear of an afterworld. And on such fear, he knew, was based all of mankind's mental ailments.

The next morning he arrived at his office ready for a new day's work. Miss Allen was already there. She had an open newspaper on the desk before her. She greeted him with excitement and horror.

"—a most *dreadful* thing last night, doctor!" she said. "I can hardly believe it. You remember that little Mrs. Williams who came here yesterday afternoon?"

"Yes, of course. Why?"

"Oh, it's terrible! Last night a fire broke out in Mrs. Rand's home, and—"

"What!" Dr. Barton's face paled. "Let me see!" He clutched the newspaper, found the account.

—firemen had the conflagation under control and all members of the Rand family were rescued. The housekeeper, a Mrs. Williams, was the only victim. She was seen to climb from her bedroom window to the fire escape and make her way down to within a few steps of safety.

Then, apparently overcome by the heat, she stopped and deliberately stepped back into the heart of the fire. Observers believe she must have died instantly—

Died instantly! That scream! That sudden change in manner!

"What is it, Dr. Barton?" cried Miss Allen. "Oh, Dr. Barton, what *is* it?"

But Dr. Barton, philosopher and scientist, did not hear. He did not even know that his trembling hands had dropped the paper, that his eyes were bleak and staring, nor that from his throat there bubbled such soft and meaningless laughter as often echoed from the cells of the big white building on the Hill—

What Robert Bloch and Ray Bradbury were to Weird Tales *during the 1940s—the writers who did the most to set the tone of the magazine—Sprague de Camp and Theodore Sturgeon were to* Unknown. *Others wrote as much, or almost—but none seemed to hit as often just the key that made* Unknown *the delight it was. And, where de Camp worked best in the novel/novelette length, which gave him scope for a wry examination of the consequences of his distortions of reality (and for plenty of action, generally with swords), Sturgeon did his best work in short stories. Though I've tried to avoid "overexposed" stories here, it's true that this one has been anthologized before—but not to the extent that almost all of Sturgeon's other* Unknown *pieces have been. Anyhow, it's good. And if you've read it already, read it again. I read it twice in getting up this book, and it was funny each time. Can you say that about* War and Peace?

It might be noted (in fact, I'm noting it) that Sturgeon turned out more stories than the magazine could accommodate under his name, and he had a couple published under variants of "E. Hunter Waldo," a label which, for some reason, has become, as far as librarians are concerned, his real one; so that all his listings are something like "STURGEON, Theodore; See Waldo, E." (Robert Heinlein wrote a story called Waldo, *which doesn't help matters at all.) One reader wrote in in praise of a Waldo story, comparing it favorably to Sturgeon's work; "Waldo" replied saying that it was written "consciously in the style of Sturgeon." So is this one, and who could want more?*

Yesterday Was Monday

Theodore Sturgeon

Harry Wright rolled over and said something spelled "Bzzzzhha-a-aw!" He chewed a bit on a mouthful of dry air and spat it out, opened one eye to see if it really would open, opened the other and closed the first, closed the second, swung his feet onto the floor, opened them again and stretched. This was a daily occurrence, and the only thing that made it remarkable at all was that he did it on a Wednesday morning, and—

Yesterday was Monday.

Oh, he knew it was Wednesday all right. It was partly that, even though he knew yesterday was Monday, there was a gap between Monday and now; and that must have been Tuesday. When you fall asleep and lie there all night without dreaming, you know, when you wake up, that time has passed. You've done nothing that you can re-remember; you've had no particular thoughts, no way to gauge time, and yet you know that some hours have passed. So it was with Harry Wright. Tuesday had gone wherever your eight hours went last night.

But he hadn't slept through Tuesday. Oh no. He never slept, as a matter of fact, more than six hours at a stretch, and there was no particular reason for him doing so now. Monday was the day before yesterday; he had turned in and slept his usual stretch, he had awakened, and it was Wednesday.

It *felt* like Wednesday. There was a Wednesdayish feel to the air.

Harry put on his socks and stood up. He wasn't fooled. He knew what day it was. "What happened to yesterday?" he muttered. "Oh—yesterday was Monday." That sufficed until he got his pajamas off. "Monday," he mused, reaching for his underwear, "was quite a while back, seems as though." If he had been the worrying type, he would have started then and there. But he wasn't. He was an easygoing sort, the kind of man that gets himself into a rut and stays there until he is pushed out. That was why he was an automobile mechanic at twenty-three dollars a week; that's why he had been one for eight years now, and would be from now on, if he could only find Tuesday and get back to work.

Guided by his reflexes, as usual, and with no mental effort at all, which was also usual, he finished washing, dressing, and making his bed. His alarm clock, which never alarmed because he was of such regular habits, said, as usual, six twenty-two when he paused on the way out, and gave his room the once-over. And there was a certain something about the place that made even this phlegmatic character stop and think.

It wasn't finished.

The bed was there, and the picture of Joe Louis. There were the two chairs sharing their usual seven legs, the split table, the pipe-organ bedstead, the beige wallpaper with the two swans over and over and over, the tiny corner sink, the tilted bureau. But none of them were finished. Not that there were any holes in anything. What paint there had been in the first place was still there. But there was an odor of old cut lumber, a subtle, insistent air of building, about the room and everything in it. It was indefinable, inescapable, and Harry Wright stood there caught up in it, wondering. He glanced suspiciously around but saw nothing he could really be suspicious of. He shook his head, locked the door and went out into the hall.

On the steps a little fellow, just over three feet tall, was gently stroking the third step from the top with a razor-sharp chisel, shaping up a new scar in the dirty wood. He looked up as Harry approached, and stood up quickly.

"Hi," said Harry, taking in the man's leather coat, his peaked cap, his wizened, bright-eyed little face. "Whatcha doing?"

"Touch-up," piped the little man. "The actor in the third floor front has a nail in his right heel. He came in late Tuesday night and cut the wood here. I have to get it ready for Wednesday."

"This is Wednesday," Harry pointed out.

"Of course. Always has been. Always will be."

Harry let that pass, started on down the stairs. He had achieved his amazing bovinity by making a practice of ignoring things he could not understand. But one thing bothered him—

"Did you say that feller in the third floor front was an actor?"

"Yes. They're all actors, you know."

"You're nuts, friend," said Harry bluntly. "That guy works on the docks."

"Oh yes—that's his part. That's what he acts."

"No kiddin'. An' what does he do when he isn't acting?"

"But he— Well, that's all he does do! That's all any of the actors do!"

"Gee— I thought he looked like a reg'lar guy, too," said Harry. "An actor? 'Magine!"

"Excuse me," said the little man, "but I've got to get back to work. We mustn't let anything get by us, you know. They'll be through Tuesday before long, and everything must be ready for them."

Harry thought: this guy's crazy nuts. He smiled uncertainly and went down to the landing below. When he looked back the man was cutting skillfully into the stair, making a neat little nail scratch. Harry shook his head. This was a screwy morning. He'd be glad to get back to the shop. There was a '39 sedan down there with a busted rear spring. Once he got his mind on that he could forget this nonsense. That's all that matters to a man in a rut. Work, eat, sleep, pay day. Why even try to think anything else out?

The street was a riot of activity, but then it always was. But not quite this way. There were automobiles and trucks and buses around, aplenty, but none of them were moving. And none of them were quite complete. This was Harry's own field; if there was anything he didn't know about motor vehicles, it wasn't very important. And through that medium he began to get the general idea of what was going on.

Swarms of little men who might have been twins of the one he had spoken to were crowding around the cars, the sidewalks, the stores and buildings. All were working like mad with every tool imaginable. Some were touching up the finish of the cars with fine wire brushes, laying on networks of microscopic cracks and scratches. Some, with ball peens and mallets, were denting fenders skillfully, bending bumpers in an artful crash pattern, spider-webbing safety-glass windshields. Others were aging top dressing with high-pressure, needlepoint sandblasters. Still others were pumping dust into upholstery, sandpapering the dashboard finish around light switches, throttles, chokes, to give a finger-worn appearance. Harry stood aside as a half dozen of the workers scampered down the street bearing a fender which they riveted to a 1930 coupé. It was freshly bloodstained.

Once awakened to this highly unusual activity, Harry stopped, slightly open-mouthed, to watch what else was going on. He saw the same process being industriously accomplished with the houses and stores. Dirt was being laid on plate-glass windows over a coat of clear sizing. Woodwork was being cleverly scored and the paint peeled to make it look correctly weather-beaten, and dozens of leather-clad laborers were on their hands and knees, poking dust and dirt into the cracks between the paving blocks. A line of them went down the sidewalk, busily chewing gum and spitting it out; they were followed by another crew who carefully placed the wads according to diagrams they carried, and stamped them flat.

Harry set his teeth and muscled his rocking brain into something like its normal position. "I ain't never seen a day like this or crazy people like this," he said, "but I ain't gonna let it be any of my affair. I got my job to go to." And trying vainly to ignore the hundreds of little, hard-working figures, he went grimly on down the street.

When he got to the garage he found no one there but more swarms of stereotyped little people climbing over the place, dulling the paint work, cracking the cement flooring, doing their hurried, efficient little tasks of aging. He noticed, only because he was so familiar with the garage, that they were actually *making* the marks that had been there as long as he had known the place. "Hell with it," he gritted, anxious to submerge himself into his own world of wrenches and grease guns. "I got my job; this is none o' my affair."

He looked about him, wondering if he should clean these interlopers out of the garage. Naw—not his affair. He was hired to repair cars, not to police the joint. Long as they kept away from him—and, of course, animal caution told him that he was far, far outnumbered. The absence of the boss and the other mechanics was no surprise to Harry; he always opened the place.

He climbed out of his street clothes and into coveralls, picked up a tool case and walked over to the sedan, which he had left up on the hydraulic rack yester— that is, Monday night. And that is when Harry Wright lost his temper. After all, the car was his job, and he didn't like having anyone else mess with a job he had started. So when he saw his job— his '39 sedan—resting steadily on its wheels over the rack, which was down under the floor, and when he saw that the rear spring was repaired, he began to burn. He dived under the car and ran deft fingers over the rear wheel suspensions. In spite of his anger at this unprecedented occurrence, he had to admit to himself that the job had been done well. "Might have done it myself," he muttered.

A soft clank and a gentle movement caught his attention. With a roar he reached out and grabbed the leg of one of the ubiquitous little men, wriggled out from under the car, caught his culprit by his leather collar, and dangled him at arm's length.

"What are you doing to my job?" Harry bellowed.

The little man tucked his chin into the front of his shirt to give his windpipe a chance, and said, "Why, I was just finishing up that spring job."

"Oh. So you were just finishing up on that spring job," Harry whispered, choked with rage. Then, at the top of his voice, "Who told you to touch that car?"

"Who told me? What do you—Well, it just had to be done, that's all. You'll have to let me go. I must tighten up those two bolts and lay some dust on the whole thing."

"You must *what?* You get within six feet o' that car and I'll twist your head offn your neck with a Stillson!"

"But— It has to be done!"

"You won't do it! Why, I oughta—"

"Please let me go! If I don't leave that car the way it was Tuesday night—"

"When was Tuesday night?"

"The last act, of course. Let me go, or I'll call the district supervisor!"

"Call the devil himself. I'm going to spread you on the sidewalk outside; and heaven help you if I catch you near here again!"

The little man's jaw set, his eyes narrowed, and he whipped

his feet upward. They crashed into Wright's jaw; Harry dropped him and staggered back. The little man began squealing, "Supervisor! Supervisor! Emergency!"

Harry growled and started after him; but suddenly, in the air between him and the midget workman, a long white hand appeared. The empty air was swept back, showing an aperture from the garage to blank, blind nothingness. Out of it stepped a tall man in a single loose-fitting garment literally studded with pockets. The opening closed behind the man.

Harry cowered before him. Never in his life had he seen such noble, powerful features, such strength of purpose, such broad shoulders, such a deep chest. The man stood with the backs of his hands on his hips, staring at Harry as if he were something somebody forgot to sweep up.

"That's him," said the little man shrilly. "He is trying to stop me from doing the work!"

"Who are you?" asked the beautiful man, down his nose.

"I'm the m-mechanic on this j-j— Who wants to know?"

"Iridel, supervisor of the district of Futura, wants to know."

"Where in hell did you come from?"

"I did not come from hell. I came from Thursday."

Harry held his head. "What *is* all this?" he wailed. "Why is today Wednesday? Who are all these crazy little guys? What happened to Tuesday?"

Iridel made a slight motion with his finger, and the little man scurried back under the car. Harry was frenzied to hear the wrench busily tightening bolts. He half started to dive under after the little fellow, but Iridel said, "Stop!" and when Iridel said, "Stop!" Harry stopped.

"This," said Iridel calmly, "is an amazing occurrence." He regarded Harry with unemotional curiosity. "An actor on stage before the sets are finished. Extraordinary."

"What stage?" asked Harry. "What are you doing here anyhow, and what's the idea of all these little guys working around here?"

"You ask a great many questions, actor," said Iridel. "I shall answer them, and then I shall have a few to ask you. These little men are stage hands— I am surprised that you didn't realize that. They are setting the stage for Wednesday. Tuesday? That's going on now."

"Arrgh!" Harry snorted. "How can Tuesday be going on when today's Wednesday?"

"Today isn't Wednesday, actor."

"Huh?"

"Today is Tuesday."

Harry scratched his head. "Met a feller on the steps this mornin'—one of these here stage hands of yours. He said this was Wednesday."

"It *is* Wednesday. Today is Tuesday. Tuesday is today. 'Today' is simply the name for the stage set which happens to be in use. 'Yesterday' means the set that has just been used; 'Tomorrow' is the set that will be used after the actors have finished with 'today.' This is Wednesday. Yesterday was Monday; today is Tuesday. See?"

Harry said, "No."

Iridel threw up his long hands. "My, you actors are stupid. Now listen carefully. This is Act Wednesday, Scene 6:22. That means that everything you see around you here is being readied for 6:22 a. m. on Wednesday. Wednesday isn't a time; it's a place. The actors are moving along toward it now. I see you still don't get the idea. Let's see ... ah. Look at that clock. What does it say?"

Harry Wright looked at the big electric clock on the wall over the compressor. It was corrected hourly and highly accurate, and it said 6:22. Harry looked at it amazed. "Six tw— but my gosh, man, that's what time I left the house. I walked here, an' I been here ten minutes already!"

Iridel shook his head. "You've been here no time at all, because there is no time until the actors make their entrances."

Harry sat down on a grease drum and wrinkled up his brains with the effort he was making. "You mean that this time proposition ain't something that moves along all the time? Sorta—well, like a road. A road don't go no place—You just go places along it. Is that it?"

"That's the general idea. In fact, that's a pretty good example. Suppose we say that it's a road; a highway built of paving blocks. Each block is a day; the actors move along it, and go through day after day. And our job here—mine and the little men—is to ... well, pave that road. This is the clean-up gang here. They are fixing up the last little details, so that everything will be ready for the actors."

Harry sat still, his mind creaking with the effects of this information. He felt as if he had been hit with a lead pipe, and the shock of it was being drawn out infinitely. This was the craziest-sounding thing he had ever run into. For no reason at all he remembered a talk he had had once with a drunken aviation mechanic who had tried to explain to him how the air flowing over an airplane's wings makes the machine go up in the air. He hadn't understood a word of the man's discourse, which was all about eddies and chords and cambers and foils, dihedrals and the Bernouilli effect. That didn't make any difference; the things flew whether he understood how or not; he knew that because he had seen them. This guy Iridel's lecture was the same sort of thing. If there was nothing in all he said, how come all these little guys were working around here? Why wasn't the clock telling time? Where was Tuesday?

He thought he'd get that straight for good and all. "Just where is Tuesday?" he asked.

"Over there," said Iridel, and pointed. Harry recoiled and fell off the drum; for when the man extended his hand, it *disappeared!*

Harry got up off the floor and said tautly, "Do that again."

"What? Oh— Point toward Tuesday? Certainly." And he pointed. His hand appeared again when he withdrew it.

Harry said, "My gosh!" and sat down again on the drum, sweating and staring at the supervisor of the district of Futura. "You point, an' your hand—ain't," he breathed. "What direction is that?"

"It is a direction like any other direction," said Iridel. "You know yourself there are four directions—forward, sideward, upward, and"—he pointed again, and again his hand vanished —"*that* way!"

"They never tol'e me that in school," said Harry. "Course, I was just a kid then, but—"

Iridel laughed. "It is the fourth dimension—it is *duration*. The actors move through length, breadth, and height, anywhere they choose to within the set. But there is another movement—one they can't control—and that is duration."

"How soon will they come ... eh ... here?" asked Harry, waving an arm. Iridel dipped into one of his numberless pockets and pulled out a watch. "It is now eight thirty-seven Tuesday morning," he said. "They'll be here as soon as they finish the act, and the scenes in Wednesday that have already been prepared."

Harry thought again for a moment, while Iridel waited patiently, smiling a little. Then he looked up at the supervisor and asked, "Hey—this 'actor' business—what's that all about?"

"Oh—that. Well, it's a play, that's all. Just like any play—put on for the amusement of an audience."

"I was to a play once," said Harry. "Who's the audience?"

Iridel stopped smiling. "Certain— Ones who may be amused," he said. "And now I'm going to ask you some questions. How did you get here?"

"Walked."

"You *walked* from Monday night to Wednesday moning?"

"Naw— From the house to here."

"Ah— But how did you get to Wednesday, six twenty-two?"

"Well I— Damfino. I just woke up an' came to work as usual."

"This is an extraordinary occurrence," said Iridel, shaking his head in puzzlement. "You'll have to see the producer."

"Producer? Who's he?"

"You'll find out. In the meantime, come along with me. I can't leave you here; you're too close to the play. I have to make my rounds anyway."

Iridel walked toward the door. Harry was tempted to stay and find himself some more work to do, but when Iridel glanced back at him and motioned him out, Harry followed. It was suddenly impossible to do anything else.

Just as he caught up with the supervisor, a little worker ran up, whipping off his cap.

"Iridel, sir," he piped, "the weather makers put .006 of one percent too little moisture in the air on this set. There's three sevenths of an ounce too little gasoline in the storage tanks under here."

"How much is in the tanks?"

"Four thousand two hundred and seventy-three gallons, three pints, seven and twenty-one thirty-fourths ounces."

Iridel grunted. "Let it go this time. That was very sloppy work. Someone's going to get transferred to Limbo for this."

"Very good, sir," said the little man. "Long as you know we're not responsible." He put on his cap, spun around three times and rushed off.

"Lucky for the weather makers that the amount of gas in that tank doesn't come into Wednesday's script," said Iridel. "If anything interferes with the continuity of the play, there's the devil to pay. Actors haven't sense enough to cover up, either. They are liable to start whole series of miscues because of a little thing like that. The play might flop and then we'd all be out of work."

"Oh," Harry oh-ed. "Hey, Iridel—what's the idea of that patchy-looking place over there?"

Iridel followed his eyes. Harry was looking at a corner lot. It was tree-lined and overgrown with weeds and small saplings. The vegetation was true to form around the edges of the lot, and around the path that ran diagonally through it; but the spaces in between were a plane surface. Not a leaf nor a blade of grass grew there; it was naked-looking, blank, and absolutely without any color whatever.

"Oh, that," answered Iridel. "There are only two characters in Act Wednesday who will use that path. Therefore it is as grown-over as it should be. The rest of the lot doesn't enter into the play, so we don't have to do anything with it."

"But— Suppose someone wandered off the path on Wednesday," Harry offered.

"He'd be due for a surprise, I guess. But it could hardly happen. Special prompters are always detailed to spots like that, to keep the actors from going astray or missing any cues."

"Who are they—the prompters, I mean?"

"Prompters? G.A.'s—Guardian Angels. That's what the script writers call them."

"I heard o' them," said Harry.

"Yes, they have their work cut out for them," said the supervisor. "Actors are always forgetting their lines when they shouldn't, or remembering them when the script calls for a lapse. Well, it looks pretty good here. Let's have a look at Friday."

"Friday? You mean to tell me you're working on Friday already?"

"Of course! Why, we work years in advance! How on earth do you think we could get our trees grown otherwise? Here—step in!" Iridel put out his hand, seized empty air, drew it aside to show the kind of absolute nothingness he had first appeared from, and waved Harry on.

"Y-you want me to go in there?" asked Harry diffidently.

"Certainly. Hurry, now!"

Harry looked at the section of void with a rather weak-kneed look, but could not withstand the supervisor's strange compulsion. He stepped through.

And it wasn't so bad. There were no whirling lights, no sensations of falling, no falling unconscious. It was just like stepping into another room—which is what had happened. He found himself in a great round chamber, whose roundness was touched a bit with the indistinct. That is, it had curved walls and a domed roof, but there was something else about it. It seemed to stretch off in that direction toward which Iridel had so astonishingly pointed. The walls were lined with an amazing array of control machinery—switches and ground-glass screens, indicators and dials, knurled knobs, and levers. Moving deftly before them was a crew of men, each looking exactly like Iridel except that their garments had no pockets. Harry stood wide-eyed, hypnotized by the enormous complexity of the controls and the ease with which the men worked among them. Iridel touched his shoulder. "Come with me," he said. "The producer is in now; we'll find out what is to be done with you."

They started across the floor. Harry had not quite time to wonder how long it would take them to cross that enormous room, for when they had taken perhaps a dozen steps they found themselves at the opposite wall. The ordinary laws of space and time simply did not apply in the place.

They stopped at a door of burnished bronze, so very highly polished that they could see through it. It opened and Iridel pushed Harry through. The door swung shut. Harry, panic-stricken lest he be separated from the only thing in this weird world he could begin to get used to, flung himself against the great bronze portal. It bounced him back, head over heels, into the middle of the floor. He rolled over and got up to his hands and knees.

He was in a tiny room, one end of which was filled by a colossal teakwood desk. The man sitting there regarded him with amusement. "Where'd you blow in from?" he asked; and his voice was like the angry bee sound of an approaching hurricane.

"Are you the producer?"

"Well, I'll be darned," said the man, and smiled. It seemed to fill the whole room with light. He was a big man, Harry noticed; but in this deceptive place, there was no way of telling how big. "I'll be most verily darned. An actor. You're a persistent lot, aren't you? Building houses for me that I almost never go into. Getting together and sending requests for better parts. Listening carefully to what I have to say and then ignoring or misinterpreting my advice. Always asking for just one more chance, and when you get it, messing that up too. And now one of you crashes the gate. What's your trouble, anyway?"

There was something about the producer that bothered Harry, but he could not place what it was, unless it was the fact that the man awed him and he didn't know why. "I woke up in Wednesday," he stammered, "and yesterday was Tuesday. I mean Monday. I mean—" He cleared his throat and started over. "I went to sleep Monday night and woke up Wednesday, and I'm looking for Tuesday."

"What do you want me to do about it?"

"Well—couldn't you tell me how to get back there? I got work to do."

"Oh—I get it," said the producer. "You want a favor from me. You know, someday, some one of you fellows is going to come to me wanting to give me something, free and for nothing, and then I am going to drop quietly dead. Don't I have enough trouble running this show without taking up time and space by doing favors for the likes of you?" He drew a couple of breaths and then smiled again. "However— I have always tried to be just, even if it is a tough job sometimes. Go on out and tell Iridel to show you the way back. I think I know what happened to you; when you made your exit from the last act you played in, you somehow managed to walk out behind the wrong curtain when you reached the wings. There's going to be a prompter sent to Limbo for this. Go on now—beat it."

Harry opened his mouth to speak, thought better of it and scuttled out the door, which opened before him. He stood in the huge control chamber, breathing hard. Iridel walked up to him.

"Well?"

"He says for you to get me out of here."

"All right," said Iridel. "This way." He led the way to a curtained doorway much like the one they had used to come in. Beside it were two dials, one marked in days, and the other in hours and minutes.

"Monday night good enough for you?" asked Iridel.

"Swell," said Harry.

Iridel set the dials for 9:30 p. m. on Monday. "So long, actor. Maybe I'll see you again some time."

"So long," said Harry. He turned and stepped through the door.

He was back in the garage, and there was no curtained doorway behind him. He turned to ask Iridel if this would enable him to go to bed again and do Tuesday right from the start, but Iridel was gone.

The garage was a blaze of light. Harry glanced up at the clock— It said fifteen seconds after nine-thirty. That was funny; everyone should be home by now except Slim Jim, the night man, who hung out until four in the morning serving up gas at the pumps outside. A quick glance around sufficed. This might be Monday night, but it was a Monday night he hadn't known.

The place was filled with the little men again!

Harry sat on the fender of a convertible and groaned. "Now what have I got myself into?" he asked himself.

He could see that he was at a different place-in-time from the one in which he had met Iridel. There, they had been working to build, working with a precision and nicety that was a pleasure to watch. But here—

The little men were different, in the first place. They were tired-looking, sick, slow. There were scores of overseers about, and Harry winced with one of the little fellows when one of the men in white lashed out with a long whip. As the Wednesday crews worked, so the Monday gangs slaved. And the work they were doing was different. For here they were breaking down, breaking up, carting away. Before his eyes, Harry saw sections of paving lifted out, pulverized, toted away by the sackload by lines of trudging, browbeaten little men. He saw great beams upended to support the roof, while bricks were pried out of the walls. He heard the gang working on the roof, saw patches of roofing torn away. He saw walls and roof both melt away under that driving, driven onslaught, and before he knew what was happening he was standing alone on a section of the dead white plain he had noticed before on the corner lot.

It was too much for his overburdened mind; he ran out into the night, breaking through lines of laden slaves, through neat and growing piles of rubble, screaming for Iridel. He ran for a long time, and finally dropped down behind a stack of lumber out where the Unitarian church used to be, dropped because he could go no farther. He heard footsteps and tried to make himself smaller. They came on steadily;

one of the overseers rounded the corner and stood looking at him. Harry was in deep shadow, but he knew the man in white could see in the dark.

"Come out o' there," grated the man. Harry came out.

"You the guy was yellin' for Iridel?"

Harry nodded.

"What makes you think you'll find Iridel in Limbo?" sneered his captor. "Who are you, anyway?"

Harry had learned by this time. "I'm an actor," he said in a small voice. "I got into Wednesday by mistake, and they sent me back here."

"What for?"

"Huh? Why— I guess it was a mistake, that's all."

The man stepped forward and grabbed Harry by the collar. He was about eight times as powerful as a hydraulic jack. "Don't give me no guff, pal," said the man. "Nobody gets sent to Limbo by mistake, or if he didn't do somethin' up there to make him deserve it. Come clean, now."

"I didn't do nothin'." Harry wailed. "I asked them the way back, and they showed me a door, and I went through it and came here. That's all I know. Stop it, you're choking me!"

The man dropped him suddenly. "Listen, babe, you know who I am? Hey?" Harry shook his head. "Oh—you don't. Well, I'm Gurrah!"

"Yeah?" Harry said, not being able to think of anything else at the moment.

Gurrah puffed out his chest and appeared to be waiting for something more from Harry. When nothing came, he walked up to the mechanic, breathed in his face. "Ain't scared, huh? Tough guy, huh? Never heard of Gurrah, supervisor of Limbo an' the roughest, toughest son of the devil from Incidence to Eternity, huh?"

Now Harry was a peaceable man, but if there was anything he hated, it was to have a stranger breathe his bad breath pugnaciously at him. Before he knew it had happened, Gurrah was sprawled eight feet away, and Harry was standing alone rubbing his left knuckles—quite the more surprised of the two.

Gurrah sat up, feeling his face. "Why, you ... you hit me!" he roared. He got up and came over to Harry. "You hit me!" he said softly, his voice slightly out of focus in amazement. Harry wished he hadn't—wished he was in bed or in Futura or dead or something. Gurrah reached out with a heavy fist and—patted him on the shoulder. "Hey," he said, suddenly friendly, "you're all right. Heh! Took a poke at me, didn't you? Be damned! First time in a month o' Mondays anyone ever made a pass at me. Last was a feller named Orton. I killed 'im." Harry paled.

Gurrah leaned back against the lumber pile. "Dam'f I didn't enjoy that, feller. Yeah. This is a hell of a job they palmed off on me, but what can you do? Breakin' down— breakin' down. No sooner get through one job, workin' top speed, drivin' the boys till they bleed, than they give you the devil for not bein' halfway through another job. You'd think I'd been in the business long enough to know what it was all about, after more than eight hundred an' twenty million acts, wouldn't you? Heh. Try to tell *them* that. Ship a load of dog houses up to Wednesday, sneakin' it past backstage nice as you please. They turn right around and call me up. 'What's the matter with you, Gurrah? Them dog houses is no good. We sent you a list o' worn-out items two acts ago. One o' the items was dog houses. Snap out of it or we send someone back there who can read an' put you on a toteline.' That's what I get—act in and act out. An' does it do any good to tell 'em that my aid got the message an' dropped dead before he got it to me? No. Uh-uh. If I say anything about that, they tell me to stop workin' 'em to death. If I do that, they kick because my shipments don't come in fast enough."

He paused for breath. Harry had a hunch that if he kept Gurrah in a good mood it might benefit him. He asked, "What's your job, anyway?"

"Job?" Gurrah howled. "Call this a job? Tearin' down the sets, shippin' what's good to the act after next, junkin' the rest?" He snorted.

Harry asked, "You mean they use the same props over again?"

"That's right. They don't last, though. Six, eight acts, maybe. Then they got to build new ones and weather them and knock 'em around to make 'em look as if they was used."

There was silence for a time. Gurrah, having got his bitterness off his chest for the first time in literally ages, was feeling pacified. Harry didn't know how to feel. He finally broke the ice. "Hey, Gurrah— How'm I goin' to get back into the play?"

"What's it to me? How'd you— Oh, that's right, you walked in from the control room, huh? That it?"

Harry nodded.

"An' how," growled Gurrah, "did you get inta the control room?"

"Iridel brought me."

"Then what?"

"Well, I went to see the producer, and—"

"Th' *producer!* Holy— You mean you walked right in and—" Gurrah mopped his brow. "What'd he say?"

"Why—he said he guessed it wasn't my fault that I woke up in Wednesday. He said to tell Iridel to ship me back."

"An' Iridel threw you back to Monday." And Gurrah threw back his shaggy head and roared.

"What's funny," asked Harry, a little peeved.

"Iridel," said Gurrah. "Do you realize that I've been trying for fifty thousand acts or more to get something on that pretty ol' heel, and he drops you right in my lap. Pal, I can't thank you enough! He was supposed to send you back into the play, and instead o' that you wind up in yesterday! Why, I'll blackmail him till the end of time!" He whirled exultantly, called to a group of bedraggled little men who were staggering under a cornerstone on their way to the junkyard. "Take it easy, boys!" he called. "I got ol' Iridel by the short hair. No more busted backs! No more snotty messages! *Haw haw haw!*"

Harry, a little amazed at all this, put in a timid word, "Hey —Gurrah. What about me?"

Gurrah turned. "You? Oh. *Tel-e-phone!*" At his shout two little workers, a trifle less bedraggled than the rest, trotted up. One hopped up and perched on Gurrah's right shoulder; the other draped himself over the left, with his head forward. Gurrah grabbed the latter by the neck, brought the man's head close and shouted into his ear, "Give me Iridel!" There was a moment's wait, then the little man on his other shoulder spoke in Iridel's voice, into Gurrah's ear, "Well?"

"Hiyah, fancy pants!"

"Fancy— I beg your— Who is this?"

"It's Gurrah, you futuristic parasite. I got a couple things to tell you."

"Gurrah! How—*dare* you talk to me like that! I'll have you—"

"You'll have me in your job if I tell all I know. You're a wart on the nose of progress, Iridel."

"What is the meaning of this?"

"The meaning of this is that you had instructions sent to you by the producer an' you muffed them. Had an actor there, didn't you? He saw the boss, didn't he? Told you he was to be sent back, didn't he? Sent him right over to me instead of to the play, didn't you? You're slippin', Iridel. Gettin' old. Well, get off the wire. I'm callin' the boss, right now."

"The boss? Oh—don't do that, old man. Look, let's talk this thing over. Ah—about that shipment of three-legged dogs I was wanting you to round up for me; I guess I can do without them. Any little favor I can do for you—"

—"you'll damn well do, after this. You better, Goldilocks." Gurrah knocked the two small heads together, breaking the connection and probably the heads, and turned grinning to Harry. "You see," he explained, "that Iridel feller is a damn good supervisor, but he's a stickler for detail. He sends people to Limbo for the silliest little mistakes. He never forgives anyone and he never forgets a slip. He's the cause of half the misery back here, with his hurry-up orders. Now things are gonna be different. The boss has wanted to give Iridel a does of his own medicine for a long time now, but Irrie never gave him a chance."

Harry said patiently, "About me getting back now—"

"My fran'!" Gurrah bellowed. He delved into a pocket and pulled out a watch like Iridel's. "It's eleven forty on Tuesday," he said. "We'll shoot you back there now. You'll have to dope out your own reasons for disappearing. Don't spill too much, or a lot of people will suffer for it—you the most. Ready?"

Harry nodded; Gurrah swept out a hand and opened the curtain to nothingness. "You'll find yourself quite a ways from where you started," he said, "because you did a little moving around here. Go ahead."

"Thanks," said Harry.

Gurrah laughed. "Don't thank me, chum. You rate all the thanks! Hey—if, after you kick off, you don't make out so good up there, let them toss you over to me. You'll be treated good; you've my word on it. Beat it; luck!"

Holding his breath, Harry Wright stepped through the doorway.

He had to walk thirty blocks to the garage, and when he got there the boss was waiting for him.

"Where you been, Wright?"

"I—lost my way."

"Don't get wise. What do you think this is—vacation time? Get going on the spring job. Damn it, it won't be finished now till tomorra."

Harry looked him straight in the eye and said, "Listen. It'll be finished tonight. I happen to know." And, still grinning, he went back into the garage and took out his tools.

Both Ray Bradbury and Isaac (later Good Doctor) Asimov picked this story as among the ten best in Unknown's first year. Asimov said in his letter to the magazine, "I'm getting so that I'm practically nuts over anything De Camp writes. He is such easy and interesting reading that I lose my perspective and go off into torrents of praise at the slightest provocation." Most readers seemed to share that feeling, for if it is possible to imagine a "typical" writer for such a quicksilver entity as Unknown, *Sprague de Camp would probably be it. At any rate, if people remember* Unknown *at all, they remember the Harold Shea stories (which he wrote with Fletcher Pratt),* The Wheels of If, Divide and Rule, *and* Lest Darkness Fall. *De Camp loved to put ordinary, sometimes crass, people in extraordinary situations—a psychologist in the world of Norse mythology, a 20th-century historian in crumbling Rome, a New York D. A. in a series of "probability worlds." In this story, he's reversed things a touch, bringing an extraordinary being into an ordinary—and extremely crass—world. But Clarence Gaffney was well able to handle himself. He should have been—he'd had enough experience....*

The Gnarly Man

L. Sprague de Camp

Dr. Matilda Saddler first saw the gnarly man on the evening of June 14, 1946, at Coney Island.

The spring meeting of the Eastern Section of the American Anthropological Association had broken up, and Dr. Saddler had had dinner with two of her professional colleagues, Blue of Columbia and Jeffcott of Yale. She mentioned that she had never visited Coney, and meant to go there that evening. She urged Blue and Jeffcott to come along, but they begged off.

Watching Dr. Saddler's retreating back, Blue of Columbia cackled: "The Wild Woman from Wichita. Wonder if she's hunting another husband?" He was a thin man with a small gray beard and a who-the-hell-are-you-sir expression.

"How many has she had?" asked Jeffcott of Yale.

"Two to date. Don't know why anthropologists lead the most disorderly private lives of any scientists. Must be that they study the customs and morals of all these different peoples, and ask themselves, 'If the Eskimos can do it, why can't we?' I'm old enough to be safe, thank God."

"I'm not afraid of her," said Jeffcott. He was in his early forties and looked like a farmer uneasy in store clothes. "I'm so very thoroughly married."

"Yeah? Ought to have been at Stanford a few years ago, when she was there. Wasn't safe to walk across the campus, with Tuthill chasing all the females and Saddler all the males."

Dr. Saddler had to fight her way off the subway train, as the adolescents who infest the platform of the B. M. T.'s Stillwell Avenue station are probably the worst-mannered people on earth, possibly excepting the Dobu Islanders, of the western Pacific. She didn't much mind. She was a tall, strongly built woman in her late thirties, who had been kept in trim by the outdoor rigors of her profession. Besides, some of the inane remarks in Swift's paper on acculturation among the Arapaho Indians had gotten her fighting blood up.

Walking down Surf Avenue toward Brighton Beach, she looked at the concessions without trying them, preferring to watch the human types that did and the other human types that took their money. She did try a shooting gallery, but found knocking tin owls off their perch with a .22 too easy to be much fun. Long-range work with an army rifle was her idea of shooting.

The concession next to the shooting gallery would have been called a side show if there had been a main show for it to be a side show to. The usual lurid banner proclaimed the uniqueness of the two-headed calf, the bearded woman, Arachne the spider girl, and other marvels. The pièce de resistance was Ungo-Bungo, the ferocious ape-man, captured in the Congo at a cost of twenty-seven lives. The picture showed an enormous Ungo-Bungo squeezing a hapless Negro in each hand, while others sought to throw a net over him.

Dr. Saddler knew perfectly well that the ferocious ape-man would turn out to be an ordinary Caucasian with false hair on his chest. But a streak of whimsicality impelled her to go in. Perhaps, she thought, she could have some fun with her colleagues about it.

The spieler went through his leather-lunged harangue. Dr. Saddler guessed from his expression that his feet hurt. The tattooed lady didn't interest her, as her decorations obviously had no cultural significance, as they have among the Polynesians. As for the ancient Mayan, Dr. Saddler thought it in questionable taste to exhibit a poor microcephalic idiot that way. Professor Yoki's legerdemain and fire eating weren't bad.

There was a curtain in front of Ungo-Bungo's cage. At the appropriate moment there were growls and the sound of a length of chain being slapped against a metal plate. The spieler wound up on a high note: "—ladies and gentlemen, the one and only UNGO-BUNGO!" The curtain dropped.

The ape-man was squatting at the back of his cage. He dropped his chain, got up, and shuffled forward. He grasped two of the bars and shook them. They were appropriately loose and rattled alarmingly. Ungo-Bungo snarled at the patrons, showing his even, yellow teeth.

Dr. Saddler stared hard. This was something new in the ape-man line. Ungo-Bungo was about five feet three, but very massive, with enormous hunched shoulders. Above and below his blue swimming trunks thick, grizzled hair covered him from crown to ankle. His short, stout-muscled arms ended in big hands with thick, gnarled fingers. His neck projected slightly forward, so that from the front he seemed to have but little neck at all.

His face—well, thought Dr. Saddler, she knew all the living races of men, and all the types of freak brought about by glandular maladjustment, and none of them had a face like *that*. It was deeply lined. The forehead between the short scalp hair and the brows on the huge supraorbital ridges receded sharply. The nose, although wide, was not apelike; it was a shortened version of the thick, hooked Armenoid nose, so often miscalled Jewish. The face ended in a long upper lip and a retreating chin. And the yellowish skin apparently belonged to Ungo-Bungo.

The curtain was whisked up again.

Dr. Saddler went out with the others, but paid another dime, and soon was back inside. She paid no attention to the spieler, but got a good position in front of Ungo-Bungo's cage before the rest of the crowd arrived.

Ungo-Bungo repeated his performance with mechanical precision. Dr. Saddler noticed that he limped a little as he came forward to rattle the bars, and that the skin under his mat of hair bore several big whitish scars. The last joint of his left ring finger was missing. She noted certain things about the proportions of his shin and thigh, of his forearm and upper arm, and his big splay feet.

Dr. Saddler paid a third dime. An idea was knocking at her mind somewhere. If she let it in, either she was crazy or physical anthropology was haywire or—something. But she knew that if she did the sensible thing, which was to go home, the idea would plague her from now on.

After the third performance she spoke to the spieler. "I think your Mr. Ungo-Bungo used to be a friend of mine. Could you arrange for me to see him after he finishes?"

The spieler checked his sarcasm. His questioner was so obviously not a—not the sort of dame who asks to see guys after they finish.

"Oh, him," he said. "Calls himself Gaffney—Clarence Aloysius Gaffney. That the guy you want?"

"Why, yes."

"I guess you can." He looked at his watch. "He's got four more turns to do before we close. I'll have to ask the boss. He popped through a curtain and called, "Hey, Morrie!" Then he was back. "It's O. K. Morrie says you can wait in his office. Foist door to the right."

Morrie was stout, bald, and hospitable. "Sure, sure," he said, waving his cigar. "Glad to be of soivice, Miss Saddler. Chust a min while I talk to Gaffney's manager." He stuck his head out. "Hey, Pappas! Lady wants to talk to your ape-man later. I meant *lady*. O. K." He returned to orate on the difficulties besetting the freak business. "You take this Gaffney, now. He's the best damn ape-man in the business; all that hair rilly grows outa him. And the poor guy rilly has a face like that. But do people believe it? No! I hear 'em going out, saying about how the hair is pasted on, and the whole thing is a fake. It's mawtifying." He cocked his head, listening. "That rumble wasn't no rolly-coaster; it's gonna rain. Hope it's over by tomorrow. You wouldn't believe the way a rain can knock ya receipts off. If you drew a coive, it would be like this." He drew his finger horizontally through space, jerking it down sharply to indicate the effect of rain. "But as I said, people don't appreciate what you try to do for 'em. It's not just the money; I think of myself as an ottist. A creative ottist. A show like this got to have balance and propawtion, like any other ott—"

It must have been an hour later when a slow, deep voice at the door said: "Did somebody want to see me?"

The gnarly man was in the doorway. In street clothes, with

the collar of his raincoat turned up and his hat brim pulled down, he looked more or less human, though the coat fitted his great, sloping shoulders badly. He had a thick, knobby walking stick with a leather loop near the top end A small, dark man fidgeted behind him.

"Yeah," said Morrie, interrupting his lecture. "Clarence, this is Miss Saddler. Miss Saddler, this is Mr. Gaffney, one of our outstanding creative ottists."

"Pleased to meetcha," said the gnarly man. "This is my manager, Mr. Pappas."

Dr. Saddler explained, and said she'd like to talk to Mr Gaffney if she might. She was tactful; you had to be to pry into the private affairs of Naga headhunters, for instance The gnarly man said he'd be glad to have a cup of coffee with Miss Saddler; there was a place around the corner that they could reach without getting wet.

As they started out, Pappas followed, fidgeting more and more. The gnarly man said: "Oh, go home to bed, John Don't worry about me." He grinned at Dr. Saddler. The effect would have been unnerving to anyone but an anthropologist. "Every time he sees me talking to anybody, he thinks it's some other manager trying to steal me." He spoke general American, with a suggestion of Irish brogue in the lowering of the vowels in words like "man" and "talk." "I made the lawyer who drew up our contract fix it so it can be ended on short notice."

Pappas departed, still looking suspicious. The rain had practically ceased. The gnarly man stepped along smartly despite his limp.

A woman passed with a fox terrier on a leash. The dog sniffed in the direction of the gnarly man, and then to all appearances went crazy, yelping and slavering. The gnarly man shifted his grip on the massive stick and said quietly, "Better hang onto him, ma'am." The woman departed hastily. "They just don't like me," commented Gaffney. "Dogs, that is."

They found a table and ordered their coffee. When the gnarly man took off his raincoat, Dr. Saddler became aware of a strong smell of cheap perfume. He got out a pipe with a big knobby bowl. It suited him, just as the walking stick did. Dr. Saddler noticed that the deep-sunk eyes under the beetling arches were light hazel.

"Well?" he said in his rumbling drawl.

She began her questions.

"My parents were Irish," he answered. "But I was born in South Boston . . . let's see . . . forty-six years ago. I can get you a copy of my birth certificate. Clarence Aloysius Gaffney, May 2, 1900." He seemed to get some secret amusement out of that statement.

"Were either of your parents of your somewhat unusual physical type?"

He paused before answering. He always did, it seemed. "Uh-huh. Both of 'em. Glands, I suppose."

"Were they both born in Ireland?"

"Yep. County Sligo." Again that mysterious twinkle.

She thought. "Mr. Gaffney, you wouldn't mind having some photographs and measurements made, would you? You could use the photographs in your business."

"Maybe." He took a sip. "Ouch! Gazooks, that's hot!"

"What?"

"I said the coffee's hot."

"I mean, before that."

The gnarly man looked a little embarrassed. "Oh, you mean the 'gazooks'? Well, I . . . uh . . . once knew a man who used to say that."

"Mr. Gaffney, I'm a scientist, and I'm not trying to get anything out of you for my own sake. You can be frank with me."

There was something remote and impersonal in his stare that gave her a slight spinal chill. "Meaning that I haven't been so far?"

"Yes. When I saw you I decided that there was something extraordinary in your background. I still think there is. Now, if you think I'm crazy, say so and we'll drop the subject. But I want to get to the bottom of this."

He took his time about answering. "That would depend." There was another pause. Then he said: "With your connections, do you know any really first-class surgeons?"

"But . . . yes, I know Dunbar."

"The guy who wears a purple gown when he operates? The guy who wrote a book on 'God, Man, and the Universe'?"

"Yes. He's a good man, in spite of his theatrical mannerisms. Why? What would you want of him?"

"Not what you're thinking. I'm satisfied with my . . . uh . . . unusual physical type. But I have some old injuries— broken bones that didn't knit properly—that I want fixed up.

He'd have to be a good man, though. I have a couple of thousand dollars in the savings bank, but I know the sort of fees those guys charge. If you could make the necessary arrangements—"

"Why, yes, I'm sure I could. In fact, I could guarantee it. Then I *was* right? And you'll—" She hesitated.

"Come clean? Uh-huh. But remember, I can still prove I'm Clarence Aloysius if I have to."

"Who *are* you, then?"

Again there was a long pause. Then the gnarly man said: "Might as well tell you. As soon as you repeat any of it, you'll have put your professional reputation in my hands, remember.

"First off, I wasn't born in Massachusetts. I was born on the upper Rhine, near Mommenheim. And I was born, as nearly as I can figure out, about the year 50,000 B. C."

Matilda Saddler wondered whether she'd stumbled on the biggest thing in anthropology, or whether this bizarre personality was making Baron Munchausen look like a piker.

He seemed to guess her thoughts. "I can't prove that, of course. But so long as you arrange about that operation, I don't care whether you believe me or not."

"But . . . but . . . *how?*"

"I think the lightning did it. We were out trying to drive some bison into a pit. Well, this big thunderstorm came up, and the bison bolted in the wrong direction. So we gave up and tried to find shelter. And the next thing I knew I was lying on the ground with the rain running over me, and the rest of the clan standing around wailing about what had they done to get the storm god sore at them, so he made a bull's-eye on one of their best hunters. They'd never said *that* about me before. It's funny how you're never appreciated while you're alive.

"But I was alive, all right. My nerves were pretty well shot for a few weeks, but otherwise I was O. K., except for some burns on the soles of my feet. I don't know just what happened, except I was reading a couple of years ago that scientists had located the machinery that controls the replacement of tissue in the medulla oblongata. I think maybe the lightning did something to my medulla to speed it up. Anyway, I never got any older after that. Physically, that is. I was thirty-three at the time, more or less. We didn't keep track of ages. I look older now, because the lines in your face are bound to get sort of set after a few thousand years, and because our hair was always gray at the ends. But I can still tie an ordinary *Homo sapiens* in a knot if I want to."

"Then you're . . . you mean to say you're . . . you're trying to tell me you're—"

"A Neanderthal man? *Homo neanderthalensis?* That's right."

Matilda Saddler's hotel room was a bit crowded, with the gnarly man, the frosty Blue, the rustic Jeffcott, Dr. Saddler herself, and Harold McGannon, the historian. This McGannon was a small man, very neat and pink-skinned. He looked more like a New York Central director than a professor. Just now his expression was one of fascination. Dr. Saddler looked full of pride; Professor Jeffcott looked interested but puzzled; Dr. Blue looked bored—he hadn't wanted to come in the first place. The gnarly man, stretched out in the most comfortable chair and puffing his overgrown pipe, seemed to be enjoying himself.

McGannon was formulating a question. "Well, Mr.—Gaffney? I suppose that's your name as much as any."

"You might say so," said the gnarly man. "My original name meant something like Shining Hawk. But I've gone under hundreds of names since then. If you register in a hotel as 'Shining Hawk,' it's apt to attract attention. And I try to avoid that."

"Why?" asked McGannon.

The gnarly man looked at his audience as one might look at willfully stupid children. "I don't like trouble. The best way to keep out of trouble is not to attract attention. That's why I have to pull up stakes and move every ten or fifteen years. People might get curious as to why I never got any older."

"Pathological liar," murmured Blue. The words were barely audible, but the gnarly man heard them.

"You're entitled to your opinion, Dr. Blue," he said affably. "Dr. Saddler's doing me a favor, so in return I'm letting you all shoot questions at me. And I'm answering. I don't give a damn whether you believe me or not."

McGannon hastily threw in another question. "How is it that you have a birth certificate, as you say you have?"

"Oh, I knew a man named Clarence Gaffney once. He got killed by an automobile, and I took his name."

"Was there any reason for picking this Irish background?"

"Are you Irish, Dr. McGannon?"

"Not enough to matter."

"O. K. I didn't want to hurt any feelings. It's my best bet. There are real Irishmen with upper lips like mine."

Dr. Saddler broke in. "I meant to ask you, Clarence." She put a lot of warmth into his name. "There's an argument as to whether your people interbred with mine, when mine overran Europe at the end of the Mousterian. Some scientists have thought that some modern Europeans, especially along the west coast of Ireland, might have a little Neanderthal blood."

He grinned slightly. "Well—yes and no. There never was any back in the stone age, as far as I know. But these long-lipped Irish are my fault."

"How?"

"Believe it or not, but in the last fifty centuries there have been some women of your species that didn't find me too repulsive. Usually there were no offspring. But in the sixteenth century I went to Ireland to live. They were burning too many people for witchcraft in the rest of Europe to suit me at that time. And there was a woman. The result this time was a flock of hybrids—cute little devils, they were. So the Irishmen who look like me are my descendants."

"What did happen to your people?" asked McGannon. "Were they killed off?"

The gnarly man shrugged. "Some of them. We weren't at all warlike. But then the tall ones, as we called them, weren't either. Some of the tribes of the tall ones looked on us as legitimate prey, but most of them let us severely alone. I guess they were almost as scared of us as we were of them. Savages as primitive as that are really pretty peaceable people. You have to work so hard to keep fed, and there are so few of you, that there's no object in fighting wars. That comes later, when you get agriculture and livestock, so you have something worth stealing.

"I remember that a hundred years after the tall ones had come, there were still Neanderthalers living in my part of the country. But they died out. I think it was that they lost their ambition. The tall ones were pretty crude, but they were so far ahead of us that our things and our customs seemed silly. Finally we just sat around and lived on the scraps we could beg from the tall ones' camps. You might say we died of an inferiority complex."

"What happened to you?" asked McGannon.

"Oh, I was a god among my own people by then, and naturally I represented them in their dealings with the tall ones. I got to know the tall ones pretty well, and they were willing to put up with me after all my own clan were dead. Then in a couple of hundred years they'd forgotten all about my people, and took me for a hunchback or something. I got to be pretty good at flint working, so I could earn my keep. When metal came in, I went into that, and finally into blacksmithing. If you'd put all the horseshoes I've made in a pile, they'd—well, you'd have a damn big pile of horseshoes, anyway."

"Did you . . . ah . . . limp at that time?" asked McGannon.

"Uh-huh. I busted my leg back in the Neolithic. Fell out of a tree, and had to set it myself, because there wasn't anybody around. Why?"

"Vulcan," said McGannon softly.

"Vulcan?" repeated the gnarly man. "Wasn't he a Greek god or something?"

"Yes. He was the lame blacksmith of the gods."

"You mean you think that maybe somebody got the idea from me? That's an interesting theory. Little late to check up on it, though."

Blue leaned forward and said crisply: "Mr. Gaffney, no real Neanderthal man could talk as fluently and entertainingly as you do. That's shown by the poor development of the frontal lobes of the brain and the attachments of the tongue muscles."

The gnarly man shrugged again. "You can believe what you like. My own clan considered me pretty smart, and then you're bound to learn something in fifty thousand years."

Dr. Saddler beamed. "Tell them about your teeth, Clarence."

The gnarly man grinned. "They're false, of course. My own lasted a long time, but they still wore out somewhere back in the Paleolithic. I grew a third set, and they wore out, too. So I had to invent soup."

"You *what?*" It was the usually taciturn Jeffcott.

"I had to invent soup, to keep alive. You know, the bark-dish-and-hot-stones method. My gums got pretty tough after a while, but they still weren't much good for chewing hard stuff. So after a few thousand years I got pretty sick of soup and mushy foods generally. And when metal came in I began experimenting with false teeth. Bone teeth in copper plates. You might say I invented them, too. I tried often to sell them, but they never really caught on until around 1750 A. D. I was living in Paris then, and I built up quite a little business before I moved on." He pulled the handkerchief out of his breast pocket to wipe his forehead; Blue made a face as the wave of perfume reached him.

"Well, Mr. Shining Hawk," snapped Blue with a trace of sarcasm, "how do you like our machine age?"

The gnarly man ignored the tone of the question. "It's not bad. Lots of interesting things happen. The main trouble is the shirts."

"Shirts?"

"Uh-huh. Just try to buy a shirt with a twenty neck and a twenty-nine sleeve. I have to order 'em special. It's almost as bad with hats and shoes. I wear an eight and one half hat and a thirteen shoe." He looked at his watch. "I've got to get back to Coney to work."

McGannon jumped up. "Where can I get in touch with you again, Mr. Gaffney? There's lots of things I'd like to ask you."

The gnarly man told him. "I'm free mornings. My working hours are two to midnight on weekdays, with a couple of hours off for dinner. Union rules, you know."

"You mean there's a union for you show people?"

"Sure. Only they call it a guild. They think they're artists, you know. Artists don't have unions; they have guilds. But it amounts to the same thing."

Blue and Jeffcott saw the gnarly man and the historian walking slowly toward the subway together. Blue said: "Poor old Mac! Always thought he had sense. Looks like he's swallowed this Gaffney's ravings, hook, line, and sinker."

"I'm not so sure," said Jeffcott, frowning. "There's something funny about the business."

"What?" barked Blue. "Don't tell me that *you* believe this story of being alive fifty thousand years? A caveman who uses perfume! Good God!"

"N-no," said Jeffcott. "Not the fifty thousand part. But I don't think it's a simple case of paranoia or plain lying, either. And the perfume's quite logical, if he were telling the truth."

"Huh?"

"Body odor. Saddler told us how dogs hate him. He'd have a smell different from ours. We're so used to ours that we don't even know we have one, unless somebody goes without a bath for a month. But we might notice his if he didn't disguise it."

Blue snorted. "You'll be believing him yourself in a minute. It's an obvious glandular case, and he's made up this story to fit. All that talk about not caring whether we believe him or not is just bluff. Come on, let's get some lunch. Say, see the way Saddler looked at him every time she said 'Clarence'? Like a hungry wolf. Wonder what she thinks she's going to do with him?"

Jeffcott thought. "I can guess. And if he *is* telling the truth, I think there's something in Deuteronomy against it."

The great surgeon made a point of looking like a great surgeon, to pince-nez and Vandyke. He waved the X-ray negatives at the gnarly man, pointing out this and that.

"We'd better take the leg first," he said. "Suppose we do that next Thursday. When you've recovered from that we can tackle the shoulder. It'll all take time, you know."

The gnarly man agreed, and shuffled out of the little private hospital to where McGannon awaited him in his car. The gnarly man described the tentative schedule of operations, and mentioned that he had made arrangements to quit his job. "Those two are the main thing," he said. "I'd like to try professional wrestling again some day, and I can't unless I get this shoulder fixed so I can raise my left arm over my head."

"What happened to it?" asked McGannon.

The gnarly man closed his eyes, thinking. "Let me see. I get things mixed up sometimes. People do when they're only fifty years old, so you can imagine what it's like for me.

"In 42 B. C. I was living with the Bituriges in Gaul. You remember that Cæsar shut up Werkinghetorich—Vercingetorix to you—in Alesia, and the confederacy raised an army of relief under Caswollon."

"Caswollon?"

The gnarly man laughed shortly. "I meant Wercaswollon. Caswollon was a Briton, wasn't he? I'm always getting those two mixed up.

"Anyhow, I got drafted. That's all you can call it; I didn't want to go. It wasn't exactly *my* war. But they wanted me because I could pull twice as heavy a bow as anybody else.

"When the final attack on Cæsar's ring of fortifications came, they sent me forward with some other archers to provide a covering fire for their infantry. At least, that was the plan. Actually, I never saw such a hopeless muddle in my life. And before I even got within bowshot, I fell into one of the Romans' covered pits. I didn't land on the point of the stake, but I fetched up against the side of it and busted my shoulder. There wasn't any help, because the Gauls were too busy running away from Cæsar's German cavalry to bother about wounded men."

The author of "God, Man, and the Universe" gazed after his departing patient. He spoke to his head assistant: "What do you think of him?"

"I think it's so," said the assistant. "I looked over those X rays pretty closely. That skeleton never belonged to a human being. And it has more healed fractures than you'd think possible."

"Hm-m-m," said Dunbar. "That's right, he wouldn't be human, would he? Hm-m-m. You know, if anything happened to him—"

The assistant grinned understandingly. "Of course, there's the S. P. C. A."

"We needn't worry about *them*. Hm-m-m." He thought, you've been slipping; nothing big in the papers for a year. But if you published a complete anatomical description of a Neanderthal man—or if you found out why his medulla functions the way it does—Hm-m-m. Of course, it would have to be managed properly—"

"Let's have lunch at the Natural History Museum," said McGannon. "Some of the people there ought to know you."

"O. K.," drawled the gnarly man. "Only I've still got to get back to Coney afterward. This is my last day. Tomorrow, Pappas and I are going up to see our lawyer about ending our contract. Guy named Robinette. It's a dirty trick on poor old John, but I warned him at the start that this might happen."

"I suppose we can come up to interview you while you're . . . ah . . . convalescing? Fine. Have you ever been to the museum, by the way?"

"Sure," said the gnarly man. "I get around."

"What did you . . . ah . . . think of their stuff in the Hall of the Age of Man?"

"Pretty good. There's a little mistake in one of those big wall paintings. The second horn on the woolly rhinoceros ought to slant forward more. I thought of writing them a letter. But you know how it is. They'd say: 'Were you there?' and I'd say, 'Uh-huh,' and they'd say, 'Another nut.' "

"How about the pictures and busts of Paleolithic men?"

"Pretty good. But they have some funny ideas. They always show us with skins wrapped around our middles. In summer we didn't wear skins, and in winter we hung them around our shoulders, where they'd do some good.

"And then they show those tall ones that you call Cro-Magnon men clean-shaven. As I remember, they all had whiskers. What would they shave with?"

"I think," said McGannon, "that they leave the beards off the busts to . . . ah . . . show the shape of the chins. With the beards they'd all look too much alike."

"Is that the reason? They might say so on the labels." The gnarly man rubbed his own chin, such as it was. "I wish beards would come back into style. I look much more human with a beard. I got along fine in the sixteenth century when everybody had whiskers.

"That's one of the ways I remember when things happened, by the haircuts and whiskers that people had. I remember when a wagon I was driving in Milan lost a wheel and spilled flour bags from hell to breakfast. That must have been in the sixteenth century, before I went to Ireland, because I remember that most of the men in the crowd that collected had beards. Now—wait a minute—maybe that was the fourteenth. There were a lot of beards then, too."

"Why, why didn't you keep a diary?" asked McGannon with a groan of exasperation.

The gnarly man shrugged characteristically. "And pack around six trunks full of paper every time I moved? No, thanks."

"I . . . ah . . . don't suppose you could give me the real story of Richard III and the princes in the tower?"

"Why should I? I was just a poor blacksmith, or farmer, or something most of the time. I didn't go around with the big shots. I gave up all my ideas of ambition a long time before that. I had to, being so different from other people. As far as I can remember, the only real king I ever got a good look at was Charlemagne, when he made a speech in Paris one day. He was just a big, tall man with Santa Claus whiskers and a squeaky voice."

Next morning McGannon and the gnarly man had a session with Svedberg at the museum. Then McGannon drove Gaffney around to the lawyer's office, on the third floor of a seedy office building in the West Fifties. James Robinette looked something like a movie actor and something like a chipmunk. He looked at his watch and said to McGannon: "This won't take long. If you'd like to stick around, I'd be glad to have lunch with you." The fact was that he was feeling just a trifle queasy about being left with this damn queer client, this circus freak or whatever he was, with his barrel body and his funny slow drawl.

When the business had been completed, and the gnarly man had gone off with his manager to wind up his affairs at Coney, Robinette said: "Whew! I thought he was a halfwit, from his looks. But there was nothing half-witted about the way he went over those clauses. You'd have thought the damn contract was for building a subway system. What *is* he, anyhow?"

McGannon told him what he knew.

The lawyer's eyebrows went up. "Do you *believe* his yarn? Oh, I'll take tomato juice and filet of sole with tartar sauce —only without the tartar sauce—on the lunch, please."

"The same for me. Answering your question, Robinette, I do. So does Saddler. So does Svedberg up at the museum. They're both topnotchers in their respective fields. Saddler and I have interviewed him, and Svedberg's examined him physically. But it's just opinion. Fred Blue still swears it's a hoax or . . . ah . . . some sort of dementia. Neither of us can prove anything."

"Why not?"

"Well .. ah ... how are you going to prove that he was, or was not, alive a hundred years ago? Take one case: Clarence says he ran a sawmill in Fairbanks, Alaska, in 1906 and '07, under the name of Michael Shawn. How are you going to find out whether there was a sawmill operator in Fairbanks at that time? And if you did stumble on a record of a Michael Shawn, how would you know whether he and Clarence were the same? There's not a chance in a thousand that there'd be a photograph or a detailed description that you could check with. And you'd have an awful time trying to find anybody who remembered him at this late date.

"Then, Svedberg poked around Clarence's face, yesterday, and said that no *Homo sapiens* ever had a pair of zygomatic arches like that. But when I told Blue that, he offered to produce photographs of a human skull that did. I know what'll happen. Blue will say that the arches are practically the same, and Svedberg will say that they're obviously different. So there we'll be."

Robinette mused, "He does seem damned intelligent for an ape-man."

"He's not an ape-man, really. The Neanderthal race was a separate branch of the human stock; they were more primitive in some ways and more advanced in others than we are. Clarence may be slow, but he usually grinds out the right answer. I imagine that he was . . . ah . . . brilliant, for one of his kind, to begin with. And he's had the benefit of so much experience. He knows an incredible lot. He knows us; he sees through us and our motives."

The little pink man puckered up his forehead. "I do hope nothing happens to him. He's carrying around a lot of priceless information in that big head of his. Simply priceless. Not much about war and politics; he kept clear of those as a matter of self-preservation. But little things, about how people lived and how they thought thousands of years ago. He gets his periods mixed up sometimes, but he gets them straightened out if you give him time.

"I'll have to get hold of Pell, the linguist. Clarence knows dozens of ancient languages, such as Gothic and Gaulish. I was able to check him on some of them, like vulgar Latin; that was one of the things that convinced me. And there are archeologists and psychologists—

"If only something doesn't happen to scare him off. We'd never find him. I don't know. Between a man-crazy female scientist and a publicity-mad surgeon—I wonder how it'll work out—"

The gnarly man innocently entered the waiting room of Dunbar's hospital. He, as usual, spotted the most comfortable chair and settled luxuriously into it.

Dunbar stood before him. His keen eyes gleamed with anticipation behind their pince-nez. "There'll be a wait of about half an hour, Mr. Gaffney," he said. "We're all tied up now, you know. I'll send Mahler in; he'll see that you have anything you want." Dunbar's eyes ran lovingly over the gnarly man's stumpy frame. What fascinating secrets mightn't he discover once he got inside it?

Mahler appeared, a healthy-looking youngster. Was there anything Mr. Gaffney would like? The gnarly man paused as usual to let his massive mental machinery grind. A vagrant impulse moved him to ask to see the instruments that were to be used on him.

Mahler had his orders, but this seemed a harmless enough request. He went and returned with a tray full of gleaming steel. "You see," he said, "these are called scalpels."

Presently the gnarly man asked: "What's this?" He picked up a peculiar-looking instrument.

"Oh, that's the boss's own invention. For getting at the mid-brain."

"Mid-brain? What's that doing here?"

"Why, that's for getting at your— That must be there by mistake—"

Little lines tightened around the queer hazel eyes. "Yeah?" He remembered the look Dunbar had given him, and Dunbar's general reputation. "Say, could I use your phone a minute?"

"Why . . . I suppose . . . what do you want to phone for?"

"I want to call my lawyer. Any objections?"

"No, of course not. But there isn't any phone here."

"What do you call that?" The gnarly man got up and walked toward the instrument in plain sight on a table. But Mahler was there before him, standing in front of it.

"This one doesn't work. It's being fixed."

"Can't I try it?"

"No, not till it's fixed. It doesn't work, I tell you."

The gnarly man studied the young physician for a few seconds. "O. K., then I'll find one that does." He started for the door.

"Hey, you can't go out now!" cried Mahler.

"Can't I? Just watch me!"

"Hey!" It was a full-throated yell. Like magic more men in white coats appeared.

Behind them was the great surgeon. "Be reasonable, Mr. Gaffney," he said. "There's no reason why you should go out now, you know. We'll be ready for you in a little while."

"Any reason why I shouldn't?" The gnarly man's big face swung on his thick neck, and his hazel eyes swiveled. All the exits were blocked. "I'm going."

"Grab him!" said Dunbar.

The white coats moved. The gnarly man got his hands on the back of a chair. The chair whirled, and became a dissolving blur as the men closed on him. Pieces of chair flew about the room, to fall with the dry, sharp *ping* of short lengths of wood. When the gnarly man stopped swinging, having only a short piece of the chair back left in each fist, one assistant was out cold. Another leaned whitely against the wall and nursed a broken arm.

"Go on!" shouted Dunbar when he could make himself heard. The white wave closed over the gnarly man, then broke. The gnarly man was on his feet, and held young Mahler by the ankles. He spread his feet and swung the shrieking Mahler like a club, clearing the way to the door. He turned, whirled Mahler around his head like a hammer thrower, and let the now mercifully unconscious body fly. His assailants went down in a yammering tangle.

One was still up. Under Dunbar's urging he sprang after the gnarly man. The latter had gotten his stick out of the umbrella stand in the vestibule. The knobby upper end went *whoosh* past the assistant's nose. The assistant jumped back and fell over one of the casualties. The front door slammed, and there was a deep roar of "Taxi!"

"Come on!" shrieked Dunbar. "Get the ambulance out!"

James Robinette was sitting in his office, thinking the thoughts that lawyers do in moments of relaxation, when there was a pounding of large feet in the corridor, a startled protest from Miss Spevak in the outer office, and the strange client of the day before was at Robinette's desk, breathing hard.

"I'm Gaffney," he growled between gasps. "Remember me? I think they followed me down here. They'll be up any minute. I want your help."

"They? Who's they?" Robinette winced at the impact of that damn perfume.

The gnarly man launched into his misfortunes. He was going well when there were more protests from Miss Spevak, and Dr. Dunbar and four assistants burst into the office.

"He's ours," said Dunbar, his glasses agleam.

"He's an ape-man," said the assistant with the black eye.

"He's a dangerous lunatic," said the assistant with the cut lip.

"We've come to take him away," said the assistant with the torn coat.

The gnarly man spread his feet and gripped his stick like a baseball bat by the small end.

Robinette opened a desk drawer and got out a large pistol. "One move toward him and I'll use this. The use of extreme violence is justified to prevent commission of a felony, to wit: kidnaping."

The five men backed up a little. Dunbar said: "This isn't kidnaping. You can only kidnap a person, you know. He isn't a human being, and I can prove it."

The assistant with the black eye snickered. "If he wants protection, he better see a game warden instead of a lawyer."

"Maybe that's what *you* think," said Robinette. "You

aren't a lawyer. According to the law, he's human. Even corporations, idiots, and unborn children are legally persons, and he's a damn sight more human than they are."

"Then he's a dangerous lunatic," said Dunbar.

"Yeah? Where's your commitment order? The only persons who can apply for one are: (a) close relatives and (b) public officials charged with the maintenance of order. You're neither."

Dunbar continued stubbornly: "He ran amuck in my hospital and nearly killed a couple of my men, you know. I guess that gives us some rights."

"Sure," said Robinette. "You can step down to the nearest station and swear out a warrant." He turned to the gnarly man. "Shall we throw the book at 'em, Gaffney?"

"I'm all right," said that individual, his speech returning to its normal slowness. "I just want to make sure these guys don't pester me any more."

"O. K. Now listen, Dunbar. One hostile move out of you and we'll have a warrant out for you for false arrest, assault and battery, attempted kidnaping, criminal conspiracy, and disorderly conduct. *And* we'll slap on a civil suit for damages for sundry torts, to wit: assault, deprivation of civil rights, placing in jeopardy of life and limb, menace, and a few more I may think of later."

"You'll never make that stick," snarled Dunbar. "We have all the witnesses."

"Yeah? And wouldn't the great Evan Dunbar look sweet defending such actions? Some of the ladies who gush over your books might suspect that maybe you weren't such a damn knight in shining armor. We can make a prize monkey of you, and you know it."

"You're destroying the possibility of a great scientific discovery, you know, Robinette."

"To hell with that. My duty is to protect my client. Now beat it, all of you, before I call a cop." His left hand moved suggestively to the telephone.

Dunbar grasped at a last straw. "Hm-m-m. Have you got a permit for that gun?"

"Damn right. Want to see it?"

Dunbar sighed. "Never mind. You *would* have." His greatest opportunity for fame was slipping out of his fingers. He drooped toward the door.

The gnarly man spoke up. "If you don't mind, Dr. Dunbar, I left my hat at your place. I wish you'd send it to Mr. Robinette here. I have a hard time getting hats to fit me."

Dunbar looked at him silently and left with his cohorts.

The gnarly man was giving the lawyer further details when the telephone rang. Robinette answered: "Yes. . . . Saddler? Yes, he's here. . . . Your Dr. Dunbar was going to murder him so he could dissect him. . . . O. K." He turned to the gnarly man. "Your friend Dr. Saddler is looking for you. She's on her way up here."

"Zounds!" said Gaffney. "I'm going."

"Don't you want to see her? She was phoning from around the corner. If you go out now you'll run into her. How did she know where to call?"

"I gave her your number. I suppose she called the hospital and my boardinghouse, and tried you as a last resort. This door goes into the hall, doesn't it? Well, when she comes in the regular door I'm going out this one. And I don't want you saying where I've gone. It's nice to have known you, Mr. Robinette."

"Why? What's the matter? You're not going to run out now, are you? Dunbar's harmless, and you've got friends. I'm your friend."

"You're durn tootin' I'm going to run out. There's too much trouble. I've kept alive all these centuries by staying away from trouble. I let down my guard with Dr. Saddler, and went to the surgeon she recommended. First he plots to take me apart to see what makes me tick. If that brain instrument hadn't made me suspicious, I'd have been on my way to the alcohol jars by now. Then there's a fight, and it's just pure luck I didn't kill a couple of those internes, or whatever they are, and get sent up for manslaughter. Now Matilda's after me with a more-than-friendly interest. I know what it means when a woman looks at you that way and calls you 'dear.' I wouldn't mind if she weren't a prominent person of the kind that's always in some sort of garboil. That would mean more trouble, sooner or later. You don't suppose I *like* trouble, do you?"

"But look here, Gaffney, you're getting steamed up over a lot of damn—"

"Ssst!" The gnarly man took his stick and tiptoed over to the private entrance. As Dr. Saddler's clear voice sounded in the outer office, he sneaked out. He was closing the door behind him when the scientist entered the inner office.

Matilda Saddler was a quick thinker. Robinette hardly had time to open his mouth when she flung herself at and through the private door with a cry of "Clarence!"

Robinette heard the clatter of feet on the stairs. Neither the pursued nor the pursuer had waited for the creaky elevator. Looking out the window, he saw Gaffney leap into a taxi. Matilda Saddler sprinted after the cab, calling: "Clarence! Come back!" But the traffic was light and the chase correspondingly hopeless.

They did hear from the gnarly man once more. Three months later Robinette got a letter whose envelope contained, to his vast astonishment, ten ten-dollar bills. The single sheet was typed, even to the signature.

DEAR MR. ROBINETTE:

I do not know what your regular fees are, but I hope that the inclosed will cover your services to me of last June.

Since leaving New York I have had several jobs. I pushed a hack—as we say—in Chicago, and I tried out as pitcher on a bush league baseball team. Once I made my living by knocking over rabbits and things with stones, and I can still throw fairly well. Nor am I bad at swinging a club, such as a baseball bat. But my lameness makes me too slow for a baseball career, and it will be some time before I try any remedial operations again.

I now have a job whose nature I cannot disclose because I do not wish to be traced. You need pay no attention to the postmark; I am not living in Kansas City, but had a friend post this letter there.

Ambition would be foolish for one in my peculiar position. I am satisfied with a job that furnishes me with the essentials, and allows me to go to an occasional movie, and a few friends with whom I can drink beer and talk.

I was sorry to leave New York without saying good-by to Dr. Harold McGannon, who treated me very nicely. I wish you would explain to him why I had to leave as I did. You can get in touch with him through Columbia University.

If Dunbar sent you my hat as I requested, please mail it to me: General Delivery, Kansas City, Mo. My friend will pick it up. There is not a hat store in this town where I live that can fit me. With best wishes, I remain,

Yours sincerely,
SHINING HAWK
Alias CLARENCE ALOYSIUS GAFFNEY.

Unknown *made the field of "modern" fantasy—horrors in hallways, magic in the metropolis—peculiarly its own; but it didn't neglect the traditional heroic fantasy of the kind made famous by Edgar Rice Burroughs and Robert E. Howard. Norvell Page's stories of Prester John, for instance, had satisfactory amounts of cloven skulls and deep-drinking swords and all that kind of thing. But it was Fritz Leiber's stories of "unhistoried Lankhmar" which captured the imagination of most readers. The team of the agile Gray Mouser and the northman Fafhrd took on enchanters, thieves, the dead and undead, with exemplary aplomb and a cheerful eye for the main chance; and in this story they're at their best. (For any who have wondered, I've consulted with the author about the proper pronunciation of* Fafhrd; *if there were a verb to* foffer, *the Northman's name would be pronounced like its past participle:* foffered.*)*

The Bleak Shore

Fritz Leiber

"So you think a man can cheat death and outwit doom?" said the small, pale man, whose bulging forehead was shadowed by a black cowl.

The Gray Mouser, holding the dice box ready for a throw, paused and quickly looked sideways at the questioner.

"I said that a cunning man can cheat death for a long time."

The tavern room in ancient Lankhmar, chief city of the unhistoried land of Lankhmar, bustled with pleasantly raucous excitement. Fighting men predominated, and the clank of swordsmen's harness mingled with the thump of tankards, providing a background for the shrill laughter of the women. Swaggering guardsmen elbowed the hired bravoes of the young lords. Grinning slaves bearing open wine jars dodged nimbly between. In one corner a slave girl was dancing, the jingle of her silver anklet bells inaudible in the din. Outside the small, tight-shuttered windows a dry, whistling wind from the south filled the air with dust that eddied between the cobblestones and hazed the stars. But here all was jovial confusion.

The Gray Mouser was one of a dozen at the gaming table. He was dressed all in gray—jerkin, silken shirt, and mouseskin cap—but his dark, flashing eyes and inscrutable smile made him seem more alive than any of the others, save for the huge copper-haired barbarian next him, who roared frequent laughter and drank tankards of the sour, heavy wine of Lankhmar as if it were beer.

"They say you're a skillful swordsman and have come close to death many times," continued the small, pale man in the black robe, his thin lips barely parting as he spoke the words.

But the Mouser had made his throw, and the odd dice of Lankhmar had stopped with the symbols of the eel and serpent uppermost, and he was raking in triangular golden coins. The barbarian answered for him.

"Yes, the gray one handles a sword daintily enough—almost as well as myself. He's also a great cheat at dice."

"Are you, then, Fafhrd the Northerner," said the other, "and do you, too, think a man can cheat death, be he ever so cunning a cheat at dice?"

The barbarian showed his white teeth in a grin and peered puzzledly at the small, pale man whose somber appearance and manner contrasted so strangely with the revelers thronging the low-ceilinged tavern fumy with wine.

"You guess right again," he said in a bantering tone. "I am Fafhrd the Northerner, and ready to put my wits against any doom." He nudged his companion. "Look, Mouser, what do you think of this little black-coated mouse who's sneaked in through a crack in the floor and wants to talk with you and me about death."

The man in black did not seem to notice the jesting insult. Again his bloodless lips hardly moved, yet his words were unaffected by the surrounding clamor, and impinged on the ears of Fafhrd and the Gray Mouser with peculiar clarity.

"It is said you two came close to death in the Forbidden City of the Black Idols, and in the stone trap of Angarngi, and on the misty island in the Sea of Monsters. It is also said that you have walked with doom on the Cold Waste and through the Mazes of Klesht. But who may be sure of these things, and whether death and doom were truly near? Who knows but what you are both braggarts who have boasted once too often? Now I have heard tell that death sometimes calls to a man in a voice only he can hear. Then he must rise and leave his friends and go to whatever place death shall bid him, and there meet his doom. Has death ever called to you in such a fashion?"

Fafhrd might have laughed, but did not. The Mouser had a witty rejoiner on the tip of his tongue, but instead he heard himself saying: "In what words might death call?"

"That would depend," said the small man. "He might look at two such as you and say 'The Bleak Shore.' Nothing more than that. 'The Bleak Shore.' And you would have to go."

This time Fafhrd tried to laugh, but the laugh never came. Both of them could only meet the gaze of the small man with the white, bulging forehead, stare stupidly into his cold, cavernous eyes. Around them the tavern roared with mirth at some jest. A drunken guardsman was bellowing a song. The gamblers called impatiently to the Mouser to stake his next wager. A giggling woman in red and gold stumbled past the small, pale man, almost brushing the black cowl that covered his pate. But he did not move. And Fafhrd and the Gray Mouser continued to stare—fascinatedly, helplessly —into his chill, black eyes, which now seemed to them twin tunnels leading into a far and evil distance. Something deeper than fear gripped them in iron paralysis. The tavern became faint and soundless, as if viewed through many thicknesses of glass. They saw only the eyes and what lay beyond the eyes, something desolate, drear, and deadly.

"The Bleak Shore," he repeated, "and they would have to go."

Then those in the tavern saw Fafhrd and the Gray Mouser rise, and without sign or word of leave-taking, walk together to the low oaken door. A guardsman cursed as the huge Northerner blindly shoved him out of the way. There were a few shouted questions and mocking comments—the Mouser had been winning—but these were quickly hushed, for all perceived something strange and alien in the manner of the two. Of the small, pale, black-robed man none took notice. They saw the door open. They heard the dry moaning of the wind and a hollow flapping that probably came from the awnings. They saw an eddy of dust swirl up from the threshold. Then the door was closed and Fafhrd and the Mouser were gone.

No one saw them on their way to the great stone docks

that bank the River Hlal from one end of Lankhmar to the other. No one saw Fafhrd's north-rigged, red-sailed sloop cast off and slip out into the current that slides down to the squally Inner Sea. The night was dark and the dust kept men indoors. But the next day they were gone, and the boat with them, and its Mingol crew of four—these being slave prisoners, sworn to life service, whom Fafhrd and the Mouser had brought back from their foray against the Forbidden City of the Black Idols.

About a fortnight later a tale came back to Lankhmar from Earth's End, the little harbor town that lies farthest of all towns to the west, on the very margin of the shipless Outer Sea; a tale of how a north-rigged sloop had come into port to take on an unusually large amount of food and water —unusually large because there were only six in the crew: a sullen, white-skinned northern barbarian; an unsmiling little man in gray; and four squat, stolid, black-haired Mingols. Afterward the sloop had sailed straight into the sunset. The people of Earth's End had watched the red sail until nightfall, shaking their heads at its audacious progress. When this tale was repeated in Lankhmar, there were others who shook their heads, and some who spoke significantly of the peculiar behavior of the two companions on the night of their departure. And as the weeks dragged out into months and the months slowly succeeded one another, there were many who talked of Fafhrd and the Gray Mouser as two dead men.

Then Ourph the Mingol appeared and told his curious story to the dockmen of Lankhmar. There was some difference of opinion as to the validity of the story, for although Ourph spoke the soft language of Lankhmar moderately well, he was an outsider, and after he was gone, no one could prove that he was or was not one of the four Mingols who had sailed with the north-rigged sloop. Moreover, his story did not answer several puzzling questions, which is one of the reasons that many thought it untrue.

"They were mad," said Ourph, "or else under a curse, those two men, the great one and the small one. I suspected it when they spared our lives under the very walls of the Forbidden City. I knew it for certain when they sailed west and west and west, never reefing, never changing course, always keeping the star of the ice fields on our right hand. They talked little, they slept little, they laughed not at all. Ola, they were cursed!

As for us four—Teevs, Larlt, Ouwenyis, and I—we were ignored but not abused. We had our amulets to keep off evil magics. We were sworn slaves to the death. We were men of the Forbidden City. We made no mutiny.

"For many days we sailed. The sea was stormless and empty around us, and small, very small; it looked as if it bent down out of sight to the north and the south and the awful west, as if the sea ended an hour's sail from where we were. And then it began to look that way to the east, too. But the great Northerner's hand rested on the steering oar like a curse, and the small gray one's hand was as firm. We four sat mostly in the bow, for there was little enough sail-tending, and diced our destinies at night and morning, and gambled for our amulets and money and clothes—we would have played for our hides and bones, were we not slaves.

"To keep track of the days, I tied a cord round my right thumb and moved it over a finger each day until it passed from right little finger to left little finger and came to my left thumb. Then I put it on Teev's right thumb. When it came to his left thumb he gave it to Larlt. So we numbered the days and knew them. And each day the sky became emptier and the sea smaller, until it seemed that the end of the sea was but a bowshot away from our stem and sides and stern. Teevs said that we were upon an enchanted patch of water that was being drawn through the air toward the red star that is Hell. Surely Teevs may have been right. There cannot be so much water to the west. I have crossed the Inner Sea and the Sea of Monsters—and I say so.

"It was when the cord was around Larlt's left ring finger that the great storm came at us from the southeast. For three days it blew stronger and stronger, smiting the water into great seething waves; crags and gullies piled mast-high with foam. No other men have seen such waves nor should see them; they are not churned for us or for our oceans. Then I had further proof that our masters were under a curse. They took no notice of the storm; they let it reef their sails for them. They took no notice when Teevs was washed overboard, when we were half swamped and filled to the gunwales with spume, our bailing buckets foaming like tankards of beer. They stood in the stern, both braced against the steering oar, both drenched by the following waves, staring straight ahead, seeming to hold converse with creatures that only the bewitched can hear. Ola! They were accursed! Some evil demon was preserving their lives for a dark reason of his own. How else came we safe through the storm?

"For when the cord was on Larlt's left thumb, the towering waves and briny foam gave way to a great black sea swell that the whistling gale from the west rippled but did not whiten. When the dawn came and we first saw it, Ouwenyis cried out that we were riding by magics upon a sea of black sand; and Larlt averred that we were fallen during the storm into the ocean of sulphurous oil that some say lies under the earth—for Larlt has seen the black, bubbling lakes of the Far East; and I remembered what Teevs had said and wondered if our patch of water had not been carried through the thin air and plunged into a wholly different sea on a wholly different world. But the small gray one heard our talk and dipped a bucket over the side and soused us with it, so that we knew our hull was still in water and that the water still was salt—wherever that water might be.

"And then he bid us patch the sails and make the sloop shipshape. By midday we were flying west at a speed even greater than we had made during the storm, but so long were the swells and so swift did they move with us that we could only climb five or six in a whole day. By the Black Idols, but they were long!

"And so the cord moved across Ouwenyis' fingers. But the clouds were as leaden dark above us as was the strange sea heavy around our hull, and we knew not if the light that came through them was that of the sun or of some wizard moon, and when we caught sight of the stars they seemed strange. And still the white hand of the Northerner lay heavy on the steering oar, and still he and the gray one stared straight ahead. But on the third day of our flight across that black expanse the Northerner broke silence. A mirthless, terrible smile twisted his lips, and I heard him mutter 'The Bleak Shore.' Nothing more than that. The gray one nodded, as if there were some portentous magic in the words. Four times I heard the words pass the Northerner's lips, so that they were imprinted on my memory.

"The days grew darker and colder, and the clouds slid lower and lower, threatening, like the roof of a great cavern. And when the cord was on Ouwenyis' pointing finger we saw a leaden and motionless extent ahead of us, looking like the swells, but rising above them, and we knew that we were come to 'The Bleak Shore.'

"Higher and higher that shore rose, until we could distinguish the towering basalt crags, rounded like the sea swell, studded here and there with gray boulders, whitened in spots as if by the droppings of birds—yet we saw no birds. Above the cliffs were the dark clouds, and below them was a strip of pale sand, nothing more. Then the Northerner bent the steering oar and sent us straight in, as though he intended our destruction; but at the last moment he passed us at mast length by a rounded reef that hardly rose above the crest of the swell and found us harbor room. We sent the anchor over and rode safe.

"Then the Northerner and the gray one, moving like men in a dream, accoutered themselves, a shirt of light chain mail and a rounded, uncrested helmet for each—both helmets and shirts white with salt from the foam and spray of the storm. And they bound their swords to their sides, and wrapped great cloaks about them, and took a little food and a little water, and bade us unship the small boat. And I rowed them ashore and they stepped out onto the beach and walked toward the cliffs. Then, although I was much frightened, I cried out after them, 'Where are you going? Shall we follow? What shall we do?' For several moments there was no reply. Then, without turning his head, the gray one answered, his voice a low, hoarse whisper. And he said, 'Do not follow. We are dead men. Go back if you can.'

"And I shuddered and bowed my head to his words and rowed out to the ship. Ouwenyis and Larlt and I watched them climb the high, rounded crags. They grew smaller and smaller, until the Northerner was no more than a tiny, slim beetle and his gray companion almost invisible, save when they crossed a whitened space. Then a wind came down from the crags and blew the swell away from the shore, and we knew we could make sail. But we stayed—for were we not sworn slaves? And am I not a Mingol?

"As evening darkened, the wind blew stronger, and our desire to depart—if only to drown in the unknown sea—became greater. For we did not like the strangely rounded basalt crags of The Bleak Shore; we did not like it that we saw no gulls or hawks or birds of any kind in the leaden air, no seaweed on the beach. And we all three began to catch glimpses of something shimmering and black at the summit of the cliffs. Yet it was not until the third hour of night that we upped anchor and left The Bleak Shore behind.

"There was another great storm after we were out several days, and perhaps it hurled us back into the seas we know. Ouwenyis was washed overboard and Larlt went mad from thirst, and toward the end I knew not myself what was happening. Only I was cast up on the southern coast near Quarmall and, after many difficulties, am come here to Lankhmar. But my dreams are haunted by those black cliffs and by visions of the whitening bones of my masters, and their grinning skulls staring empty-eyed at something strange and deadly."

Unconscious of the fatigue that stiffened his muscles, the Gray Mouser wormed his way past the last boulder, finding shallow handholds and footholds at the juncture of the granite and black basalt, and finally stood erect on the top of the rounded crags that walled The Bleak Shore. He was aware that Fafhrd the Northerner stood at his side, a vague, hulking figure in whitened chain-mail vest and helmet. But he saw Fafhrd vaguely, as if through many thicknesses of glass. The only things he saw clearly—and it seemed he had been looking at them for an eternity—were two cavernous, tunnellike black eyes, and beyond them something desolate and deadly, which had once been far away but was now close at hand. So it had been, ever since he had risen from the gaming table in the low-ceilinged tavern in Lankhmar. Vaguely he remembered the staring people of Earth's End, the foam and fury of the storm, the curve of the black sea swell, and the look of terror on the face of Ourph the Mingol; these memories, too, came to him as if through many thicknesses of glass. Dimly he realized that he and his companions were under a curse, and that they were now come to the source of that curse.

For the flat landscape that spread out before them was without sign of life. In front of them the basalt dipped down to form a large hollow floored with black sand—tiny particles of iron ore. In the sand were half embedded more than two-score of what seemed to the Gray Mouser to be inky-black, oval boulders of various sizes. But they were too perfectly rounded, too regular in form, and slowly it was borne in on the Mouser's consciousness that they were not boulders, but monstrous black eggs, a few small, some so large that a man could not have clasped his arms around them, one huge as a hemispherical tent.

Scattered over the sand were bones, large and small. The Mouser recognized the tusked skull of a boar, and two smaller ones—wolves. There was the skeleton of some great predatory cat, crouched as if for attack. Beside it lay the bones of a horse, and beyond them the rib case of a man or ape. The bones lay all around the huge black eggs—a whitely gleaming circle.

From somewhere a toneless voice sounded, thin but clear, like a command, saying: "For warriors, a warrior's doom."

The Mouser knew the voice, for it had been echoing in his ears for weeks, ever since it had first come from the lips of a pale, bulging-foreheaded little man in a black robe sitting near him in a tavern in Lankhmar.

Then he saw that what lay before him was not utterly lifeless. Movement of a sort had come to The Bleak Shore. A crack had appeared in one of the great black eggs, and then in another, and the cracks were branching, widening as bits of shell fell to the black, sandy floor.

The Mouser knew that this was happening in answer to the voice. He knew this was the end to which the thin voice had called him across the Outer Sea. Powerless to move farther, he dully watched the slow progress of this monstrous birth. Under the darkening, leaden sky he watched twin deaths hatching out for him and his companion.

The first hint to their nature came in the form of a long, swordlike claw which struck out through a crack, widening it farther. Fragments of shell fell more swiftly.

The two creatures which emerged in the gathering dusk were monstrous even to the Mouser's drugged mind. Shambling things, erect like men but taller, with reptilian heads boned and crested like helmets, feet clawed like a lizard's, shoulders topped with bony spikes, forelimbs each terminating in a single yard-long claw. In the semidarkness they seemed like hideous caricatures of fighting men, armored and bearing swords. Dusk did not hide the yellow of their blinking eyes.

Then the voice called again: "For warriors, a warrior's doom."

At those words the bonds of paralysis dropped from the Mouser. For an instant he thought he was waking from a dream. But then he saw the new-hatched creatures racing toward them, a shrill, eager screeching issuing from their long muzzles. From beside him he heard a quick, rasping sound as Fafhrd's sword whipped from its scabbard. Then the Mouser drew his own blade, and a moment later it crashed against a steellike claw which thrust at his throat. Simultaneously, Fafhrd parried a like blow from the other monster.

What followed was nightmare. Claws that were swords slashed and stabbed. Not so swiftly that they could not be parried, though there were four against two. Counterthrusts glanced off impenetrable bony armor. Both creatures suddenly wheeled, striking at the Mouser. Fafhrd drove in from the side, saving him. Slowly the two companions were driven back toward where the crag sheered off. The beasts seemed tireless, creatures of bone and metal rather than flesh. The Mouser foresaw the end. He and Fafhrd might hold them off for a while longer, but eventually fatigue would supervene; their parries would become slower, weaker; the beasts would have them.

As if in anticipation of this, the Mouser felt a claw nick his wrist. It was then that he remembered the dark, cavernous eyes that had drawn them across the Outer Sea, the voice that had loosed doom upon them. He was gripped with a strange, mad rage—not against the beasts but their master. From down in the black, sanded hollow he seemed to see the black, dead eyes staring at him. Then he lost control of his actions. When the two monsters next attempted a double attack on Fafhrd he did not turn to help, but instead dodged past and dashed down into the hollow, toward the embedded eggs.

Left to face the monsters alone, Fafhrd fought like a madman himself, his great sword whistling as his last resources of energy jolted his muscles. He hardly noticed when one of the beasts turned back to pursue his comrade.

The Mouser stood among the eggs, facing one of a glossier hue and smaller than most. Vindictively he brought his sword crashing down upon it. The blow numbed his hand. It shattered open.

Then the Mouser knew the source of the evil of The Bleak Shore, spawned by hell knew what alien creature, lying here like a foul blot, spreading death and calling men to doom. Behind him he heard the scrabbling steps and eager screeching of the monster chosen for his destruction. But he did not turn. Instead, he raised his sword and brought it down whirring on the half-embryonic creature gloating in secret over the men he had called to death, down on the bulging forehead of the small pale man with the thin lips.

Then he waited for the finishing blow of the claw. It did not come. Turning, he saw the monster sprawled motionless on the black sand. Around him, the deadly eggs were crumbling to dust. Silhouetted against the lesser darkness of the sky, he saw Fafhrd stumbling toward him, sobbing out vague words of relief and wonder in a deep, throaty voice. Death was gone from The Bleak Shore, the curse cut off at the root. From out of the night sounded the exultant cry of a sea bird, and Fafhrd and the Mouser thought of the long, trackless road leading back to Lankhmar.

One question you might ask, if you ask that kind of question, is: who does magic happen to? King's sons, yes; goatherds, and virtuous maidens, certainly; sometimes nowadays, writers, honeymooners, melancholy fellows in boarding houses, and of course Mad Scientists. That, at any rate, was the way it was up to the first issue of Unknown, *in March, 1939. Readers who stopped shuddering after finishing Eric Frank Russell's* Sinister Barrier, *the lead story, discovered a new kind of hero, or straight man, for fantasy in Greenberg the concessionaire, who learned the importance of H2O the hard way.*

Trouble With Water

H. L. Gold

Greenberg did not deserve his surroundings. He was the first fisherman of the season, which guaranteed him a fine catch; he sat in a dry boat—one without a single leak—far out on a lake that was ruffled only enough to agitate his artificial fly. The sun was warm, the air was cool; he sat comfortably on a cushion; he had brought a hearty lunch; and two bottles of beer hung over the stern in the cold water.

Any other man would have been soaked with joy to be fishing on such a splendid day. Normally, Greenberg himself would have been ecstatic, but instead of relaxing and waiting for a nibble, he was plagued by worries.

This short, slightly gross, definitely bald, eminently respectable businessman lived a gypsy life. During the summer he lived in a hotel with kitchen privileges in Rockaway; winters he lived in a hotel with kitchen privileges in Florida; and in both places he operated concessions. For years now, rain had fallen on schedule every week end, and there had been storms and floods on Decoration Day, July 4th and Labor Day. He did not love his life, but it was a way of making a living.

He closed his eyes and groaned. If he had only had a son

instead of his Rosie! Then things would have been mighty different—

For one thing, a son could run the hot dog and hamburger griddle, Esther could draw beer, and he would make soft drinks. There would be small difference in the profits, Greenberg admitted to himself; but at least those profits could be put aside for old age, instead of toward a dowry for his miserably ugly, dumpy, pitifully eager Rosie.

"All right—so what do I care if she don't get married?" he had cried to his wife a thousand times. "I'll support her. Other men can set up boys in candy stores with soda fountains that have only two spigots. Why should I have to give a boy a regular International Casino?"

"May your tongue rot in your head, you no-good piker!" she would scream. "It ain't right for a girl to be an old maid. If we have to die in the poor-house, I'll get my poor Rosie a husband. Every penny we don't need for living goes to her dowry!"

Greenberg did not hate his daughter, nor did he blame her for his misfortunes; yet, because of her, he was fishing with a broken rod that he had to tape together.

That morning his wife opened her eyes and saw him packing his equipment. She instantly came awake. "Go ahead!" she shrilled—speaking in a conversational tone was not one of her accomplishments—"Go fishing, you loafer! Leave me here alone. I can connect the beer pipes and the gas for soda water. I can buy ice cream, frankfurters, rolls, sirup, and watch the gas and electric men at the same time. Go ahead—go fishing!"

"I ordered everything," he mumbled soothingly. "The gas and electric won't be turned on today. I only wanted to go fishing—it's my last chance. Tomorrow we open the concession. Tell the truth, Esther, can I go fishing after we open?"

"I don't care about that. Am I your wife or ain't I, that you should go ordering everything without asking me—"

He defended his actions. It was a tactical mistake. While she was still in bed, he should have picked up his equipment and left. By the time the argument got around to Rosie's dowry, she stood facing him.

"For myself I don't care," she yelled. "What kind of a monster are you that you can go fishing while your daughter eats her heart out? And on a day like this yet! You should only have to make supper and dress Rosie up. A lot you care that a nice boy is coming to supper tonight and maybe take Rosie out, you no-good father, you!"

From that point it was only one hot protest and a shrill curse to find himself clutching half a broken rod, with the other half being flung at his head.

Now he sat in his beautifully dry boat on an excellent game lake far out on Long Island, desperately aware that any average fish might collapse his taped rod.

What else could he expect? He had missed his train; he had had to wait for the boathouse proprietor; his favorite dry fly was missing; and, since morning, not a fish struck at the bait. Not a single fish!

And it was getting late. He had no more patience. He ripped the cap off a bottle of beer and drank it, in order to gain courage to change his fly for a less sporting bloodworm. It hurt him, but he wanted a fish.

The hook and the squirming worm sank. Before it came to rest, he felt a nibble. He sucked in his breath exultantly and snapped the hook deep into the fish's mouth. Sometimes, he thought philosophically, they just won't take artificial bait. He reeled in slowly.

"Oh, Lord," he prayed, "a dollar for charity—just don't let the rod bend in half where I taped it!"

It was sagging dangerously. He looked at it unhappily and raised his ante to five dollars; even at that price it looked impossible. He dipped his rod into the water, parallel with the line, to remove the strain. He was glad no one could see him do it. The line reeled in without a fight.

"Have I—God forbid!—got an eel or something not kosher?" he mumbled. "A plague on you—why don't you fight?"

He did not really care what it was—even an eel—anything at all.

He pulled in a long, pointed, brimless green hat.

For a moment he glared at it. His mouth hardened. Then, viciously, he yanked the hat off the hook, threw it on the floor and trampled on it. He rubbed his hands together in anguish.

"All day I fish," he wailed, "two dollars for train fare, a dollar for a boat, a quarter for bait, a new rod I got to buy—and a five-dollar-mortgage charity has got on me. For what? For you, you hat, you!"

Out in the water an extremely civil voice asked politely: "May I have my hat, please?"

Greenberg glowered up. He saw a little man come swimming vigorously through the water toward him: small arms crossed with enormous dignity, vast ears on a pointed face propelling him quite rapidly and efficiently. With serious determination he drove through the water, and, at the starboard rail, his amazing ears kept him stationary while he looked gravely at Greenberg.

"You are stamping on my hat," he pointed out without anger.

To Greenberg this was highly unimportant. "With the ears you're swimming," he grinned in a superior way. "Do you look funny!"

"How else could I swim?" the little man asked politely.

"With the arms and legs, like a regular human being, of course."

"But I am not a human being. I am a water gnome, a relative of the more common mining gnome. I cannot swim with my arms, because they must be crossed to give an appearance of dignity suitable to a water gnome; and my feet are used for writing and holding things. On the other hand, my ears are perfectly adapted for propulsion in water. Consequently, I employ them for that purpose. But please, my hat—there are several matters requiring my immediate attention, and I must not waste time."

Greenberg's unpleasant attitude toward the remarkably civil gnome is easily understandable. He had found someone he could feel superior to, and, by insulting him, his depressed ego could expand. The water gnome certainly looked inoffensive enough, being only two feet tall.

"What you got that's so important to do, Big Ears?" he asked nastily.

Greenberg hoped the gnome would be offended. He was not, since his ears, to him, were perfectly normal, just as you would not be insulted if a member of a race of atrophied beings were to call you "Big Muscles." You might even feel flattered.

"I really must hurry," the gnome said, almost anxiously. "But if I have to answer your questions in order to get back my hat—we are engaged in restocking the Eastern waters with fish. Last year there was quite a drain. The bureau of fisheries is coöperating with us to some extent, but, of course, we cannot depend too much on them. Until the population rises to normal, every fish has instructions not to nibble."

Greenberg allowed himself a smile, an annoyingly skeptical smile.

"My main work," the gnome went on resignedly, "is control of the rainfall over the Eastern seaboard. Our fact-finding committee, which is scientifically situated in the meteorological center of the continent, coördinates the rainfall needs of the entire continent; and when they determine the amount of rain needed in particular spots of the East, I make it rain to that extent. Now may I have my hat, please?"

Greenberg laughed coarsely. "The first lie was big enough —about telling the fish not to bite. You make it rain like I'm President of the United States!" He bent toward the gnome slyly. "How's about proof?"

"Certainly, if you insist." The gnome raised his patient, triangular face toward a particularly clear blue spot in the sky, a trifle to one side of Greenberg. "Watch that bit of the sky."

Greenberg looked up humorously. Even when a small dark cloud rapidly formed in the previously clear spot, his grin remained broad. It could have been coincidental. But then large drops of undeniable rain fell over a twenty-foot circle; and Greenberg's mocking grin shrank and grew sour.

He glared hatred at the gnome, finally convinced. "So you're the dirty crook who makes it rain on week ends!"

"Usually on week ends during the summer," the gnome admitted. "Ninety-two percent of water consumption is on weekdays. Obviously we must replace that water. The week ends, of course, are the logical time."

"But, you thief!" Greenberg cried hysterically, "you murderer! What do you care what you do to my concession with your rain? It ain't bad enough business would be rotten even without rain, you got to make floods!"

"I'm sorry," the gnome replied, untouched by Greenberg's rhetoric. "We do not create rainfall for the benefit of men. We are here to protect the fish.

"Now please give me my hat. I have wasted enough time, when I should be preparing the extremely heavy rain needed for this coming week end."

Greenberg jumped to his feet in the unsteady boat. "Rain this week end—when I can maybe make a profit for a change! A lot you care if you ruin business. May you and your fish die a horrible, lingering death."

And he furiously ripped the green hat to pieces and hurled them at the gnome.

"I'm really sorry you did that," the little fellow said calmly, his huge ears treading water without the slightest increase of pace to indicate his anger. "We Little Folk have no tempers to lose. Nevertheless, occasionally we find it necessary to discipline certain of your people, in order to retain our dignity. I am not malignant; but, since you hate water and those who live in it, water and those who live in it will keep away from you."

With his arms still folded in great dignity, the tiny water gnome flipped his vast ears and disappeared in a neat surface dive.

Greenberg glowered at the spreading circles of waves. He did not grasp the gnome's final restraining order; he did not even attempt to interpret it. Instead he glared angrily out of the corner of his eye at the phenomenal circle of rain that fell from a perfectly clear sky. The gnome must have remembered it at length, for a moment later the rain stopped. Like shutting off a faucet, Greenberg unwillingly thought.

"Good-by, week-end business," he growled. "If Esther finds out I got into an argument with the guy who makes it rain—"

He made an underhand cast, hoping for just one fish. The line flew out over the water; then the hook arched upward and came to rest several inches above the surface, hanging quite steadily and without support in the air.

"Well, go down in the water, damn you!" Greenberg said viciously, and he swished his rod back and forth to pull the hook down from its ridiculous levitation. It refused.

Muttering something incoherent about being hanged before

he'd give in, Greenberg hurled his useless rod at the water. By this time he was not surprised when it hovered in the air above the lake. He merely glanced red-eyed at it, tossed out the remains of the gnome's hat, and snatched up the oars.

When he pulled back on them to row to land, they did not touch the water—naturally. Instead they flashed unimpeded through the air, and Greenberg tumbled into the bow.

"A-ha!" he grated. "Here's where the trouble begins." He bent over the side. As he had suspected, the keel floated a remarkable distance above the lake.

By rowing against the air, he moved with maddening slowness toward shore, like a medieval conception of a flying machine. His main concern was that no one should see him in his humiliating position.

At the hotel he tried to sneak past the kitchen to the bathroom. He knew that Esther waited to curse him for fishing the day before opening, but more especially on the very day that a nice boy was coming to see her Rosie. If he could dress in a hurry, she might have less to say—

"Oh, there you are, you good-for-nothing!"

He froze to a halt.

"Look at you!" she screamed shrilly. "Filthy—you stink from fish!"

"I didn't catch anything, darling," he protested timidly.

"You stink anyhow. Go take a bath, may you drown in it! Get dressed in two minutes or less, and entertain the boy when he gets here. Hurry!"

He locked himself in, happy to escape her voice, started the water in the tub, and stripped from the waist up. A hot bath, he hoped, would rid him of his depressed feeling.

First, no fish; now, rain on week ends! What would Esther say—if she knew, of course. And, of course, he would not tell her.

"Let myself in for a lifetime of curses!" he sneered. "Ha!"

He clamped a new blade into his razor, opened the tube of shaving cream, and stared objectively at the mirror. The dominant feature of the soft, chubby face that stared back was its ugly black stubble; but he set his stubborn chin and glowered. He really looked quite fierce and indomitable. Unfortunately, Esther never saw his face in that uncharacteristic pose, otherwise she would speak more softly.

"Herman Greenberg never gives in!" he whispered between savagely hardened lips. "Rain on week ends, no fish—anything he wants; a lot I care! Believe me, he'll come crawling to me before I go to him."

He gradually became aware that his shaving brush was not getting wet. When he looked down and saw the water dividing into streams that flowed around it, his determined face slipped and grew desperately anxious. He tried to trap the water—by catching it in his cupped hands, by creeping up on it from behind, as if it were some shy animal, and shoving his brush at it—but it broke and ran away from his touch. Then he jammed his palm against the faucet. Defeated, he heard it gurgle back down the pipe, probably as far as the main.

"What do I do now?" he groaned. "Will Esther give it to me if I don't take a shave! But how? . . . I can't shave without water."

Glumly, he shut off the bath, undressed and stepped into the tub. He lay down to soak. It took a moment of horrified stupor to realize that he was completely dry and that he lay in a waterless bathtub. The water, in one surge of revulsion, had swept out onto the floor.

"Herman, stop splashing!" his wife yelled. "I just washed that floor. If I find one little puddle I'll murder you!"

Greenberg surveyed the instep-deep pool over the bathroom floor. "Yes, my love," he croaked unhappily.

With an inadequate washrag he chased the elusive water, hoping to mop it all up before it could seep through to the apartment below. His washrag remained dry, however, and he knew that the ceiling underneath was dripping. The water was still on the floor.

In despair, he sat on the edge of the bathtub. For some time he sat in silence. Then his wife banged on the door, urging him to come out. He started and dressed moodily.

When he sneaked out and shut the bathroom door tightly on the flood inside, he was extremely dirty and his face *was* raw where he had experimentally attempted to shave with a dry razor.

"Rosie!" he called in a hoarse whisper. "Sh! Where's mamma?"

His daughter sat on the studio couch and applied nail-polish to her stubby fingers. "You look terrible," she said in a conversational tone. "Aren't you going to shave?"

He recoiled at the sound of her voice, which, to him, roared out like a siren. "Quiet, Rosie! Sh!" And for further emphasis, he shoved his lips out against a warning finger. He heard his wife striding heavily around the kitchen. "Rosie," he cooed, "I'll give you a dollar if you'll mop up the water I spilled in the bathroom."

"I can't papa," she stated firmly. "I'm all dressed."

"Two dollars, Rosie—all right, two and a half, you blackmailer."

He flinched when he heard her gasp in the bathroom; but, when she came out with soaked shoes, he fled downstairs. He wandered aimlessly toward the village.

Now he was in for it, he thought; screams from Esther, tears from Rosie—plus a new pair of shoes for Rosie and two and a half dollars. It would be worse, though, if he could not get rid of his whiskers—

Rubbing the tender spots where his dry razor had raked his face, he mused blankly at a drugstore window. He saw nothing to help him, but he went inside anyhow and stood hopefully at the drug counter. A face peered at him through a space scratched in the wall case mirror, and the druggist came out. A nice-looking, intelligent fellow, Greenberg saw at a glance.

"What you got for shaving that I can use without water?" he asked.

"Skin irritation, eh?" the pharmacist replied. "I got something very good for that."

"No. It's just— Well, I don't like to shave with water."

The druggist seemed disappointed. "Well, I got brushless shaving cream." Then he brightened. "But I got an electric razor—much better."

"How much?" Greenberg asked cautiously.

"Only fifteen dollars, and it lasts a lifetime."

"Give me the shaving cream," Greenberg said coldly.

With the tactical science of a military expert, he walked around until some time after dark. Only then did he go back to the hotel, to wait outside. It was after seven, he was getting hungry, and the people who entered the hotel he knew as permanent summer guests. At last a stranger passed him and ran up the stairs.

Greenberg hesitated for a moment. The stranger was scarcely a boy, as Esther had definitely termed him, but Greenberg reasoned that her term was merely wish-fulfillment, and he jauntily ran up behind him.

He allowed a few minutes to pass, for the man to introduce

himself and let Esther and Rosie don their company manners. Then, secure in the knowledge that there would be no scene until the guest left, he entered.

He waded through a hostile atmosphere, urbanely shook hands with Sammie Katz, who was a doctor—probably, Greenberg thought shrewdly, in search of an office—and excused himself.

In the bathroom he carefully read the direction for using brushless shaving cream. He felt less confident when he realized that he had to wash his face thoroughly with soap and water, but without benefit of either, he spread the cream on, patted it, and waited for his beard to soften. It did not, as he discovered while shaving. He wiped his face dry. The towel was sticky and black, with whiskers suspended in paste, and, for that, he knew, there would be more hell to pay. He shrugged resignedly. He would have to spend fifteen dollars for an electric razor after all; this foolishness was costing him a fortune!

That they were waiting for him before beginning supper, was, he knew, only a gesture for the sake of company. Without changing her hard, brilliant smile, Esther whispered: "Wait! I'll get you later—"

He smiled back, his tortured, slashed face creasing painfully. All that could be changed by his being enormously pleasant to Rosie's young man. If he could slip Sammie a few dollars—more expense, he groaned—to take Rosie out, Esther would forgive everything.

He was too engaged in beaming and putting Sammie at ease to think of what would happen after he ate caviar canapes. Under other circumstances Greenberg would have been repulsed by Sammie's ultra-professional waxed mustache—an offensively small, pointed thing—and his commercial attitude toward poor Rosie; but Greenberg regarded him as a potential savior.

"You open an office yet, Doctor Katz?"

"Not yet. You know how things are. Anyhow, call me Sammie."

Greenberg recognized the gambit with satisfaction, since it seemed to please Esther so much. At one stroke Sammie had ingratiated himself and begun bargaining negotiations.

Without another word, Greenberg lifted his spoon to attack the soup. It would be easy to snare this eager doctor. A *doctor!* No wonder Esther and Rosie were so puffed with joy.

In the proper company way, he pushed his spoon away from him. The soup spilled onto the tablecloth.

"Not so hard, you dope," Esther hissed.

He drew the spoon toward him. The soup leaped off it like a live thing and splashed over him—turning, just before contact, to fall on the floor. He gulped and pushed the bowl away. This time the soup poured over the side of the plate and lay in a huge puddle on the table.

"I didn't want any soup anyhow," he said in a horrible attempt at levity. Lucky for him, he thought wildly, that Sammie was there to pacify Esther with his smooth college talk—not a bad fellow, Sammie, in spite of his mustache; he'd come in handy at times.

Greenberg lapsed into a paralysis of fear. He was thirsty after having eaten the caviar, which beats herring any time as a thirst raiser. But the knowledge that he could not touch water without having it recoil and perhaps spill, made his thirst a monumental craving. He attacked the problem cunningly.

The others were talking rapidly and rather hysterically. He waited until his courage was equal to his thirst; then he leaned over the table with a glass in his hand. "Sammie, do you mind—a little water, huh?"

Sammie poured from a pitcher while Esther watched for more of his tricks. It was to be expected, but still he was shocked when the water exploded out of the glass directly at Sammie's only suit.

"If you'll excuse me," Sammie said angrily, "I don't like to eat with lunatics."

And he left, though Esther cried and begged him to stay. Rosie was too stunned to move. But when the door closed, Greenberg raised his agonized eyes to watch his wife stalk murderously toward him.

Greenberg stood on the boardwalk outside his concession and glared blearily at the peaceful, blue, highly unpleasant ocean. He wondered what would happen if he started at the edge of the water and strode out. He could probably walk right to Europe on dry land.

It was early—much too early for business—and he was tired. Neither he nor Esther had slept; and it was practically certain that the neighbors hadn't either. But above all he was incredibly thirsty.

In a spirit of experimentation, he mixed a soda. Of course its high water content made it slop onto the floor. For breakfast he had surreptitiously tried fruit juice and coffee, without success.

With his tongue dry to the point of furriness, he sat weakly on a boardwalk bench in front of his concession. It was Friday morning, which meant that the day was clear, with a promise of intense heat. Had it been Saturday, it naturally would have been raining.

"This year," he moaned, "I'll be wiped out. If I can't mix sodas, why should beer stay in a glass for me? I thought I could hire a boy for ten dollars a week to run the hot-dog griddle; I could make sodas, and Esther could draw beer. All I can do is make hot dogs, Esther can still draw beer; but twenty or maybe twenty-five a week I got to pay a sodaman. I won't even come out square—a fortune I'll lose!"

The situation really was desperate. Concessions depend on too many factors to be anything but capriciously profitable.

His throat was fiery and his soft brown eyes held a fierce glaze when the gas and electric were turned on, the beer pipes connected, the tank of carbon dioxide hitched to the pump, and the refrigerator started.

Gradually, the beach was filling with bathers. Greenberg writhed on his bench and envied them. They could swim and drink without having liquids draw away from them as if in horror. They were not thirsty—

And then he saw his first customers approach. His business experience was that morning customers buy only soft drinks. In a mad haste he put up the shutters and fled to the hotel.

"Esther!" he cried. "I got to tell you! I can't stand it—"

Threateningly, his wife held her broom like a baseball bat. "Go back to the concession, you crazy fool. Ain't you done enough already?"

He could not be hurt more than he had been. For once he did not cringe. "You got to help me, Esther."

"Why didn't you shave, you no-good bum? Is that any way—"

"That's what I got to tell you. Yesterday I got into an argument with a water gnome—"

"A what?" Esther looked at him suspiciously.

"A water gnome," he babbled in a rush of words. "A little

man so high, with big ears that he swims with, and he makes it rain—"

"Herman!" she screamed. "Stop that nonsense. You're crazy!"

Greenberg pounded his forehead with his fist. "I *ain't* crazy. Look, Esther. Come with me into the kitchen."

She followed him readily enough, but her attitude made him feel more helpless and alone than ever. With her fists on her plump hips and her feet set wide, she cautiously watched him try to fill a glass of water.

"Don't you see?" he wailed. "It won't go in the glass. It spills over. It runs away from me."

She was puzzled. "What happened to you?"

Brokenly, Greenberg told of his encounter with the water gnome, leaving out no single degrading detail. "And now I can't touch water," he ended. "I can't drink it. I can't make sodas. On top of it all, I got such a thirst, it's killing me."

Esther's reaction was instantaneous. She threw her arms around him, drew his head down to her shoulder, and patted him comfortingly as if he were a child. "Herman, my poor Herman!" she breathed tenderly. "What did we ever do to deserve such a curse?"

"What shall I do, Esther?" he cried helplessly.

She held him at arm's length. "You got to go to a doctor," she said firmly. "How long can you go without drinking? Without water you'll die. Maybe sometimes I am a little hard on you, but you know I love you—"

"I know, mamma," he sighed. "But how can a doctor help me?"

"Am I a doctor that I should know? Go anyhow. What can you lose?"

He hesitated. "I need fifteen dollars for an electric razor," he said in a low, weak voice.

"So?" she replied. "If you got to, you got to. Go, darling. I'll take care of the concession."

Greenberg no longer felt deserted and alone. He walked almost confidently to a doctor's office. Manfully, he explained his symptoms. The doctor listened with professional sympathy, until Greenberg reached his description of the water gnome.

Then his eyes glittered and narrowed. "I know just the thing for you, Mr. Greenberg," he interrupted. "Sit there until I come back."

Greenberg sat quietly. He even permitted himself a surge of hope. But it seemed only a moment later that he was vaguely conscious of a siren screaming toward him; and then he was overwhelmed by the doctor and two internes who pounced on him and tried to squeeze him into a bag.

He resisted, of course. He was terrified enough to punch wildly. "What are you doing to me?" he shrieked. "Don't put that thing on me!"

"Easy now," the doctor soothed. "Everything will be all right."

It was on that humiliating scene that the policeman, required by law to accompany public ambulances, appeared. "What's up?" he asked.

"Don't stand there, you fathead," an interne shouted. "This man's crazy. Help us get him into this strait jacket."

But the policeman approached indecisively. "Take it easy, Mr. Greenberg. They ain't gonna hurt you while I'm here. What's it all about?"

"Mike!" Greenberg cried, and clung to his protector's sleeve. "They think I'm crazy—"

"Of course he's crazy," the doctor stated. "He came in here with a fantastic yarn about a water gnome putting a curse on him."

"What kind of a curse, Mr. Greenberg?" Mike asked cautiously.

"I got into an argument with the water gnome who makes it rain and takes care of the fish," Greenberg blurted. "I tore up his hat. Now he won't let water touch me. I can't drink, or anything—"

The doctor nodded. "There you are. Absolutely insane."

"Shut up." For a long moment Mike stared curiously at Greenberg. Then: "Did any of you scientists think of testing him? Here, Mr. Greenberg." He poured water into a paper cup and held it out.

Greenberg moved to take it. The water backed up against the cup's far lip; when he took it in his hand, the water shot out into the air.

"Crazy, is he?" Mike asked with heavy irony. "I guess you don't know there's things like gnomes and elves. Come with me, Mr. Greenberg."

They went out together and walked toward the boardwalk. Greenberg told Mike the entire story and explained how, besides being so uncomfortable to him personally, it would ruin him financially.

"Well, doctors can't help you," Mike said at length. "What do they know about the Little Folk? And I can't say I blame you for sassing the gnome. You ain't Irish or you'd have spoke with more respect to him. Anyhow, you're thirsty. Can't you drink *anything?*"

"Not a thing," Greenberg said mournfully.

They entered the concession. A single glance told Greenberg that business was very quiet, but even that could not lower his feelings more than they already were. Esther clutched him as soon as she saw them.

"Well?" she asked anxiously.

Greenberg shrugged in despair. "Nothing. He thought I was crazy."

Mike stared at the bar. Memory seemed to struggle behind his reflective eyes. "Sure," he said after a long pause. "Did you try beer, Mr. Greenberg? When I was a boy my old mother told me all about elves and gnomes and the rest of the Little Folk. She knew them, all right. They don't touch alcohol, you know. Try drawing a glass of beer—"

Greenberg trudged obediently behind the bar and held a glass under the spigot. Suddenly his despondent face brightened. Beer creamed into the glass—and stayed there! Mike and Esther grinned at each other as Greenberg threw back his head and furiously drank.

"Mike!" he crowed. "I'm saved. You got to drink with me!"

"Well—" Mike protested feebly.

By late afternoon, Esther had to close the concession and take her husband and Mike to the hotel.

The following day, being Saturday, brought a flood of rain. Greenberg nursed an imposing hang-over that was constantly aggravated by his having to drink beer in order to satisfy his recurring thirst. He thought of forbidden icebags and alkaline drinks in an agony of longing.

"I can't stand it!" he groaned. "Beer for breakfast—phooey!"

"It's better than nothing," Esther said fatalistically.

"So help me, I don't know if it is. But, darling, you ain't mad at me on account of Sammie, are you?"

She smiled gently, "Poo! Talk dowry and he'll come back quick."

"That's what I thought. But what am I going to do about my curse?"

Cheerfully, Mike furled an umbrella and strode in with a little old woman, whom he introduced as his mother. Greenberg enviously saw evidence of the effectiveness of icebags and alkaline drinks, for Mike had been just as high as he the day before.

"Mike told me about you and the gnome," the old lady said. "Now I know the Little Folk well, and I don't hold you to blame for insulting him, seeing you never met a gnome before. But I suppose you want to get rid of your curse. Are you repentant?"

Greenberg shuddered. "Beer for breakfast! Can you ask?"

"Well, just you go to this lake and give the gnome proof."

"What kind of proof?" Greenberg asked eagerly.

"Bring him sugar. The Little Folk love the stuff—"

Greenberg beamed. "Did you hear that, Esther? I'll get a barrel—"

"They love sugar, but they can't eat it," the old lady broke in. "It melts in water. You got to figure out a way so it won't. Then the little gentleman'll know you're repentant for real."

"A-ha!" Greenberg cried. "I knew there was a catch!"

There was a sympathetic silence while his agitated mind attacked the problem from all angles. Then the old lady said in awe: "The minute I saw your place I knew Mike had told the truth. I never seen a sight like it in my life—rain coming down, like the flood, everywhere else; but all around this place, in a big circle, it's dry as a bone!"

While Greenberg scarcely heard her, Mike nodded and Esther seemed peculiarly interested in the phenomenon. When he admitted defeat and came out of his reflected stupor, he was alone in the concession, with only a vague memory of Esther's saying she would not be back for several hours.

"What am I going to do?" he muttered. "Sugar that won't melt—" He drew a glass of beer and drank it thoughtfully. "Particular they got to be yet. Ain't it good enough if I bring simple sirup—that's sweet."

He pottered about the place, looking for something to do. He could not polish the fountain on the bar, and the few frankfurters boiling on the griddle probably would go to waste. The floor had already been swept. So he sat uneasily and worried his problem.

"Monday, no matter what," he resolved, "I'll go to the lake. It don't pay to go tomorrow. I'll only catch a cold because it'll rain."

At last Esther returned, smiling in a strange way. She was extremely gentle, tender and thoughtful; and for that he was appreciative. But that night and all day Sunday he understood the reason for her happiness.

She had spread word that, while it rained in every other place all over town, their concession was miraculously dry. So, besides a headache that made his body throb in rhythm to its vast pulse, Greenberg had to work like six men satisfying the crowd who mobbed the place to see the miracle and enjoy the dry warmth.

How much they took in will never be known. Greenberg made it a practice not to discuss such personal matters. But it is quite definite that not even in 1929 had he done so well over a single week end.

Very early Monday morning he was dressing quietly, not to disturb his wife. Esther, however, raised herself on her elbow and looked at him doubtfully.

"Herman," she called softly, "do you really have to go?"

He turned, puzzled. "What do you mean—do I have to go?"

"Well—" She hesitated. Then: "Couldn't you wait until the end of the season, Herman, darling?"

He staggered back a step, his face working in horror. "What kind of an idea is that for my own wife to have?" he croaked. "Beer I have to drink instead of water. How can I stand it? Do you think I *like* beer? I can't wash myself. Already people don't like to stand near me; and how will they act at the end of the season? I go around looking like a bum because my beard is too tough for an electric razor, and I'm all the time drunk—the first Greenberg to be a drunkard. I want to be respected—"

"I know, Herman, darling," she sighed. "But I thought for the sake of our Rosie— Such a business we've never done like we did this week end. If it rains every Saturday and Sunday, but not on our concession, we'll make a *fortune!*"

"Esther!" Herman cried, shocked. "Doesn't my health mean anything?"

"Of course, darling. Only I thought maybe you could stand it for—"

He snatched his hat, tie and jacket, and slammed the door. Outside, though, he stood indeterminedly. He could hear his wife crying, and he realized that, if he succeeded in getting the gnome to remove the curse, he would forfeit an opportunity to make a great deal of money.

He finished dressing more slowly. Esther was right, to a certain extent. If he could tolerate his waterless condition—

"No!" he gritted decisively. "Already my friends avoid me. It isn't right that a respectable man like me should always be drunk and not take a bath. So we'll make less money. Money isn't everything—"

And with great determination he went to the lake.

But that evening, before going home, Mike walked out of his way to stop in at the concession. He found Greenberg sitting on a chair, his head in his hands, and his body rocking slowly in anguish.

"What is it, Mr. Greenberg?" he asked gently.

Greenberg looked up. His eyes were dazed. "Oh, you, Mike," he said blankly. Then his gaze cleared, grew more intelligent, and he stood up and led Mike to the bar. Silently, they drank beer. "I went to the lake today," he said hollowly. "I walked all around it hollering like mad. The gnome didn't stick his head out of the water once."

"I know," Mike nodded sadly. "They're busy all the time."

Greenberg spread his hands imploringly. "So what can I do? I can't write him a letter or send him a telegram; he ain't got a door to knock on or a bell for me to ring. How do I get him to come up and talk?"

His shoulders sagged. "Here, Mike. Have a cigar. You been a real good friend, but I guess we're licked."

They stood in an awkward silence. Finally Mike blurted: "Real hot, today. A regular scorcher."

"Yeah. Esther says business was pretty good, if it keeps up."

Mike fumbled at the Cellophane wrapper. Greenberg said: "Anyhow, suppose I did talk to the gnome. What about the sugar?"

The silence dragged itself out, became tense and uncomfortable. Mike was distinctly embarrassed. His brusque nature was not adapted for comforting discouraged friends.

With immense concentration he rolled the cigar between his fingers and listened for a rustle.

"Day like this's hell on cigars," he mumbled, for the sake of conversation. "Dries them like nobody's business. This one ain't, though."

"Yeah," Greenberg said abstractedly. "Cellophane keeps them—"

They looked suddenly at each other, their faces clean of expression.

"Holy smoke!" Mike yelled.

"Cellophane on sugar!" Greenberg choked out.

"Yeah," Mike whispered in awe. "I'll switch my day off with Joe, and I'll go to the lake with you tomorrow. I'll call for you early."

Greenberg pressed his hand, too strangled by emotion for speech. When Esther came to relieve him, he left her at the concession with only the inexperienced griddle boy to assist her, while he searched the village for cubes of sugar wrapped in Cellophane.

The sun had scarcely risen when Mike reached the hotel, but Greenberg had long been dressed and stood on the porch waiting impatiently. Mike was genuinely anxious for his friend. Greenberg staggered along toward the station, his eyes almost crossed with the pain of a terrific hang-over.

They stopped at a cafeteria for breakfast. Mike ordered orange juice, bacon and eggs, and coffee half-and-half. When he heard the order, Greenberg had to gag down a lump in his throat.

"What'll you have?" the counterman asked.

Greenberg flushed. "Beer," he said hoarsely.

"You kidding me?" Greenberg shook his head, unable to speak. "Want anything with it? Cereal, pie, toast—"

"Just beer." And he forced himself to swallow it. "So help me," he hissed at Mike, "another beer for breakfast will kill me!"

"I know how it is," Mike said around a mouthful of food.

On the train they attempted to make plans. But they were faced by a phenomenon that neither had encountered before, and so they got nowhere. They walked glumly to the lake, fully aware that they would have to employ the empirical method of discarding tactics that did not work.

"How about a boat?" Mike suggested.

"It won't stay in the water with me in it. And you can't row it."

"Well, what'll we do then?"

Greenberg bit his lip and stared at the beautiful blue lake. There the gnome lived, so near to them. "Go through the woods along the shore, and holler like hell. I'll go the opposite way. We'll pass each other and meet at the boathouse. If the gnome comes up, yell for me."

"O. K.," Mike said, not very confidently.

The lake was quite large and they walked slowly around it, pausing often to get the proper stance for particularly emphatic shouts. But two hours later, when they stood opposite each other with the full diameter of the lake between them, Greenberg heard Mike's hoarse voice: "Hey, gnome!"

"Hey, gnome!" Greenberg yelled. "Come on up!"

An hour later they crossed paths. They were tired, discouraged, and their throats burned; and only fishermen disturbed the lake's surface.

"The hell with this," Mike said. "It ain't doing any good. Let's go back to the boathouse."

"What'll we do?" Greenberg rasped. "I can't give up!"

They trudged back around the lake, shouting half-heartedly. At the boathouse, Greenberg had to admit that he was beaten. The boathouse owner marched threateningly toward him.

"Why don't you maniacs get away from here?" he barked. "What's the idea of hollering and scaring away the fish? The guys are sore—"

"We're not going to holler any more," Greenberg said. "It's no use."

When they bought beer and Mike, on an impulse, hired a boat, the owner cooled off with amazing rapidity, and went off to unpack bait.

"What did you get a boat for?" Greenberg asked. "I can't ride in it."

"You're not going to. You're gonna walk."

"Around the lake again?" Greenberg cried.

"Nope. Look, Mr. Greenberg. Maybe the gnome can't hear us through all that water. Gnomes ain't hardhearted. If he heard us and thought you were sorry, he'd take his curse off you in a jiffy."

"Maybe." Greenberg was not convinced. "So where do I come in?"

"The way I figure it, some way or other you push water

away, but the water pushes you away just as hard. Anyhow, I hope so. If it does, you can walk on the lake." As he spoke, Mike had been lifting large stones and dumping them on the bottom of the boat. "Give me a hand with these."

Any activity, however useless, was better than none, Greenberg felt. He helped Mike fill the boat until just the gunwales were above water. Then Mike got in and shoved off.

"Come on," Mike said. "Try to walk on the water."

Greenberg hesitated. "Suppose I can't?"

"Nothing'll happen to you. You can't get wet; so you won't drown."

The logic of Mike's statement reassured Greenberg. He stepped out boldly. He experienced a peculiar sense of accomplishment when the water hastily retreated under his feet into pressure bowls, and an unseen, powerful force buoyed him upright across the lake's surface. Though his footing was not too secure, with care he was able to walk quite swiftly.

"Now what?" he asked, almost happily.

Mike had kept pace with him in the boat. He shipped his oars and passed Greenberg a rock. "We'll drop them all over the lake—make it damned noisy down there and upset the place. That'll get him up."

They were more hopeful now, and their comments, "Here's one that'll wake him," and "I'll hit him right on the noodle with this one," served to cheer them still further. And less than half the rocks had been dropped when Greenberg halted, a boulder in his hands. Something inside him wrapped itself tightly around his heart and his jaw dropped.

Mike followed his awed, joyful gaze. To himself, Mike had to admit that the gnome, propelling himself through the water with his ears, arms folded in tremendous dignity, was a funny sight.

"Must you drop rocks and disturb us at our work?" the gnome asked.

Greenberg gulped. "I'm sorry, Mr. Gnome," he said nervously. "I couldn't get you to come up by yelling."

The gnome looked at him. "Oh. You are the mortal who was disciplined. Why did you return?"

"To tell you that I'm sorry, and I won't insult you again."

"Have you proof of your sincerity?" the gnome asked quietly.

Greenberg fished furiously in his pocket and brought out

a handful of sugar wrapped in Cellophane, which he tremblingly handed to the gnome.

"Ah, very clever, indeed," the little man said, unwrapping a cube and popping it eagerly into his mouth. "Long time since I've had some."

A moment later Greenberg spluttered and floundered under the surface. Even if Mike had not caught his jacket and helped him up, he could almost have enjoyed the sensation of being able to drown.

Someone lately asked a lot of people what the happiest day in their life had been; and, rather depressingly, the majority answer was "my high-school graduation." As old H. P. Lovecraft used to say, there are things Man was not meant to know; and I suspect this is one of them. Jimmy Childers had a respectably eventful Best Day—but whether, in the end, he would have settled for a high-school graduation instead, is open to question. . . .

Doubled and Redoubled

Malcolm Jameson

The very first thing that startled Jimmy Childers that extraordinary, repetitive June day was the alarm clock going off. It shouldn't have gone off. He remembered distinctly setting it at "Silent" when he went to bed the night before, and thumbing his nose derisively at it. He was a big shot now; he could get down to the office, along with the Westchesterites, at a quarter of ten, not at nine, as heretofore.

He rose on an elbow and hurled a pillow at the jangling thing, then flopped back onto the pillow for a moment's luxurious retrospect.

Ah, what a day yesterday had been! The perfect day. The kind that happens only in fiction, or the third act of plays, when every problem is solved and every dream comes true all at once. He grinned happily. This time yesterday he had been a poor wage slave, a mere clerk; today he was head of a department. Until last evening the course of true love, as practiced by himself and Genevieve, had run anything but smoothly; this morning she was his bride-to-be. Twenty-four hours ago the name of Jimmy Childers was known only to a few hundred persons; all today's papers would carry his pictures and the commendations of the police and the mayor. Yesterday—

But why go on? Today was another day. Jimmy pulled himself together and got out of bed, making a slightly wry face as he did so. One only reached the utmost pinnacle once in his life; today, after yesterday, could only be anticlimactic. At ten he must hit the grit again. It would be a new kind of a grind, pitched on a higher level with higher and fresher ambitions, but a grind nevertheless. And so thinking, he reached for his clothes.

And that was when Jimmy Childers received jolts number two, three and so on! For the neatly wrapped packages delivered late yesterday afternoon from Livingston & Laird were not on the chair where he had placed them for the night. Nor was the nice, new pigskin wallet and the two hundred-odd dollars he had kept out as spending money from his race-track haul, anywhere to be seen. Even the empty jeweler's box that had contained Genevieve's ring was gone. Burglars!

Jimmy frowned in puzzlement. His door was spring-locked, but it was bolted, too. There was no transom, and the window was inaccessible from any other. It didn't make sense. He thought he would hardly make a row about it yet. Moreover, he was consoled by the thought that before going on his shopping spree yesterday, he had dropped by the bank and deposited a flat thousand. For reassurance, he slipped a hand into the inner pocket of his dangling coat and drew forth the little blue book.

The book was here, but the entry was not! Jimmy's eyes popped in unbelief. The last entry was May 15th, and for the usual ten dollars. Yet he remembered clearly Mr. Kleib's pleasantries as he chalked up the one-grand deposit. Why, it was only yesterday!

He glanced up at the calendar that hung behind the door. Each night he crossed the current day off. Last night he had not crossed it, but encircled it in a triple circle of red—the day of days! He suddenly went a little sick at the stomach as the rectangle of black figures stared back at him. The fourteenth of June was neither crossed off nor encircled. Jimmy Childers sat down and scratched his head, bewildered and dazed. Had he dreamed all that he thought had happened? Could it be that today was the fourteenth, and not the day after? Trembling a little, he finished dressing.

For a time he pondered his strange feelings. He tried to account for the disappearance of the things he had bought, remembering that the boys rooming down the hall had a way of borrowing without always telling. They *might* have come in last evening while he was out. As to the loss of the wallet, a pickpocket might have lifted that, and he had to recall occasions when he had been crowded or jostled. He gave it up. There was only the old hag on Riverside Drive, who had held out a scrawny, clutching hand for alms. Surely she couldn't have been the thief! He smiled to recollect her fawning gratitude when in his exuberance he had unexpectedly given her a five-spot, and her mumbling as she tottered on her way.

No. None of it fitted. As a matter of fact, now that he was going into such details, he remembered distinctly getting home *after that,* and putting the wallet and empty ring box on his dresser, winding the clock, and the rest. He sighed deeply. It was all so screwy.

He walked briskly from the house. He had decided to say nothing about his loss to Mrs. Tankersley. Upon second thought, he would wait until he got to his office, then he would ring up the police commissioner personally. Hadn't he told him only yesterday that if he ever needed anything just give him a buzz? Jimmy felt very grandiose with his new connections. He had completely conquered his jitters when he stopped at the tobacco stand on the corner.

"Gimme a pack," he said "and extra matches."

The clerk handed the cigarettes over, and then in a low, confidential voice added, "I gotta hot one for you today— Swiss Rhapsody in the first at Aqueduct. She's sure fire, even if she's a long shot. The dope is straight from Eddie Kelly—"

"Wake up," laughed Jimmy Childers, "that was yesterday!" He started to add, "Don't you remember my dropping by here last night and handing you a 'C' for the tip?" but for some reason choked it. The fellow evidently didn't remember it, or something. The situation was cockeyed again. So Jimmy said that much and stopped.

The clerk shook his head. "Not this nag. She hasn't been running."

"O. K.," said Childers, on a sudden impulse, and digging into his watch pocket he fished out four crumpled dollar bills. That was what he had to live on the rest of the week. "Two bucks—on the nose."

"You ain't making a mistake, pal," said the clerk.

The words startled Jimmy Childers more than anything else that had happened. Syllable for syllable the last exchange of sentences were identical with what had passed between them yesterday this time. Jimmy had the queer feeling, which comes over one at times, he was reliving something that had already happened. Hastily he pocketed his cigarettes and backed out of the place.

Downstairs in the subway station he snatched a paper and just made the crowded train, squeezing in the middle door into a solid mass of humanity. He was anxious to see whether his exploit in foiling the Midtown Bank robbery had made the first page or not, but it was not for several stations that he had the opportunity to open up his paper. Then he muttered savagely in dissatisfaction. The dealer had worked off yesterday's paper on him! He had read it all before—June 14th, PARIS FALLS. Bah!

"The young men of this generation have no manners whatever!" bleated a nagging, querulous voice behind him, and he felt a vicious dig at his ribs.

"I beg your pardon," he exclaimed, automatically nudging away to give what room he could.

"People go around sticking their elbows in other people's eyes, trying to read sensational trash!"

"I'm very sorry, madam," reiterated Jimmy Childers, making still more room. He was looking down into the snapping eyes of an acid-faced old beldam, and the sight of her made chills run up and down his spine. This very incident had occurred to him in every detail only yesterday. He felt very queer. Should he drop off and see a doctor? No, he decided, it was that damn vivid dream that still hung on to him.

Then, when the flurry caused by the tart old woman's eruption had subsided, he stole a glance over the shoulders of his neighbors. Some were reading one paper and some another, but they all had one thing in common. They were yesterday's papers! And their readers seemed content!

"Hell's bells," ejaculated Childers, "I *am* nuts."

At Thirty-fourth Street he got no shock, for the mad stampede of the office-bound herd is much the same, whatever the date. It was when he stepped into his own company's suite that fate biffed him squarely between the eyes again. Biff number one was that none of the other clerks took any special notice of him as he walked past the desks. The expected shower of congratulations did not materialize, nor for that matter, did the sour look of envy he expected to see on Miss Staunton's face. It was just like any other morning. It was just like yesterday morning, to be even more specific.

But he did not stop at his old desk in the outer office as

he always had hitherto. He walked boldly on to the private office of the manager of the foreign department. It was not until he was within a pace of it that he halted in his stride, open-mouthed. The lettering on the door was not new gold-leaf at all, but the black paint that had always been there. It said simply, "Ernest Brown, Mgr."

He stared at it a moment, then turned and slowly made his way back to his old hangout in the clerk's offices. He hung up his hat and coat and sat down at the desk he had worked at for the past five years. Presently the office boy came bearing the trays of mail. Childers watched the deck of envelopes fall onto his blotter with tense anxiety. Somewhere in that batch of mail ought to be a test of his sanity. Or was it the reverse? He couldn't be sure. That damn dream had him so mixed up, he couldn't tell reality from pipe dream any more.

"I'm going to call my shots, from now on," he told himself. With a hand that was close to trembling he pulled a pad toward him and wrote down:

> Acceptance and check for two hundred and fifty dollars in this morning's mail for a story I tossed off in my spare time and sent to the *Thursday Weekly*.

He turned the pad upside down and shot a cautious glance about the office. No one was paying him any atention. He ran through the envelopes. Yes, there it was. He almost tore the check as he snatched it out. Yes! The unexpected had happened, an impossible thing—his first effort at writing had been bought! He read the inclosed letter feverishly. Word for for word it was the one in his dream. Now he knew that yesterday had not happened. For the *Weekly* wouldn't send out two checks for the same yarn. Would the rest of the day go the same way?

It did.

At nine-thirty the messenger came and told him the boss wanted him at once. Jimmy Childers went with alacrity. For twenty-five minutes he had been sitting there, alternately chilled with fear and glowing with anticipation.

"Childers," said the Old Man, "we've watched you for some time and we like your style. Beginning tomorrow you'll have Mr. Brown's job in the foreign department. The pay will only be two hundred, but remember that we are jumping you over a lot of other people. You may take the rest of today off."

"Thank you, sir," said Jimmy Childers with every appearance of calm acceptance of his just dues as a capable employee, but all the time queer tremors were playing hob with his inner workings. "But if it's all the same, I'll hang on as I am until noon at least. I would like to clean up my present desk before I leave it."

"A very commendable spirit," said the Old Man, cracking his cold face into the first smile he had ever let Childers see. That, too, had been in the dream. Childers was not sure whether he looked forward to the rest of the day with apprehension or what. It was a little disconcerting to know beforehand just how everything would turn out.

When he got back to his desk a puckish mood seized him. "Oh, Miss Walters, will you take a letter, please."

"A-hum," he said, in his best executive manner, when she had settled beside him with her notebook. "To Mr. E. E. Frankenstein, Cylindrical Metal Castings—you know where—dear sir. In reply to your offer of this date of the position of stockmaster at your foundry, I beg to inform you that the job does not interest me and the salary you mention is ridiculous. Yours very truly—and so on and so on—the new title, you know."

"Why, Mr. Childers," exclaimed Miss Walters, "I didn't know *they* were trying to get you—"

Childers cocked an eye at the clock. He had timed it nicely. The messenger was approaching with a telegram in his hand.

"Read that to me," he said to the stenographer, with a lordly wave of the hand.

She tore the yellow envelope open and read the message aloud.

"How did you know?" she asked, wonder in her eyes.

"Hunch," he said laconically, and lit a cigarette.

"By golly," he told himself, "the dream is coming true, item by item." In succession he rang up Genevieve and made a date for that night; and then his bookmaker and doubled his bet on Swiss Rhapsody. Then he fell to thinking about the affair at the Midland Bank and that took some of the glow off. Hell, that fellow with the machine gun didn't miss him by much! Should he go through with it? He decided he would, for there were several details he had missed in the flurry of excitement in the dream. Moreover, he had pleasant memories of the fuss that was made over him afterward, not forgetting the standing reward of one thousand dollars offered by the protective agency. If he were to be married, and now he was sure he would be, any extra cash was very welcome.

He took the *Weekly*'s check and strolled out of the office. First he stopped by the haberdashers and spent a most pleasant hour selecting gay ties, a suit, hat and various other items. Then, leaving the delivery address, he made his way to the bank.

He had a very queer feeling as he went through the portals —that uncomfortable sensation of having done it all before. His upward glance at the clock and the fact that exactly 12:03 registered firmly in his memory was a part of it. But he nerved himself for the ordeal and went straight to his usual teller's window.

He had just shoved the money under the wicket and knew uneasily that goose pimples had risen all over him when the expected happened. A low, husky voice said almost in his ear.

"Stand as you are, bud. Keep your hands on that marble shelf and don't turn around. This is a stick-up."

Then the voice said to Mr. Kleib: "Shell out—everything in the cage but the silver!"

Now!

Childers deliberately and without sense of direction, except that of the voice, kicked backward with all his force. He felt something soft give and then his heel crunched against bone. There was a curse and a moan, and he heard the clatter of the gun on the floor and the soft thud as his man slid to the marble.

In that instant pandemonium reigned. A huge howler over the door began its siren wail, Tommy-guns rattled, men shouted and women screamed.

Like a flash Jimmy Childers dropped to his hands and knees just as a stream of whizzing bullets spattered against the marble cage front. He grabbed up the fallen gun and turned it on the man that was firing at him, a short, stocky thug in a light-gray suit. He saw the man drop, and as he did another rushed past, headed for the door. Jimmy let the gun fall and launched himself in a flying tackle, grabbing at the fleeing gangster's knees.

The next couple of seconds was a maelstrom of sensation

and confusion. Then he was aware of looking at the pants legs of some big man in blue, and a heavy Irish voice saying:

"Leggo, son, you've done enough. We've got him now."

Childers unwrapped his arms from the bandit's knees and got up. His heart was pounding wildly and he knew his clothes were a wreck, but it was a glorious moment and he didn't care. A circle of men were around him, men with notebooks and cameras and flashlight bulbs, snapping pictures and asking questions. Next, a big police car screamed its way to the front door, and in a moment he was receiving the unstinted congratulations of a fiery little mayor and his police commissioner.

"Nice work, Childers," said the latter. "Those eggs have been wanted a long, long time. If there is anything I can ever do for you, call on me."

Then the president of the bank came and whirled him away to the club for luncheon. What a day! Had so much ever happened to one man before in so short a space of time? And how odd that he had dreamed it all, even to the date of the vintage on the label of the sauterne the banker ordered with the lunch!

Suddenly he realized it was close to two thirty and the first at Aqueduct was probably already run. He excused himself and hastened over to Kelly's place.

"I'll take it in big bills," he said to Kelly, as he went in.

"Optimistic, ain't you?" was Kelly's rejoinder. "Didja ever hear of nine horses falling down and breaking their legs in the same race? Well, that's what it'd take to let that milkwagon nag—"

"They're off," announced the fellow with the headphones on.

"I'll still take it in big bills," said Jimmy serenely.

"I'm damned," was Kelly's only comment, a couple of minutes later.

Jimmy Childers had two free hours that somehow were not covered by the dream. He remembered vaguely that he had deposited most of his winnings and then gone for a walk in the park. That he did, but his thoughts were so in the clouds and his pulse pounding so with the sense of personal well-being and triumph that he hardly remembered jumping impulsively into a cab and going to the most famous jeweler's in the world.

Later he mounted the steps in Genevieve's house, the ring snuggling in his pocket. He knew exactly how he was to be greeted—for once the pout would be off her face and in its place jubilant excitement. For the evening papers were full of his exploits at the bank, and the reporters had brought out the fact that that morning he had been made manager of the foreign department. The auspices for a favorable reception to his umpty-teenth proposal were good, to say the least.

They went to dinner, just as he knew they would, at the most expensive place in town.

Jimmy ordered carelessly, without a glance at the card.

"Yes, sir," said the waiter, with that bow that is bestowed only on those that know their way around.

"Why, Jimmy," she tittered, "you seem to be perfectly at home here."

"Oh, yes," he said carelessly, as he flipped the folds out of his napkin. He did not see fit to tell her that in the dream of yesterday—or was it today?—it had been only after thirty minutes' study of the intricate card, to the tune of many acrimonious comments by Genevieve and the obvious disapproval of an impatient waiter, that he had picked that particular combination of food and drink. But it had been eminently satisfactory, so why not repeat?

As the evening wore on he found himself more and more eager to get to the place where that culminating kiss occurred. *That* was something he could repeat *ad infinitum*, whether in the flesh or a dream. And when it came, he was not disappointed. After that they had the little ritual of the ring, and still later his departure. His soul soared as it had never soared before.

Or rather, he reminded himself, a trifle ruefully, as it had never soared before in waking life. For after all, the day's triumphs had had just a little of the edge taken off by his certainty that they would occur.

And as he digested that thought, he concluded he would go straight home and to bed. After all, last night the only thing more he had done was stroll on the Drive, after paying the cigarstore clerk his tip, wrapped in his own glorious thoughts. No other incident had occurred worth reliving, as his pleasure at being able to give such a generous handout as a five-dollar bill was somewhat marred by the repulsiveness of the beggarly old crone who had received it.

So he went straight to his room, locked and bolted the door, and prepared for bed. Just before he turned off the light he surveyed the chair piled high with his purchases with immense satisfaction. Tomorrow he would go forth dressed as his new station in life required. His eye caught the calendar, and instead of striking out the day with his customary black cross, he encircled it twice in red. Then taking good care that the clock was wound, but not the alarm, he went to bed.

The very first thing that startled Jimmy Childers that extraordinary repetitive June day was the alarm clock going off. It shouldn't have gone off. He remembered distinctly setting it at "silent" when he went to bed the night before, and thumbing his nose derisively at it. He was a big shot now; he could get down to the office with the Westchesterites, at quarter of ten, not at nine, as heretofore.

He rose on an elbow and poised himself to hurl a pillow at the jangling thing. And then, THEN—

"Good Heaven!" he mumbled. "I've done all this before."

Angrily he bounded out of bed and choked off the offending clock. It took only a swift glance around the room to check the items some quick sense told him were missing. There were no packages from the haberdasher's, nor ring box. And the calendar stared at him unsullied by red-penciled marks. It was the morning of June 14th!

He dressed in sullen rage, grumbling at his fate. He couldn't stand many double-barreled dreams like that one—they were too exhausting. He'd better see a doctor. And yet—yet it was all so *real*. He could have sworn that all those things had actually happened to him—twice! But then he stopped, more mystified than ever. They had differed somewhat in detail, those two days. He stopped and stared at himself in the mirror and noted he appeared a bit wild-eyed.

"I'll experiment, first," he decided, and hurried out, slamming the door behind.

At the cigar stand he asked the clerk.

"How do you go about betting on the ponies?"

"I can take it," said the fellow, unenthusiastically.

"Here's two bucks," said Jimmy, "put it on Swiss Rhapsody —to win. I hope there's such a horse?"

"If you're not particular what you call a horse," said the

clerk, with an air of sneering omniscience. "I'm surprised they let her run at all."

"Why?"

"It takes her so long to finish it throws all the other races late."

"Oh," said Jimmy Childers, but he let the bet stand.

He did not waste three cents on a paper that morning. One glance at the headlines was enough. He had practically memorized its contents two days before. But when he got in the subway he was very careful to give the pasty, quarrelsome-looking old woman who blocked his path as wide a berth as possible.

"Whippersnapper!" she exclaimed venomously, noting his scrupulous avoidance of her. There was a little flurry as people glanced up and had a look at him, then they went back to the reading of their stale newspapers. Jimmy Childers groaned. Was he in some squirrel cage of fate? Did everything have to always come out the same way, no matter what his approach? He resolved to make something come out differently, no matter what the cost.

This time he opened his letter containing the literary check without a tremor, and without joy. He knew he would spend the money, and how. He knew, too, that the things he purchased with it would vanish overnight, leaving him to do it all over again tomorrow. When the messenger came to tell him the big boss wanted him at once, Childers said coldly:

"I'm busy. Anyhow, it's no farther from his desk to mine than it is from mine to his."

The messenger gaped with awe, as if wondering whether lightning would strike. Then he stumbled off toward the chief's office.

"I don't think you understand, Childers," the big boss was saying a moment later, as he stood by Jimmy's desk. "Brown has left and we're giving you his job. It pays two hundred, you know."

"Not enough," replied Childers, gruffly.

"It's all we can afford just now," said the boss pleasantly. "But that's our offer. Think it over. It will be open for a week."

Jimmy Childers stared at his retreating back.

"Gosh!" he muttered. "And I got away with that!"

He went through the bank routine with little change, although he did think something of telephoning the police a tip-off and letting it go at that, but for some unknown but compelling reason he had to go through his act personally. But the thrill was gone. His walk in the park was much less joyous, as the more he tried to digest the strangely repetitive nature of his life the last three days, the more unhappy he became.

"It's like that old song about the broken record," he muttered sourly. "All the kick's gone out of things now." He didn't even bother to go to the jeweler's to select the ring. He knew the stock number by heart. So he merely phoned for it.

The kiss that night was up to par, which was some solace, but aside from that, getting engaged was not so much fun. There was no palpitation of the heart as he hung on her words, wondering what the answer would be. He already knew damn well what the answer would be. What kind of a life was that?"

That night he threw the alarm clock out the window.

The very first thing that startled Jimmy Childers that—

"Damnation!" he growled, at the first tap of the awakening bell. He threw, not a pillow, but a heavy book, and watched with grim satisfaction as the face crystal smashed to tiny bits.

When he went out he avoided the cigar stand and took a bus, not the subway.

"Insufferable!" snorted the old hellion he sat down beside. He gasped. It was his nemesis of the subway. Apparently she had decided to vary her program a bit, too. He changed seats and listened with reddening cheeks to the titters of the other passengers.

At the office he had an unexpected telephone call. It was from the clerk at his corner cigar stand.

"Oh, Jimmy," he said, "I guess you were late this morning and didn't have time to leave your bet—so I placed one for you. Hope you don't mind?"

"What horse?" asked Childers, glumly.

"Swiss Rhapsody. She's a long shot, but—"

Jimmy hung up and stared at the phone in front of him. He just couldn't get away from this thing.

All day long he tried to ring changes on his routine, and

with astonishing minor results. But as to the major outcome there was never any difference. He was promoted, he won money, he saved the bank from robbery, he got engaged.

And the days that followed were no different. In the main, the events of June 14th had to be relived and relived until he found himself wincing at every one of the events that once had impressed him as such tremendous triumphs. Finally one day, during the hours usually devoted to the stroll in the park, he flung himself into a psychiatrist's office.

"Hm-m-m," commented the doctor, after he had smitten Childers' knees with little rubber mallets, and had scratched him on the feet and back with small prongs. "All I see are a few tremors. What's on your mind?"

"Plenty," said Jimmy savagely, and poured out his story.

"Hm-m-m," commented the doctor. "Interesting—most interesting."

He scribbled a prescription.

"Take this before you go to bed. It is simply something to make you sleep better. Then come back tomorrow at this same hour."

"Just one question, doctor."

"Yes?"

"What is today's date?"

"The fourteenth." The doctor smiled indulgently.

"And yesterday's?"

"The thirteenth. Come back tomorrow, please."

On the dot Jimmy Childers showed up at the doctor's office the next day—June the fourteenth, according to Childers' calendar. As he barged into the waiting room he was accosted with a chill:

"Name, please?"

He looked at the nurse in astonishment. Why, only the day before he had spent the best part of an hour dictating the answers of a questionnaire to her! He gave her a blank stare.

"The doctor is seen only by appointment," she added, looking at him disapprovingly.

"I . . . I made one yesterday," he stammered. "I was here . . . was examined!"

"You must be wrong," said she, sweetly. "Doctor just returned from Europe this morning."

"Oh, hell!" snarled Childers, and rushed from the place. He saw at once what a jam he was in. He had added another piece of furniture to his merry-go-round. That was all. He could vary it within limits, of course, but he would never get anywhere.

Jimmy Childers charged up and down the walks of the park in a frenzy. If only Sunday would come—something to break this vicious circle. But no, there was no way to get to Sunday. With him it was always Friday.

That night he skipped the call on Genevieve. Instead he called her up and made some flimsy, insulting excuse. All she said was:

"You old fibber. You're just shy. The ring came up and I'm *so* thrilled. Of course I'll marry you, you silly boy."

Weak and trembling he hung up. In his hand was a steamship ticket to Buenos Aires on the *Santa Mosca*, sailing at eleven p. m. He would try that on his jinx.

He got aboard all right, despite some arguments about a passport, and turned in at once, after dogging down the port and carefully locking the door. He took three of the tablets the doctor had prescribed instead of the one mentioned in the directions. If it were a dream, he ought to knock it now —different room, different bed, different environment, differtnt everything. Jimmy closed his eyes. That night, the first for many a June 14th, he went to sleep with a ray of hope.

The very first thing that startled—

"Oh, Heaven!" sighed a haggard Jimmy Childers, as he shut off the clock, "another day of it."

He went through the Red Book almost name by name. He shook his head hopelessly. He had tried almost everything from chiropractors to psychiatrists. Then he found a name that somehow he had skipped. It was under necromancers. At once he grabbed a taxi and flew to the address—a stinking hole under the Williamsburg Bridge.

"Sorry," said the macabre person he contacted, sitting placidly among his black velvet drapes in a "studio" calculated to send a strictly normal person into the heebie-jeebies, "but I only deal with the dead. That is my specialty. Now if you want a corpse raised, or anything like that—"

"No, no," said Jimmy hastily, and paid his fee and left. Outside he shuddered at the memory of the funereal atmosphere of the faker's joint. He hoped fervently that *this* episode wasn't going to get embroidered into the design. His error was in not knowing what a necromancer was. He went back to the Red Book. It just had occurred to him that perhaps under sorcerers or thaumaturgists was what he wanted.

He found a lot of them, mostly in Harlem, and made a list.

The first four were as unsatisfactory as the necromancer, a circumstance that was very trying to Jimmy, for he could visit only one a day, using the blank two hours usually spent in the park. All the rest of the time he had to devote to the tedious business of being promoted, winning money, foiling robberies or making love.

But the fifth man was very much to Jimmy Childers' liking, after he recovered from the shock of the first interview. He found him in a dilapidated office in a shabby neighborhood in Greenpoint, and on the door was crudely lettered the frank but somewhat disconcerting legend, "Master Charlatan." Nevertheless Jimmy went boldly in.

"Ah," said the seer, after gazing for a while in a crystal sphere before him. "I perceive you are the victim of a blessing that misfired."

Jimmy Childers brought his eyes back to the bald-headed, fishy-eyed fat man who had guaranteed to help him. While the master charlatan had been in his semitrance Jimmy had been examining the charts that hung about. Obviously the man he had come to was versatile in the extreme, for there were diagrams of the human palm, knobs of the human cranium, weird charts of the heavens, and all the rest of the props that go with standard charlatanry.

"Now tell me something about this original fourteenth of June," said the sage. "How long ago was it, according to your reckoning?"

"Months and months," moaned Jimmy, thinking back on the intolerable monotony of it all.

"Can you recall the exact details of the first day—I mean the very first one—the prototype?"

"I doubt it," confessed Jimmy. "You see, I've wriggled around and monkeyed with it so much that I'm all balled up."

"Try," said the wise one, calmly.

Hesitantly Jimmy Childers told his story, as best he could remember it, all the way to his going to bed the night of the genuine fourteenth of June.

"Now you begin to interest me," suddenly said the master, opening his eyes from the apparent slumber into which he had relapsed the moment Jimmy had begun talking. "Tell me

more about that beggar woman on the Drive. Was she toothless except for a single yellow fang? Did her knuckles come to about her knees? Was she blind in her left eye?"

"Yes, yes," agreed Jimmy eagerly.

"Aha!" ejaculated the seer, "I though so. Minnie the Malicious!" He made a note. "I'll report this to the Guild. She was disbarred long ago—for malpractice and incompetence."

Jimmy looked mystified.

"She used to be a practicing witch," explained the great one with a shrug, "now she is just a chiseler. You know . . . cheap curses, petty enchantments and the like. But just what did she say to you, and *most particularly*, what kind of wishes did you make just after you left her?"

"Well," admitted Jimmy, "she came up whining and asked

for a penny. I was feeling pretty high, so I gave her a five-spot."

"That was a mistake," murmured the sorcerer.

"That's all," said Jimmy, suddenly concluding. "She mumbled something, and I walked on."

"But you wished something?"

"Well, I do remember—don't forget what a wonderful day I'd had—that I was wishing every day was like that, or that I could live it over again, or something of the sort."

"Be very exact," insisted his interrogator.

"Sorry," said Jimmy.

"Let's go into the Mesmeric Department," said his consultant, leading the way into a shabby interior room. "Now sit there and keep your eye on the little jeweled light," he ordered.

It seemed only an instant before Jimmy woke up. The master charlatan was sitting in front of him placidly looking at him.

"Your exact wish," he said, "was a triple one, as I suspected. They usually are. Here are your mental words, 'Oh, I wish every day was like this one; I wish I could live it over again; I wish I'd never seen that old hag, she gives me the creeps.'"

"So what?" queried Jimmy recalling it now.

"When you gave her such a magnificent present, she mumbled out that you would have your next three wishes granted. Oddly enough, if she had been an able practitioner, nothing would have happened—"

"That doesn't make sense," objected Jimmy.

"Oh, yes it does. You see, your last wish would have had the effect of canceling the others, as you would never have met her, see?"

"It is a little involved," frowned Jimmy.

"Yes, these things have a way of getting involved," admitted the wise one. "However, since she was a low-powered witch, so to speak, only the first wish came fully true, that is, every day—for you—was like that one. By the time you had gotten to the second one some of the punch was out of it. You didn't *quite* live it over again. You had the power of varying it a little, which was a very fortunate circumstance, as otherwise you would have gone on doing it forever and ever."

"You mean I'm cured!" exclaimed Jimmy delightedly.

"Not so fast. When we come to the last wish, her power had petered out almost altogether. It did not do way with the fact that you *had* met her, but it was strong enough to cause you to avoid meeting her any more."

"I see," said Jimmy, hoping he really did.

"Now what you've got to do is to live that day over once more—the first one, mind you—including meeting Minnie; only the minute she mumbles, reverse your wish. That cancels everything."

"But I can't remember that day well enough—"

"I'll coach you," said the mesmerist. "While you were hypnotized I took it all down, every detail."

An hour later Jimmy Childers rose to go. He paid over to the magician all the money he had just collected on Swiss Rhapsody. The old man dropped it into his pocket with just the hint of a chuckle.

"By the way," asked Jimmy on the threshold, "What day is *this?*"

"That, my friend," replied the master charlatan with an oily smile, "is a mystery I'd advise you not to look into. Good day!"

Unknown was not, of course, the only magazine devoted to fantasy, nor the only good such magazine. Weird Tales, during the course of more than thirty years, published many distinguished stories, and was pretty much the only source of intelligent "supernatural" fiction around during all but seven of those years*. Weird's roster of fine writers included such greats as H. P. Lovecraft, Robert Bloch, August Derleth, Ray Bradbury, Theodore Sturgeon; and even, after the demise of Unknown, Sprague de Camp and Fletcher Pratt. Weird had its own atmosphere—mostly stronger on horror than on ingenuity—and one of its most effective regulars was Manly Wade Wellman. His stories of ghastly doings on the frontier or on the battlefields of the Civil War are among the really memorable pieces published in any magazine. When It Was Moonlight is pure Wellman, and would have been unsurprising in Weird Tales—yet it seems to fit quite well into the Unknown pattern. It may be that a really good story is at home anywhere.

When It Was Moonlight

Manly Wade Wellman

Let my heart be still a moment, and this mystery explore.
—The Raven.

His hand, as slim as a white claw, dipped a quillful of ink and wrote in one corner of the page the date—March 3, 1842. Then:

        THE PREMATURE BURIAL
            By Edgar A. Poe

He hated his middle name, the name of his miserly and spiteful stepfather. For a moment he considered crossing out

---

**Unknown's four; and the Magazine of Fantasy and Science Fiction and Beyond came up during approximately the last three years of Weird.*

even the initial; then he told himself that he was only woolgathering, putting off the drudgery of writing. And write he must, or starve—the Philadelphia *Dollar Newspaper* was clamoring for the story he had promised. Well, today he had heard a tag of gossip—his mother-in-law had it from a neighbor—that revived in his mind a subject always fascinating.

He began rapidly to write, in a fine copperplate hand:

> There are certain themes of which the interest is all-absorbing, but which are entirely too horrible for the purposes of legitimate fiction—

This would really be an essay, not a tale, and he could do it justice. Often he thought of the whole world as a vast fat cemetery, close set with tombs in which not all the occupants were at rest—too many struggled unavailingly against their smothering shrouds, their locked and weighted coffin lids. What were his own literary labors, he mused, but a struggle against being shut down and throttled by a society as heavy and grim and senseless as clods heaped by a sexton's spade?

He paused, and went to the slate mantelshelf for a candle. His kerosene lamp had long ago been pawned, and it was dark for midafternoon, even in March. Elsewhere in the house his mother-in-law swept busily, and in the room next to his sounded the quiet breathing of his invalid wife. Poor Virginia slept, and for the moment knew no pain. Returning with his light, he dipped more ink and continued down the sheet:

> To be buried while alive is, beyond question, the most terrific of these extremes which has ever fallen to the lot of mere mortality. That it has frequently, very frequently, fallen will scarcely be denied—

Again his dark imagination savored the tale he had heard that day. It had happened here in Philadelphia, in this very quarter, less than a month ago. A widower had gone, after weeks of mourning, to his wife's tomb, with flowers. Stooping to place them on the marble slab, he had heard noise beneath. At once joyful and aghast, he fetched men and crowbars, and recovered the body, all untouched by decay. At home that night, the woman returned to consciousness.

So said the gossip, perhaps exagerated, perhaps not. And

the house was only six blocks away from Spring Garden Street, where he sat.

Poe fetched out his notebooks and began to marshal bits of narrative for his composition—a gloomy tale of resurrection in Baltimore, another from France, a genuinely creepy citation from the *Chirurgical Journal* of Leipzig; a sworn case of revival, by electrical impulses, of a dead man in London. Then he added an experience of his own, romantically embellished, a dream adventure of his boyhood in Virginia Just as he thought to make an end, he had a new inspiration.

Why not learn more about that reputed Philadelphia burial and the one who rose from seeming death? It would point up his piece, give it a timely local climax, insure acceptance —he could hardly risk a rejection. Too, it would satisfy his own curiosity. Laying down the pen, Poe got up. From a peg he took his wide black hat, his old military cloak that he had worn since his ill-fated cadet days at West Point. Huddling it round his slim little body, he opened the front door and went out.

March had come in like a lion and, lionlike, roared and rampaged over Philadelphia. Dry, cold dust blew up into Poe's full gray eyes, and he hardened his mouth under the gay dark mustache. His shins felt goosefleshy; his striped trousers were unseasonably thin and his shoes badly needed mending. Which way lay his journey?

He remembered the name of the street, and something about a ruined garden. Eventually he came to the place, or what must be the place—the garden was certainly ruined, full of dry, hardy weeds that still stood in great ragged clumps after the hard winter. Poe forced open the creaky gate, went up the rough-flagged path to the stoop. He saw a bronzed nameplate—"Gauber," it said. Yes, that was the name he had heard. He swung the knocker loudly, and thought he caught a whisper of movement inside. But the door did not open.

"Nobody lives there, Mr. Poe," said someone from the street. It was a grocery boy, with a heavy basket on his arm. Poe left the doorstep. He knew the lad; indeed he owed the grocer eleven dollars.

"Are you sure?" Poe prompted.

"Well"—and the boy shifted the weight of his burden— "if anybody lived here, they'd buy from our shop, wouldn't they? And I'd deliver, wouldn't I? But I've had this job for six months, and never set foot inside that door."

Poe thanked him and walked down the street, but did not take the turn that would lead home. Instead he sought the shop of one Pemberton, a printer and a friend, to pass the time of day and ask for a loan.

Pemberton could not lend even one dollar—times were hard—but he offered a drink of Monongahela whiskey, which Poe forced himself to refuse; then a supper of crackers, cheese and garlic sausage, which Poe thankfully shared. At home, unless his mother-in-law had begged or borrowed from the neighbors, would be only bread and molasses. It was past sundown when the writer shook hands with Pemberton, thanked him with warm courtesy for his hospitality, and ventured into the evening.

Thank Heaven, it did not rain. Poe was saddened by storms. The wind had abated and the March sky was clear save for a tiny fluff of scudding cloud and a banked dark line at the horizon, while up rose a full moon the color of frozen cream. Poe squinted from under his hat brim at the shadow-pattern on the disk. Might he not write another story of a lunar voyage—like the one about Hans Pfaal, but dead serious this time? Musing thus, he walked along the dusk-filling street until he came again opposite the ruined garden, the creaky gate, and the house with the doorplate marked: "Gauber."

Hello, the grocery boy had been wrong. There was light inside the front window, water-blue light—or was there? Anyway, motion—yes, a figure stooped there, as if to peer out at him.

Poe turned in at the gate, and knocked at the door once again.

Four or five moments of silence; then he heard the old lock grating. The door moved inward, slowly and noisily. Poe fancied that he had been wrong about the blue light, for he saw only darkness inside. A voice spoke:

"Well, sir?"

The two words came huskily but softly, as though the door-opener scarcely breathed. Poe swept off his broad black hat and made one of his graceful bows.

"If you will pardon me—" He paused, not knowing whether he addressed man or woman. "This is the Gauber residence?"

"It is," was the reply, soft, hoarse and sexless. "Your business, sir?"

Poe spoke with official crispness; he had been a sergeant-major of artillery before he was twenty-one, and knew how to inject the proper note. "I am here on public duty," he announced. "I am a journalist, tracing a strange report."

"Journalist?" repeated his interrogator. "Strange report? Come in, sir."

Poe complied, and the door closed abruptly behind him, with a rusty snick of the lock. He remembered being in jail once, and how the door of his cell had slammed just so. It was not a pleasant memory. But he saw more clearly, now he was inside—his eyes got used to the tiny trickle of moonlight.

He stood in a dark hallway, all paneled in wood, with no furniture, drapes or pictures. With him was a woman, in full skirt and down-drawn lace cap, a woman as tall as he and with intent eyes that glowed as from within. She neither moved nor spoke, but waited for him to tell her more of his errand.

Poe did so, giving his name and, stretching a point, claiming to be a subeditor of the *Dollar Newspaper*, definitely assigned to the interview. "And now, madam, concerning this story that is rife concerning a premature burial—"

She had moved very close, but as his face turned toward her she drew back. Poe fancied that his breath had blown her away like a feather; then, remembering Pemberton's garlic sausage, he was chagrined. To confirm his new thought, the woman was offering him wine—to sweeten his breath.

"Would you take a glass of canary, Mr. Poe?" she invited, and opened a side door. He followed her into a room papered in pale blue. Moonglow, drenching it, reflected from that paper and seemed an artificial light. That was what he had seen from outside. From an undraped table his hostess lifted a bottle, poured wine into a metal goblet and offered it.

Poe wanted that wine, but he had recently promised his sick wife, solemnly and honestly, to abstain from even a sip of the drink that so easily upset him. Through thirsty lips he said: "I thank you kindly, but I am a temperance man."

"Oh," and she smiled. Poe saw white teeth. Then: "I am Elva Gauber—Mrs. John Gauber. The matter of which you ask I cannot explain clearly, but it is true. My husband was buried, in the Eastman Lutheran Churchyard—"

"I had heard, Mrs. Gauber, that the burial concerned a woman."

"No, my husband. He had been ill. He felt cold and quiet.

A physician, a Dr. Mechem, pronounced him dead, and he was interred beneath a marble slab in his family vault." She sounded weary, but her voice was calm. "This happened shortly after the New Year. On Valentine's Day, I brought flowers. Beneath his slab he stirred and struggled. I had him brought forth. And he lives—after a fashion—today."

"Lives today?" repeated Poe. "In this house?"

"Would you care to see him? Interview him?"

Poe's heart raced, his spine chilled. It was his peculiarity that such sensations gave him pleasure. "I would like nothing better," he assured her, and she went to another door, an inner one.

Opening it, she paused on the threshold, as though summoning her resolution for a plunge into cold, swift water. Then she started down a flight of steps.

Poe followed, unconsciously drawing the door shut behind him.

The gloom of midnight, of prison—yes, of the tomb—fell at once upon those stairs. He heard Elva Gauber gasp:

"No—the moonlight—let it in—" And then she fell, heavily and limply, rolling downstairs.

Aghast, Poe quickly groped his way after her. She lay against a door at the foot of the flight, wedged against the panel. He touched her—she was cold and rigid, without motion or elasticity of life. His thin hand groped for and found the knob of the lower door, flung it open. More dim reflected moonlight, and he made shift to drag the woman into it.

Almost at once she sighed heavily, lifted her head, and rose. "How stupid of me," she apologized hoarsely.

"The fault was mine," protested Poe. "Your nerves, your health, have naturally suffered. The sudden dark—the closeness—overcame you." He fumbled in his pocket for a tinder-box. "Suffer me to strike a light."

But she held out a hand to stop him. "No, no. The moon is sufficient." She walked to a small, oblong pane set in the wall. Her hands, thin as Poe's own, with long grubby nails, hooked on the sill. Her face, bathed in the full light of the moon, strengthened and grew calm. She breathed deeply, almost voluptuously. "I am quite recovered," she said. "Do not fear for me. You need not stand so near, sir."

He had forgotten that garlic odor, and drew back contritely. She must be as sensitive to the smell as . . . as . . . what was it that was sickened and driven away by garlic?

Poe could not remember, and he took time to note that they were in a basement, stone-walled and with a floor of dirt. In one corner water seemed to drip, forming a dank pool of mud. Close to this, set into the wall, showed a latched trapdoor of planks, thick and wide, cleated crosswise, as though to cover a window. But no window would be set so low. Everything smelt earthy and close, as through fresh air had been shut out for decades.

"Your husband is here?" he inquired.

"Yes." She walked to the shutterlike trap, unlatched it and drew it open.

The recess beyond was as black as ink, and from it came a feeble mutter. Poe followed Elva Gauber, and strained his eyes. In a little stone-flagged nook a bed had been made up. Upon it lay a man, stripped almost naked. His skin was as white as dead bone, and only his eyes, now opening, had life. He gazed at Elva Gauber and past her at Poe.

"Go away," he mumbled.

"Sir," ventured Poe formally, "I have come to hear of how you came to life in the grave—"

"It's a lie," broke in the man on the pallet. He writhed halfway to a sitting posture, laboring upward as against a crushing weight. The wash of moonlight showed how wasted and fragile he was. His face stared and snarled bare-toothed, like a skull. "A lie, I say!" he cried, with a sudden strength that might well have been his last. "Told by this monster who is not—my wife—"

The shutter-trap slammed upon his cries. Elva Gauber faced Poe, withdrawing a pace to avoid his garlic breath.

"You have seen my husband," she said. "Was it a pretty sight, sir?"

He did not answer, and she moved across the dirt to the stair doorway. "Will you go up first?" she asked. "At the top, hold the door open, that I may have—" she said "life," or, perhaps, "light." Poe could not be sure which.

Plainly she, who had almost welcomed his intrusion at first, now sought to lead him away. Her eyes, compelling as shouted commands, were fixed upon him. He felt their power, and bowed to it.

Obediently he mounted the stairs, and stood with the upper door wide. Elva Gauber came up after him. At the top her eyes again seized his. Suddenly Poe knew more than ever before about the mesmeric impulses he loved to write about.

"I hope," she said measuredly, "that you have not found your visit fruitless. I live here alone—seeing nobody, caring for the poor thing that was once my husband, John Gauber. My mind is not clear. Perhaps my manners are not good. Forgive me, and good night."

Poe found himself ushered from the house, and outside the wind was howling once again. The front door closed behind him, and the lock grated.

The fresh air, the whip of gale in his face, and the absence of Elva Gauber's impelling gaze suddenly brought him back, as though from sleep, to a realization of what had happened —or what had not happened.

He had come out, on this uncomfortable March evening, to investigate the report of a premature burial. He had seen a ghastly sick thing, that had called the gossip a lie. Somehow, then, he had been drawn abruptly away—stopped from full study of what might be one of the strangest adventures it was ever a writer's good fortune to know. Why was he letting things drop at this stage?

He decided not to let them drop. That would be worse than staying away altogether.

He made up his mind, formed quickly a plan. Leaving the doorstep, he turned from the gate, slipped quickly around the house. He knelt by the foundation at the side, just where a small oblong pane was set flush with the ground.

Bending his head, he found that he could see plainly inside, by reason of the flood of moonlight—a phenomenon, he realized, for generally an apartment was disclosed only by light within. The open doorway to the stairs, the swamp mess of mud in the corner, the out-flung trapdoor, were discernible. And something stood or huddled at the exposed niche—something that bent itself upon and above the frail white body of John Gauber.

Full skirt, white cap—it was Elva Gauber. She bent herself down, her face was touching the face or shoulder of her husband.

Poe's heart, never the healthiest of organs, began to drum and race. He pressed closer to the pane, for a better glimpse of what went on in the cellar. His shadow cut away some of the light. Elva Gauber turned to look.

Her face was as pale as the moon itself. Like the moon, it was shadowed in irregular patches. She came quickly, almost running, toward the pane where Poe crouched. He saw her, plainly and at close hand.

Dark, wet, sticky stains lay upon her mouth and cheeks. Her tongue roved out, licking at the stains—

Blood!

Poe sprang up and ran to the front of the house. He forced his thin, trembling fingers to seize the knocker, to swing it heavily again and again. When there was no answer, he pushed heavily aginst the door itself—it did not give. He moved to a window, rapped on it, pried at the sill, lifted his fist to smash the glass.

A silhouette moved beyond the pane, and threw it up. Something shot out at him like a pale snake striking—before he could move back, fingers had twisted in the front of his coat. Elva Gauber's eyes glared into his.

Her cap was off, her dark hair fallen in disorder. Blood still smeared and dewed her mouth and jowls.

"You have pried too far," she said, in a voice as measured and cold as the drip from icicles. "I was going to spare you, because of the odor about you that repelled me—the garlic. I showed you a little, enough to warn any wise person, and let you go. Now—"

Poe struggled to free himself. Her grip was immovable, like the clutch of a steel trap. She grimaced in triumph, yet she could not quite face him—the garlic still clung to his breath.

"Look in my eyes," she bade him. "Look—you cannot refuse, you cannot escape. You will die, with John—and the two of you, dying, shall rise again like me. I'll have two fountains of life while you remain—two companions after you die."

"Woman," said Poe, fighting against her stabbing gaze, "you are mad."

She snickered gustily. "I am sane, and so are you. We both know that I speak the truth. We both know the futility of your struggle." Her voice rose a little. "Through a chink in the tomb, as I lay dead, a ray of moonlight streamed and struck my eyes. I woke. I struggled. I was set free. Now at night, when the moon shines— *Ugh!* Don't breathe that herb in my face!"

She turned her head away. At that instant it seemed to Poe that a curtain of utter darkness fell and with it sank down the form of Elva Gauber.

He peered in the sudden gloom. She was collapsed across the window sill, like a discarded puppet in its booth. Her hand still twisted in the bosom of his coat, and he pried himself loose from it, finger by steely, cold finger. Then he turned to flee from this place of shadowed peril to body and soul.

As he turned, he saw whence had come the dark. A cloud had come up from its place on the horizon—the fat, sooty bank he had noted there at sundown—and now it obscured the moon. Poe paused, in midretreat, gazing.

His thoughtful eye gauged the speed and size of the cloud. It curtained the moon, would continue to curtain it for—well, ten minutes. And for that ten minutes Elva Gauber would lie motionless, lifeless. She had told the truth about the moon giving her life. Hadn't she fallen like one slain on the stairs when they were darkened? Poe began grimly to string the evidence together.

It was Elva Gauber, not her husband, who had died and gone to the family vault. She had come back to life, or a mockery of life, by touch of the moon's rays. Such light was an unpredictable force—it made dogs howl, it flogged madmen to violence, it brought fear, or black sorrow, or ecstasy. Old legends said that it was the birth of fairies, the transformation of werewolves, the motive power of broom-riding witches. It was surely the source of the strength and evil animating what had been the corpse of Elva Gauber—and he, Poe, must not stand there dreaming.

He summoned all the courage that was his, and scrambled in at the window through which slumped the woman's form. He groped across the room to the cellar door, opened it and went down the stairs, through the door at the bottom, and into the stone-walled basement.

It was dark, moonless still. Poe paused only to bring forth his tinder box, strike a light and kindle the end of a tightly twisted linen rag. It gave a feeble steady light, and he found his way to the shutter, opened it and touched the naked, wasted shoulder of John Gauber.

"Get up," he said. "I've come to save you."

The skullface feebly shifted its position to meet his gaze. The man managed to speak, moaningly:

"Useless. I can't move—unless she lets me. Her eyes keep me here—half alive. I'd have died long ago, but somehow—"

Poe thought of a wretched spider, paralyzed by the sting of a mud-wasp, lying helpless in its captive's close den until the hour of feeding comes. He bent down, holding his blazing tinder close. He could see Gauber's neck, and it was a mass of tiny puncture wounds, some of them still beaded with blood drops fresh or dried. He winced, but bode firm in his purpose.

"Let me guess the truth," he said quickly. "Your wife was brought home from the grave, came back to a seeming of life. She put a spell on you, or played a trick—made you a helpless prisoner. That isn't contrary to nature, that last. I've studied mesmerism."

"It's true," John Gauber mumbled.

"And nightly she comes to drink your blood?"

Gauber weakly nodded. "Yes. She was beginning just now, but ran upstairs. She will be coming back."

"Good," said Poe bleakly. "Perhaps she will come back to more than she expects. Have you ever heard of vampires? Probably not, but I have studied them, too. I began to guess, I think, when first she was so repelled by the odor of garlic. Vampires lie motionless by day and walk and feed at night. They are creatures of the moon—their food is blood. Come."

Poe broke off, put out his light, and lifted the man in his arms. Gauber was as light as a child. The writer carried him to the slanting shelter of the closed-in staircase, and there set him against the wall. Over him Poe spread his old cadet cloak. In the gloom, the gray of the cloak harmonized with the gray of the wall stones. The poor fellow would be well hidden.

Next Poe flung off his coat, waist-coat and shirt. Heaping his clothing in a deeper shadow of the stairway, he stood up, stripped to the waist. His skin was almost as bloodlessly pale as Gauber's, his chest and arms almost as gaunt. He dared believe that he might pass momentarily for the unfortunate man.

The cellar sprang full of light again. The cloud must be passing from the moon. Poe listened. There was a dragging sound above, then footsteps.

Elva Gauber, the blood drinker by night, had revived.

Now for it. Poe hurried to the niche, thrust himself in and pulled the trapdoor shut after him.

He grinned, sharing a horrid paradox with the blackness around him. He had heard all the fabled ways of destroying vampires—transfixing stakes, holy water, prayer, fire. But he, Edgar Allan Poe, had evolved a new way. Myriads of tales whispered frighteningly of fiends lying in wait for normal men, but who ever heard of a normal man lying in wait for a fiend? Well, he had never considered himself normal, in spirit, or brain, or taste.

He stretched out, feet together, hands crossed on his bare midriff. Thus it would be in the tomb, he found himself thinking. To his mind came a snatch of poetry by a man named Bryant, published long ago in a New England review—*Breathless darkness, and the narrow house.* It was breathless and dark enough in this hole, Heaven knew, and narrow as well. He rejected, almost hysterically, the implication of being buried. To break the ugly spell, that daunted him where thought of Elva Gauber failed, he turned sideways to face the wall, his naked arm lying across his cheek and temple.

As his ear touched the musty bedding, it brought to him once again the echo of footsteps, footsteps descending stairs. They were rhythmic, confident. They were eager.

Elva Gauber was coming to seek again her interrupted repast.

Now she was crossing the floor. She did not pause or turn aside—she had not noticed her husband, lying under the cadet cloak in the shadow of the stairs. The noise came straight to the trapdoor, and he heard her fumbling for the latch.

Light, blue as skimmed milk, poured into his nook. A shadow fell in the midst of it, full upon him. His imagination, ever outstripping reality, whispered that the shadow had weight, like lead—oppressive, baleful.

"John," said the voice of Elva Gauber in this ear, "I've come back. You know why—you know what for." Her voice sounded greedy, as though it came through loose, trembling lips. "You're my only source of strength now. I thought tonight, that a stranger—but he got away. He had a cursed odor about him, anyway."

Her hand touched the skin of his neck. She was prodding him, like a butcher fingering a doomed beast.

"Don't hold yourself away from me, John," she was commanding, in a voice of harsh mockery. "You know it won't do any good. This is the night of the full moon, and I have power for anything, anything!" She was trying to drag his arm away from his face. "You won't gain by—" She broke off, aghast. Then, in a wild-dry-throated scream:

"You're not John!"

Poe whipped over on his back, and his bird-claw hands shot out and seized her—one hand clinching upon her snaky disorder of dark hair, the other digging its fingertips into the chill flesh of her arm.

The scream quivered away into a horrible breathless rattle. Poe dragged his captive violently inward, throwing all his collected strength into the effort. Her feet were jerked from the floor and she flew into the recess, hurtling above and beyond Poe's recumbent body. She struck the inner stones with a crashing force that might break bones, and would have collapsed upon Poe; but, at the same moment, he had released her and slid swiftly out upon the floor of the cellar.

With frantic haste he seized the edge of the back-flung trapdoor. Elva Gauber struggled up on hands and knees, among the tumbled bedclothes in the niche; then Poe had slammed the panel shut.

She threw herself against it from within, yammering and wailing like an animal in a trap. She was almost as strong as he, and for a moment he thought that she would win out of the niche. But, sweating and wheezing, he bore against the planks with his shoulder, bracing his feet against the earth. His fingers found the latch, lifted it, forced it into place.

"Dark," moaned Elva Gauber from inside. "Dark—no moon—" Her voice trailed off.

Poe went to the muddy pool in the corner, thrust in his hands. The muck was slimy but workable. He pushed a double handful of it against the trapdoor, sealing cracks and edges. Another handful, another. Using his palms like trowels, he coated the boards with thick mud.

"Gauber," he said breathlessly, "how are you?"

"All right—I think." The voice was strangely strong and clear. Looking over his shoulder, Poe saw that Gauber had come upright of himself, still pale but apparently steady. "What are you doing?" Gauber asked.

"Walling her up," jerked out Poe, scooping still more mud. "Walling her up forever, with her evil."

He had a momentary flash of inspiration, a symbolic germ of a story; in it a man sealed a woman into such a nook of the wall, and with her an embodiment of active evil—perhaps in the form of a black cat.

Pausing at last to breathe deeply, he smiled to himself.

Even in the direst of danger, the most heart-breaking moment of toil and fear, he must ever be coining new plots for stories.

"I cannot thank you enough," Gauber was saying to him. "I feel that all will be well—if only she stays there."

Poe put his ear to the wall. "Not a whisper of motion, sir. She's shut off from moonlight—from life and power. Can you help me with my clothes? I feel terribly chilled."

His mother-in-law met him on the threshold when he returned to the house in Spring Garden Street. Under the white widow's cap, her strong-boned face was drawn with worry.

"Eddie, are you ill?" She was really asking if he had been drinking. A look reassured her. "No," she answered herself, "but you've been away from home so long. And you're dirty, Eddie—filthy. You must wash."

He let her lead him in, pour hot water into a basin. As he scrubbed himself, he formed excuses, a banal lie about a long walk for inspiration, a moment of dizzy weariness, a stumble into a mud puddle.

"I'll make you some nice hot coffee, Eddie," his mother-in-law offered.

"Please," he responded, and went back to his room with the slate mantelpiece. Again he lighted the candle, sat down and took up his pen.

His mind was embellishing the story inspiration that had come to him at such a black moment, in the cellar of the Gauber house. He'd work on that tomorrow. The *United States Saturday Post* would take it, he hoped. Title? He would call it simply "The Black Cat."

But to finish the present task! He dipped his pen in ink. How to begin? How to end? How, after writing and publishing such an account, to defend himself against the growing whisper of his insanity?

He decided to forget it, if he could—at least to seek healthy company, comfort, quiet—perhaps even to write some light verse, some humorous articles and stories. For the first time in his life, he had had enough of the macabre.

Quickly he wrote a final paragraph:

There are moments when, even to the sober eye of Reason, the world of our sad Humanity may assume the semblance of a Hell—but the imagination of man is no Carathis, to explore with impunity its every cavern. Alas! The grim legion of sepulchral terrors cannot be regarded as altogether fanciful—but, like the Demons in whose company Afrasiab made his voyage down the Oxus, they must sleep, or they will devour us—they must be suffered to slumber, or we will perish.

That would do for the public, decided Edgar Allan Poe. In any case, it would do for the Philadelphia *Dollar Newspaper*. His mother-in-law brought in the coffee.

Eighth Avenue in New York City is an odd street—particularly above 42nd Street: bars, a Japanese glassblower, seedy hotels, more bars, a few tattoo parlors (boarded up as a result of some curious blue law), a famous magic store, and, in establishments which have in some strange way failed and vanished, squatting gypsy fortunetellers. There is also Madison Square Garden; and in Robert Arthur's story, the ambiance of the Garden and that of the spooky Avenue mix most effectively.

Mr. Jinx

Robert Arthur

The impact upon a certain section of the New York social stratum of the lean, mahogany-complexioned, knife-faced gentleman in the black turban for a time promised to be terrific—like the concussion of a Joe Louis jab on the jaw of a third-rate contender from Upper Yawkey Falls, Idaho, or the caress of a Florida hurricane on a new bungalow development.

If only he had never crossed Millie Duane's path—

And if Millie hadn't been trying to get fifty grand belonging to Jimmy Donegan out of Roscoe Wentworth, so she and Jimmy could get married and go to Texas to raise blooded livestock and a family—

And—

But heck, that's the story! It also includes the truth about what happened to Little Pitty, the jet-eyed killer who vanished from human view in broad daylight on Eight Avenue while waiting for a convenient opportunity to put the slug on Roscoe Wentworth. As well as how Maxie Mullion came to disappear from a running bath in a locked bathroom in his penthouse thirty-one stories in the air. Both here revealed for the first time.

So to begin. With Millie, of course—

Millie Duane was a red-headed little wren three sizes bigger than a minute and twice as energetic as a thimbleful of molecules, which are the stuff science says a thimbleful of would run a battleship from New York to London—providing, of course, it didn't hit a mine on the way.

Millie had as many attractive curves as a scenic railway, and she knew more about the manly art of modified murder than Roscoe Wentworth himself, who, though he didn't invent it, patented a lot of new improvements on it. Her dad had been Miltie Duane, a fight manager and an honest one. He died when she was fifteen. Millie hated crookedness of any kind, especially in fighting, but she worked for Roscoe Wentworth because a girl had to live.

Had to live because some day a guy like Jimmy Donegan was going to come along.

Now, strictly speaking, Jimmy Donegan doesn't come into this tale at all. He's distinctly offstage motivation. Except that if you looked into Millie's blue eyes you might have seen his reflection there even when he wasn't present. If you had —or if, more prosaically, you saw his mug on the sporting page the night he won the light-heavy crown—you saw a clean-cut face, a squarish jaw, a grin, nice teeth, laughing eyes, and brown hair with something of a curl in it.

Too nice a face—anyway, Millie thought so—to be scrambled around by the impact of countless fists. Especially when Jimmy didn't particularly like fighting and only had gone into it, after getting out of agricultural college, so he could collect a stake with which to buy a farm in Texas— a ranch he could turn into a show-place breeding farm.

So that when Roscoe signed him up, and Millie saw him for the first time, right down deep inside her she knew it had happened. She was in love. And she was determined that she, with her superior knowledge of the fight business—and of Roscoe Wentworth, whose private secretary she was—was going to look out for Jimmy's interests.

Which she did, so effectively that inside a year and a half —most of the time over Roscoe Wentworth's pitiful protests —she maneuvered Jimmy into the championship before a capacity crowd at the Garden. Roscoe hadn't been ready for Jimmy to be champ yet—figuring lots of cash-bearing angles in holding him off—but Millie willed otherwise.

If it had been love at first sight for Millie, it had been ditto and double that for Jimmy. The only thing they had waited for was the championship. With that to retire on, and fifty grand—that was what they figured his savings ought to be by then—to buy the farm with, they'd get married and shake the soot of Manhattan off their shoes faster than Roscoe Wentworth could chisel a dollar from a fighter's purse. Jimmy described Texas so vividly that Millie could hear the cattle bawling, and she knew she was going to love it.

So now Jimmy was champ. And they were all ready to take up the serious business of matrimony. Except that there was a fly, a short, plump, pink-faced fly named Roscoe Wentworth, in the well-known ointment.

"Roscoe," Millie said, her voice cool and crisp, a little green glow altering the blue of her eyes, "you're a louse."

"Please, Millie," Roscoe Wentworth begged, lifting a plump hand in half-hearted protest, "you mustn't bother me now. I got troubles on my mind."

It was a June day, with a benign sun gilding the pavements of Manhattan. Roscoe, seated behind a desk big enough for a fast game of tennis, was smoking a Havana stogie with nervous puffs. In the flat safe behind him were the receipts from the previous night's bout between Bombardier Benson, the Swedish Blitzkrieg, and Neverdown Nevens, the Granite Giant. Deducing expenses and taxes, there remained fifty grand clear for Roscoe Wentworth. But this morning Roscoe could not quite summon up the *joie de vivre* the figures called for.

Ever and again, all morning long, he had found himself glancing out the broad, plate glass windows at the figure stalking back and forth across the street. Of course, Johnny Pitty—better known as "Little" Pitty—probably wouldn't really shoot him. After all, even Roscoe had thought that Neverdown was going to win last night. It had been pure accident that the Bombardier, ducking to avoid a looping right, had somehow managed to bang his frontal bone against the Granite Giant's chin.

The damage to the Swedish Blitzkrieg's skull had been negligible. But no one could dispute that Neverdown Nevens had a fractured jaw. If Little Pitty had dropped ten Gs, still, hadn't Roscoe himself lost?

But Mr. Wentworth could not put his doubts at rest. There was something feline about Little Pitty's back-and-forth stalk. Roscoe found his head swiveling first one way then the other, like a spectator at a tennis match.

Perhaps it would be best to make good to the fellow his ten thousand dollars, even though—

"Roscoe!" Millie's voice interrupted his troubled thoughts.

"Stop waggling your head back and forth and listen if you don't want me to get annoyed. I'm not here as your secretary any more. I've resigned. I'm here as Mrs. Jimmy Donegan to-be, about Jimmy's contract—and a little matter of fifty thousand dollars in lawful United States currency, legal tender for the payment of all debts, public or private."

"Now, Millie," Roscoe began placatingly, with an effort taking his eyes off Little Pitty, "I don't know what you mean. All Jimmy's contract says is that he is gonna fight three more fights for me before he retires. Or else he forfeits fifty thousand, the amount of his last purse, which I am withholding persuant to article five, paragraph B, as security for the performance of the agreed upon—"

"Yes, Roscoe"—honey dripped from Millie's curved and kissable lips—"I have had a lawyer look at the contract, and he has already told me what it says. But Roscoe, you and Jimmy had a verbal agreement that after he won the championship, he would be released from all contracts without obligation, providing he didn't fight again for somebody else."

Roscoe Wentworth mopped his brow.

"Yeah, Millie," he conceded. "But that was only a gentleman's agreement. This other contract is *signed*. Look at it like this, Millie. I, personally, spent a lot of money building Jimmy up. No, don't snort like that. It don't become a pretty girl to curl her lips so. He's a valuable propitty. Now am I gonna lose all my investment because he wants to go back to Texas an' raise hogs?"

Millie snorted again, shaking her red-gold curls in a menacing manner.

"It would be fair, *if* you had spent any money on Jimmy, which you haven't, and *if* that was all the contract said," she declared. "But the contract specifies *three fights in defense of his championship!* And I know you, Roscoe Wentworth! For every fight in defense of his title, you'd book him for three others that weren't. And suppose he lost the crown! Then he'd have to fight for you until he won it again so he could defend it, so he wouldn't lose the fifty thousand you're holding out, and that we've been planning all along to buy a stock farm with. It might take years!

"No, Roscoe, I won't stand for it. I want that contract torn up, and I want that fifty thousand of Jimmy's, right now!"

She stamped a small foot and glared at Roscoe Wentworth.

Roscoe, secure in the knowledge that if she manhandled him in any way she could go to jail for it, glared back, unyieldingly.

It was an impasse, will meeting will in a contest of strength, and how it would have turned out no one knows. For it was at that moment the tall gentleman with the beady eyes and the black turban entered, unannounced.

Mr. Jinx had arrived in town.

He came in through the door, but to Millie and Roscoe it was as if he had materialized on Roscoe's Bokhara rug. Not until he coughed did they turn and realize anyone was there.

Roscoe's eyes bugged. Even Millie stared in open-mouthed astonishment as the intruder favored them with a calm, narrow-lidded scrutiny.

The arrival of the sinister, turbaned one in New York was quite unobserved, and so far as can be determined, no one can recall noticing him before his arrival that morning in the office of the Fair-Square Sporting Club. Which is odd, for if ever there was an observable figure, it was him. It was he? Thanks. Six feet two he stood, dressed in a drape-cut suit of coffee-colored silk of a special weave that would wear till doomsday. In a way, fortunate. Otherwise his clothing was conventional, save that topping off the outfit—literally—a jet-black turban was wrapped about his high-domed head. And beneath the turban, eyes like black glass marbles gazed unwinkingly at Millie and Roscoe from either side of a hawk-beaked nose.

The curious caller carried a cane with a golden head, unpleasantly carved to look like a cobra, and on his ring finger, Millie noticed, being more observant than Roscoe Wentworth, a ring of beaten gold which held, not a jewel, but a tiny crystal globe half an inch across.

With a flourish, their visitor held out a parchment card.

"Permit me," he said, his voice deep, with a curious muted quality, like the throbbing of a temple gong in the distance. Then, as Roscoe took the proffered card, the turbaned one let his eyes rest on Millie, traveling over her from head to feet in a leisurely journey that brought a crimson flush of embarrassment to her cheeks.

His gaze only left her, after having apparently appraised—and approved of—every charm she possessed, concealed or revealed, when Roscoe Wentworth looked up from the card, on which flowing characters spelled out *The Prince Agah Shan y Pasha Rehab Neroc d'Ghengs.*

"Pronounced *Jinx*," the caller informed Roscoe somberly. "We will dispense with formality. You may call me simply —Mr. Jinx."

"Uh . . . how-do, Mr. . . . um, Jinx," Roscoe gulped. "Uh—"

"Of course. You wish to know my business here. I am in the accident . . . ah, profession."

"Uh, insurance?" Roscoe mumbled. "Sorry. Can't use any." Then his eyes swiveled toward that pacing figure in the street, momentarily forgotten. "Although, maybe—"

"Ah, no," Mr. Jinx purred, clasping both hands over the top of his cobra cane. "You misunderstand. I *cause* accidents."

"Cause accidents!" Breathing heavily, Roscoe found himself on his feet. The old protection racket! As if he hadn't just bought off the Mahoney mob by promising them inside dope on all his fights, so they could place their money right. Now this faker—

"Not faker." The deep voice was resonant in the room. "Fakir. You must not confuse the two. Now sit down. Mr. Wentworth"—and under the unwinking, snakelike gaze Roscoe found himself sitting again—"and let me explain. Briefly. I do not enjoy conversation. Although—"

The black eyes flicked for an instant to Millie. Then the turbaned one resumed.

"My profession," he went on, "is that of a causer of accidents. For a consideration I will refrain from employing my somewhat peculiar and unique talents to your disadvantage. If you do not care to retain my services—well, odd things may happen to your hirelings in their combats, and it is even possible that you yourself may suffer some unfortunate experiences. Do I make myself clear?"

"You're darn tootin' you do!" Roscoe declared, inelegantly. "Protection, huh! Well, I got protection awready. An' you're gonna get th' gate."

He pressed a buzzer. The door opened. Two large bruisers, retired from active service in the wrestling wracket—pardon me, racket—but still plenty good enough for bouncers, lumbered in. They were Murderous Mordred, the Minnesota Mauler, once champion of Mexico, and Ivan Yousapouf, the Russian Massacre, once Champion of Champions—the only title he could win.

"Throw him out!" Roscoe hollered. "Toss him on his ear so hard he bounces!"

With fire in their eyes and garlic on their breath, Wentworth's two behemoths charged. Mr. Jinx, however, made no move to avoid them. He threw himself up, folded his arms so that the hand bearing his ring was uppermost, and stared down into the transparent depth of its tiny crystal ball.

What he saw there is unknown. But what happened was immediate. The Mauler stepped on one of his own feet and fell heavily, banging his head against the desk and chipping the corner. From there he thundered to the floor and lay prone, smiling in unconsciousness—probably dreaming he was back on the mat again in the careless days of his youth.

The Massacre, continuing on, swung on Mr. Jinx. He missed and whirled around, getting in a solid blow at the base of his own skull. Like a poled ox he fell on top of the Mauler, and after a moment began to snore.

"You see?" the turbaned one asked. "It is but a minor example of my powers."

"Powers!" Millie snorted. "Those poor, punch-drunk palookas could knock themselves silly in a feather bed. Why, Ivan had a bad dream one night and bit himself in the small of the back. And got blood poisoning, too!"

"Sure!" Roscoe chimed in. "You ain't proved nothing."

Mr. Jinx did not smile. He stared at Roscoe, and his unwinking gaze probed the fat little man like a knife. Finally he nodded, the black turban moving in a slow, ominous arc.

"You have an enemy," he told Roscoe in resonant tones. "The one outside now. He wishes to kill you. You fear him. Upon him I will demonstrate my greatest power. It will not be an accident that he suffers. I will make the proof of my talents plain. I will dispose of him, once and for all, beyond the art of man to recall. He will go into limbo."

"Limbo?" Roscoe repeated doubtfully. "That's in Russia some place, ain't it?"

"Limbo," Mr. Jinx assured him, teeth flashing briefly in a cruel smile, "lies in a land between life and death. It is not a nice place."

"It still sounds like Russia to me," Roscoe murmured, uneasily, but he turned to the window to watch. Millie turned too, skepticism and doubt struggling on her countenance.

Mr. Jinx folded his arms and gazed into the crystal of his ring with such concentration that perspiration sprang out on his forehead. His lips moved, and they heard words, strange and harsh and ringing, like the muted clash of brass.

Across the street Little Pitty was staring up at the window. He saw Roscoe Wentworth and made a motion toward his pocket. The fat man would have ducked back, except for a sight that held him in a species of paralysis.

Eighth Avenue was tolerably empty, except for the little gunman. So there was no one in the way of the mustard-colored haze that began to collect at the corner of Forty-ninth Street, and swirling gently, drifted northward toward Little Pitty.

The killer did not see it. It came up from behind him, vague of outline, like a top spinning at terrific speed. And then it swirled into him. The gunman staggered backward, as if some great force had seized him, and was engulfed in the heart of the mist. For a second or so the shadowy mass whirled there, then it began to drift north again, dissolving as it moved, so that by the time it reached Fiftieth Street it was gone.

And so was Little Pitty!

"He's gone," Millie whispered, her voice queer. "Gone!"

Mr. Roscoe Wentworth stumbled backward to his swivel chair and collapsed into it.

"*Ulp!*" he gurgled. "What ha-happened to him?"

"He has been removed," Mr. Jinx murmured. "The doorway has been opened for him, and he has been drawn through into limbo. Which is a most unpleasant place where one is neither dead nor alive, but wanders homeless until doomsday."

"You can bring him back, though?" Roscoe asked.

The tall, turbaned one shook his head. "That is beyond my power. The forces I control do not extend to that. I offer one-way passage only."

And he smiled, his lips drawing back in a curious curl that made Roscoe Wentworth shudder, though the day was hot.

But disbelief still was mirrored on Millie's features.

"Just what *are* these 'powers' of yours, Mr. Jinx?" she demanded. "And who are you, anyway?"

The man in the black turban breathed on the gold head of his cobra cane and polished it gently with his palm. His lips smiled, but his eyes held no mirth.

"I am from the East," he answered, directing his whole attention upon Millie. "In my boyhood I was destined to be a priest, but found the studies boring. I took up others, less well known. My master was a magician of rather sinister repute. From him I learned the control of certain powers, such as you have seen demonstrated. In seeking to turn these to my profit, it occurred to me that here in the Western world is to be found much wealth. I have come to obtain a share of it, by placing my abilities at the service of those who may have use for them."

There was mockery in his voice now.

"It has occurred to me that what is known as the sporting world is a good place to begin. In it men are—less scrupulous. In time I shall extend my services to higher levels of society. For the present I shall deal in simple accidents and removals —such as you have witnessed. In time, when I have a sufficiency of worldly goods, I shall return to my own land. Until then"—a curious reddish flame leaped in the black eyes— "until then I shall take what I want of this Western land to which I have come, and ill will befall the man who tries to balk my purpose."

He smiled again, and again Roscoe shivered.

"You are unconvinced," the turbaned man told Millie. "In your mind lurks the suspicion that the one who vanished was my cohort, acting under my orders to deceive and frighten you."

Millie stiffened, for that was the exact suspicion in her mind.

"I shall give you further proof, then."

The tall man whirled, took up the daily paper on Roscoe's desk, opened to a picture on the sporting page of the previous night's bout. A pointed nail touched a bald head in the foreground of the news photo.

"This man," Mr. Jinx said deeply. "I do not know his name. His face I can not see. I judge him to be important—"

"Important!" Roscoe choked. "That's Maxie Mullion. Why, he's boss of the whole East Side. He has a finger in more crooked—"

"A politician!" There was distant thunder in Mr. Jinx's voice.

"But look!" Roscoe began, worriedly. "You ain't—"

"Silence!"

Quivering like a nervous jellyfish, Roscoe gulped and subsided. Placing the picture upon the desk, Mr. Jinx folded his arms and concentrated as before upon his crystal ring. For a long moment he stood so, murmuring strange words. Then he looked up.

"It is done," he announced. "You will read about it presently. For the moment I shall bid you adieu. There are other calls to be made, and I must find a suitable office. I shall have many clients. Later I shall return, for the first payment of my fees."

Black eyes rested briefly on the locked safe behind Roscoe.

"Fifty thousand dollars will be the figure," Mr. Jinx announced, as though divining the exact amount in safekeeping there.

"You won't get it!" Millie stated crisply, as Roscoe Wentworth turned a pale green with despair. "We don't like crooks or chiselers around here, and you come under those headings, whether you're a yogi, a swami, a fakir, or a faker. Besides, that fifty grand is mine—Jimmy's, I mean. And if Roscoe lets you have it, we never will be able to collect it from him. So—anyway, don't come back, unless you're looking for trouble. You may be able to buffalo poor Roscoe, but I'm not a man, and I'm not buffaloed."

"It is true you are not a man." The turbaned one's voice was bland. "And the master who taught me gave urgent warning that women should be avoided, for they have no souls, and so many of my spells are impotent against them. But there are other minor powers that are effective, and I think I can make you believe in me. And at a later date, perhaps— more. If you will but look—"

He glanced at her shapely legs. Millie followed the direction of his gaze, and saw two long runs suddenly appear in the new, off-shade silk stockings that set off her legs so well. It was as though a sharp instrument had been drawn lightly down the threads, though she had felt nothing.

While Millie still stared in speechless horror at her stockings, Mr. Jinx turned to Roscoe Wentworth.

"Remember, I shall return," he warned, as he backed to the door.

"Why, you—" Millie spluttered, choked with wrath. "You—"

But the door closed and Mr. Jinx was gone before she could express herself.

For a time after the gentleman from the Orient vanished, relative silence held the office. Relative, because it was broken by the sharp click of Millie's high heels as she strode back and forth, sparks flashing from her eyes and electricity fairly crackling from her red curls. It was broken also by the asthmatic breathing of the Mauler and the Massacre, who still encumbered the floor, and by a low moaning, as of an animal dying in extreme agony somewhere distant, coming from Roscoe.

And presently it was broken additionally by shouts from the street of newsboys proclaiming an extra.

Ivan, the Massacre, groaned and got to his feet. The Mauler opened his eyes and also hoisted himself upright.

"Geez," the Massacre groaned, blinking about him, "I feel terrible. Did he t'row me outa th' ring?"

"Was we wrasslin'?" the Mauler inquired. "I dunno— I thought—"

"Get out!" Roscoe screamed, in high passion. "Bouncers, phooey! Bring me one of them extras, an' don't come back for a week!"

The two stampeded for the door. Millie turned away from the window and faced the fight promoter, whose cigar was a frayed stub.

"He went into a restaurant," she announced. "I watched. Well?"

"Well, what?" Roscoe groaned, all three chins quivering.

"Well, what do you intend to do?" Millie stamped her foot. "Pay, I suppose!"

Roscoe stabbed at his mouth with the cigar, and missed by two inches.

"But what can I do, Millie?" he groaned. "Against a guy like him? Mr. Jinx! If he was to get mad—" Roscoe shuddered, and swallowed hard. Then his gaze fell on his safe. That recalled to mind the fifty grand Mr. Jinx was demanding. Roscoe Wentworth stiffened. There was nothing like the impending loss of a dollar to put starch in his spine.

"I got it!" he exclaimed, with relief. "It didn't any of it happen. He hypnotized us! Sure. He hypnotized me an' you an' Butch an' Ivan. Certainly I ain't gonna pay him anything. He— Well, what is it?"

The Russian Massacre, edging in, dropped a pink-sheet paper on the desk and scrambled out again.

"Just th' extra," he mumbled, and was gone, fleeing Roscoe's possible wrath. But Roscoe was paying him no more attention. His gaze was riveted upon the extra's headlines. His mouth opened. His cigar plopped to the floor.

"Glug!" he choked. "Blup!"

Millie looked over his shoulder at the headlines.

> PROMINENT POLITICIAN VANISHES FROM BATH
> *Secretary Hears Scream, Rushes to Aid. Finds Bathroom Door Locked, Water Running, Max J. Mullion Gone.*

"Then it wasn't hypnotism after all," Millie remarked, in a cool voice. "He said he could do it just from a picture, too, and he did."

Roscoe sat down with a thud.

"Wh-what," he quavered, "can we d-do, Millie?"

"Do!" Millie snorted. "Fight back at him. If you don't, you'll be practically his slave. I suppose you realize that?"

"Y-yes," Roscoe gulped. "But fight him *h-how?*"

"When you're fighting fire, fight it with more fire," Millie said obscurely, a strange, cold gleam in her blue eyes. "Set a thief to catch a thief. You men! But if you think you're going to pay Jimmy's fifty thousand dollars to that . . . that swami, you've got three more thinks coming. Now I'm going out. I'll be back. You stay here."

But Roscoe Wentworth had no intention of leaving. Even as, with unexplained determination, Millie marched out, he was reaching for the bottle in his lower left-hand drawer. When he got it, he raised the neck to his lips and held it there. For he desperately wanted to erase the mental image that had come to him, of rapacious old Maxie Mullion wandering through eternity, waiting for the crack of doom, without even a bath towel to hide behind.

When Millie returned, two hours later, Mr. Roscoe Wentworth had consumed the bottle, without apparent effect. His features were flushed and perspiration spangled his brow and triplex chin, but he still was unable to forget how Little Pitty had vanished into a mustard-colored cloud, or to put away from himself the vision of Maxie Mullion—

"Well," Millie stared briskly, "after he ate, he went to call on Bennie Barber, Nat Miller, and Colonel Worth. I expect he'll be coming back here soon."

"I know." Roscoe's voice was the plaintive moan of a beaten man. "They called me up. Said he was there. Said he'd showed a few . . . tricks. Wanted to know if I was going to pay. I said 'yes.' He wants fifty Gs from them, too.

And it's just a beginning. He let drop he was going to contact the mobs—like the Schwartz mob and the Dougal boys—about removals! Ten grand apiece. In a year he'll own this town. All of it. And anybody who holds out will go to that . . . that place. Oh, what did I ever do to deserve this, Millie?"

"Plenty," Millie stated, unfeelingly. "But that's not the point. You men! Sometimes I think all of you put together haven't as much brains or courage as just one woman. You'll let him walk all over you. You'll pay him what he wants, and be glad of the chance."

"Yeah," moaned Roscoe.

"You'll be afraid all the time."

"Yeah," Roscoe groaned.

"Your life won't be worth living."

"I know it, Millie," Roscoe said piteously. Then he looked up. Millie was gazing in a reflective manner down at the ugly runs in her stockings, and her lips were pursed.

"Millie!" Roscoe Wentworth exclaimed, clutching at a straw of hope. "You're thinking of something?"

Millie raised her eyes, so large, so blue, so innocent.

"Maybe I *could* think of something," she suggested, "if only I wasn't so upset. About Jimmy's contract, and the fifty thousand dollars."

She sighed. Roscoe sighed, too.

"You mean"—his tone was hollow—"if I was to say I'd tear up the contract and pay over the fifty thousand, you might be able to shoo off this Mr. Jinx?"

"I might," Millie answered. "I just barely might, Roscoe."

The plump little man expelled his breath gustily.

"If you would say twenty-five grand, Millie," he began, and then the opening of the office door broke off his words.

"Good afternoon," Mr. Jinx said, and his smile was catlike. "I have returned, as I promised. Shall we now discuss the business we left unfinished?"

The words were addressed to Roscoe, but his eyes were on Millie. Millie stared back for a moment, then dropped her gaze. The cat smile broadened. The black turbaned man advanced into the office, and indicated the pink sheet on Roscoe's desk.

"You have read. You are convinced?"

Roscoe gulped, but Millie spoke before he could answer.

"Of course not," she said stoutly. "I still think it's a trick.

So does he. I'm not convinced you're not a phony one little bit."

"Ah." The dark eyes rested on her with a curious expression. "You are stubborn. What proof, then, will convince you?"

"To make somebody *I* pick out disappear," Millie answered.

Mr. Jinx leaned on his cobra cane, and seemed not displeased.

"You are a practical woman," he said, almost pleasantly. "And *why* not? Name the one, and limbo shall open for him. My powers are inexhaustible. One man more or less"—and the black eyes rested fleetingly on Roscoe, with so chill a menace that that plump gentleman shivered violently—"means to me as little as the life or death of a fly."

"Well"—Millie hesitated now—"I . . . I don't, really—"

"You have chosen the test! Now name the one you wish the world relieved of!"

"All . . . all right," Millie gulped and opened her handbag. From it she took a picture, frayed at the edges, with a crease down the middle, the corners bent with soiled spots on the back. It was a blurred street scene with half a dozen figures in it.

"Th-this one," Millie stated, indicating a white splotch that was barely identifiable as the shoulder of a man in a summer suit, all the rest of him being hidden by the surrounding crowds. "I don't know his right name, or where he lives, or anything. I tried to get a picture of him once, and this was all I could get. But he's a b-blackmailer, and very ruthless, and—"

"It is enough." Mr. Jinx took the picture, letting his fingers touch her hand as he did so, and a cold electric shock tingled up Millie's arm. "It will suffice. In a moment he will be no more."

Millie licked her lips.

"It's . . . sort of drastic," she said. "But . . . well, he deserves it."

"I am glad"—and Mr. Jinx's eyes held hers—"you have not a woman's usual squeamishness about such matters. And I think that when I have set your doubts at rest, we may become—better acquainted. Much, much better acquainted. You will—appreciate me more. Now—"

"Roscoe," Millie directed, her voice crisp again, "you'd better get out that fifty thousand dollars you have."

"Well—" Roscoe began, then catching the look in her eye, hurriedly swung around. "All right," he muttered, and spun the combination. "Here it is."

He laid five packets of bills on the desk, and prepared to close the steel door again, but Millie was too quick.

"Isn't that Jimmy Donegan's contract?" she cooed, snatching out a white, legal-looking document. "Jimmy wants to read it over later. All right, Roscoe, you can close it now."

Roscoe slammed the safe shut, angrily. Millie tucked the contract in her purse and faced Mr. Jinx.

The tall man in the black turban let his eyes traverse her visible charms again, lingeringly, then he took up the blurred photo.

"In a moment," he said vibrantly, "your enemy will leave this life for another, endless and unpleasant. Please be silent now."

Millie backed away toward the window, eyes wide. The turbaned one bowed his head, and concentrated upon the tiny globe of crystal in his ring. Roscoe Wentworth, baffled and bewildered, caught Millie's urgent gestures and tiptoed toward her.

Mr. Jinx, head bowed, was murmuring unknown words as, staring into the transparent depths of the bit of crystal, he summoned up the forces which blindly obeyed his orders.

Behind the turbaned man, in the corner of the big office, something stirred. Dust whirled, and Roscoe Wentworth almost let out a squeal of terror. Millie clapped her hand over his mouth just in time, and he was silent as that dark, shadowy mass in the corner, began to take form, began to spin, faster and faster, and spinning, swept down upon the motionless Mr. Jinx.

The one from the Orient had just time to wrench his mind from its task of directing terrible forces toward the unknown one and become aware of what was happening. But it was too late to stop the powers he had loosed. The spinning shadow touched him. Something like a terrific suction pulled at him and engulfed him. He had only time to know he had been tricked, and by a woman, and then he was hurtling through invisible portals into a world whose horrors he had never fully cared to think about—

Roscoe Wentworth stared at the spot where Mr. Jinx had been only a moment before, and still seemed to hear that last cry, coming as if from a land an immeasurable distance away. Then, still strangling as he tried to get air into his lungs, he started forward. Millie was ahead of him, though, and reached the five packets of bills still lying on the desk first.

She tucked them into her purse as Roscoe drew up, baffled, and shook her head.

"You men!" her voice dripped scorn. "If it wasn't for me, he *would* have owned this city. And it was so simple, too. I just bought a camera when I left, and waited for him outside the restaurant. Then I followed him until he was in a crowd, and took a picture of his back. For five dollars the drugstore downstairs rushed me a print. I rubbed it and folded it to make it look old."

"A picture of himself!" Roscoe croaked. "You mean . . . you made him put the finger on himself, Millie?"

"Of course," Millie cooed. "He said his powers would work, even from a picture he couldn't recognize, didn't he? And proved it by that old Maxie Mullion. Any woman would have thought of that right away—especially when she saw he was sort of stuck on her. Only a man would think of giving him fifty thousand dollars when it was so easy to get rid of him forever. And another person's fifty thousand, at that!" Millie finished accusingly.

"But—" Roscoe Wentworth stammered. "But—"

"Oh, he won't come back," Millie assured him, heading for the door. "You heard him say himself it's a one-way passage. So you don't have to worry. Of course, in a way I'm sorry for him, because he did have interesting eyes. But wherever he is"—and Millie's eyes flashed fire for a moment—"he deserves it! Maybe he'll know better next time than to say a girl hasn't got a soul, and to put runs into the last pair of silk stockings she's got!"

Then the door slammed, and she was gone. To Jimmy. And shortly thereafter, to Texas.

After a time, Roscoe Wentworth's mouth stopped opening and closing like a fish's. He looked at his ravished safe and winced. Then, into his eyes came a gleam of the native guile which always enabled him to emerge triumphant from any situation.

For a moment Roscoe stared hard at the emptiness that a moment before had been Mr. Jinx. Then cautiously skirting the spot, he gained his desk and his telephone, and dialed.

"Hello," he caroled. "Hello, Benny Barber? Is Nat Miller

and Colonel Worth there? Lissen, about this Jinx fella. Yeah"
—Roscoe looked quickly at the emptiness again, and decided to stretch matters a bit—"he's here now. I been talking him into a proposition. To go away and never bother us any more. For a hundred an' fifty grand he'll do it. I already put up fifty. If you fellas are interested, an' can raise th' other hundred, send it over to my office before five. An' I'll promise you'll never see him again. I'll take th' full responsibility. You think it's worth it? I think so, too! O. K. I'll be looking for your boy."

He put down the phone, elevated his feet, and reached for the cigar box. Then, lighting it, he deliberately blew strong smoke toward the spot where the gentleman in the black turban had last been seen and began to hum a glad little tune as he pondered on what he could give Millie and Jimmy as a wedding present, for which he was willing to spend as high as five dollars even.

There are fantasy themes which never lose their fascination—omnipotence, the ever-filled purse, three wishes, selling one's soul. Unknown's writers used to delight in trying these on, so to speak, and twisting and turning them inside out to see if something new could be done with them. Tomorrow's Newspaper is a comparative newcomer to this collection of themes, but it's already had more than its share of workouts. Here Anthony Boucher has his go at it ... and comes up with a perfectly satisfactory, "fair"—and unhackneyed —solution.

Snulbug

Anthony Boucher

"That's a hell of a spell you're using," said the demon, "if I'm the best you can call up."

He wasn't much, Bill Hitchens had to admit. He looked lost in the center of that pentacle. His basic design was impressive enough—snakes for hair, curling tusks, a sharp-tipped tail, all the works—but he was something under an inch tall.

Bill had chanted the words and lit the powder with the highest hopes. Even after the feeble flickering flash and the damp fizzling *zzzt* which had replaced the expected thunder and lightning, he had still had hopes. He had stared up at the space above the pentacle waiting to be awe-struck until he had heard that plaintive little voice from the floor wailing, "Here I am."

"Nobody's wasted time and powder on a misfit like me for years," the demon went on. "Where'd you get the spell?"

"Just a little something I whipped up," said Bill modestly.

The demon grunted and muttered something about people that thought they were magicians.

"But I'm not a magician," Bill explained. "I'm a biochemist."

The demon shuddered. "I land the damnedest cases," he

mourned. "Working for that psychiatrist wasn't bad enough, I should draw a biochemist. Whatever that is."

Bill couldn't check his curiosity. "And what did you do for a psychiatrist?"

"He showed me to people who were followed by little men and told them I'd chase the little men away." The demon pantomimed shooing motions. *"Woosh woosh* all day chasing nothing."

"And did they go away?"

"Sure. Only then the people decided they'd sooner have little men than me. It didn't work so good. Nothing ever does," he added woefully. "Yours won't, either."

Bill sat down and filled his pipe. Calling up demons wasn't so terrifying, after all. Something quiet and homey about it. "Oh, yes, it will," he said. "This is foolproof."

"That's what they all think. People—" The demon wistfully eyed the match as Bill lit his pipe. "But we might as well get it over with. What do you want?"

"I want a laboratory for my embolism experiments. If this method works, it's going to mean that a doctor can spot an embolus in the bloodstream long before it's dangerous and remove it safely. My ex-boss, that screwball old occultist Reuben Choatsby, said it wasn't practical—meaning there wasn't a fortune in it for him—and fired me. Everybody else thinks I'm wacky, too, and I can't get any backing. So I need ten thousand dollars."

"There!" the demon sighed with satisfaction. "I told you it wouldn't work. That's out for me. They can't start fetching money on demand till three grades higher than me. I told you."

"But you don't," Bill grated, "appreciate all my fiendish subtlety. Look— Say, what is your name?"

The demon hesitated. "You haven't got another of those things?"

"What things?"

"Matches."

"Sure."

"Light me one, please?"

Bill tossed the burning match into the center of the pentacle. The demon scrambled eagerly out of the now cold ashes of the powder and dived into the flame, rubbing himself with the brisk vigor of a man under a needle shower. "There!" he gasped joyously. "That's more like it."

"And now what's your name?"

The demon's face fell again. "My name? You really want to know?"

"I've got to call you something."

"Oh, no, you don't. I'm going home. No money games for me."

"But I haven't explained yet what you are to do. What's your name?"

"Snulbug." The demon's voice dropped almost too low to be heard.

"Snulbug?" Bill laughed.

"Uh-huh. I've got a cavity in one tusk, my snakes are falling out, I haven't got troubles enough, I should be named Snulbug."

"All right. Now listen, Snulbug, can you travel into the future?"

"A little. I don't like it much, though. It makes you itch in the memory."

"Look, my fine snake-haired friend. It isn't a question of what you like. How would you like to be left there in that pentacle with nobody to throw matches at you?" Snulbug shuddered. "I thought so. Now you can travel into the future"

"I said a little."

"And," Bill leaned forward and puffed hard at his corncob as he asked the vital question, "can you bring back material objects?" If the answer was no, all the fine febrile fertility of his spell-making was useless. And if that was useless, Heaven alone knew how the Hitchens Embolism Diagnosis would ever succeed in ringing down the halls of history, and incidentally saving a few thousands lives annually.

Snulbug seemed more interested in the warm clouds of pipe smoke than in the question. "Sure," he said. "Within reason I can—" He broke off and stared up piteously. "You don't mean— You can't be going to pull that old gag again?"

"Look, baby. You do what I tell you and leave the worrying to me. You can bring back material objects?"

"Sure. But I warn you—"

Bill cut him off short. "Then as soon as I release you from that pentacle, you're to bring me tomorrow's newspaper."

Snulbug sat down on the burned match and tapped his forehead sorrowfully with his tail tip. "I knew it," he wailed. "I knew it. Three times already this happens to me. I've got limited powers, I'm a runt, I've got a funny name, so I should run foolish errands."

"Foolish errands?" Bill rose and began to pace about the bare attic. "Sir, if I may call you that, I resent such an imputation. I've spent weeks on this idea. Think of the limitless power in knowing the future. Think of what could be done with it: swaying the course of empire, dominating mankind. All I want is to take this stream of unlimited power, turn it into the simple channel of humanitarian research, and get me ten thousand dollars; and you call that a foolish errand!"

"That Spaniard," Snulbug moaned. "He was a nice guy, even if his spell was lousy. Had a solid, comfortable brazier where an imp could keep warm. Fine fellow. And he had to go ask to see tomorrow's newspaper— I'm warning you—"

"I know," said Bill hastily. "I've been over in my mind all the things that can go wrong. And that's why I'm laying three conditions on you before you get out of that pentacle. I'm not falling for the easy snares."

"All right." Snulbug sounded almost resigned. "Let's hear 'em. Not that they'll do any good."

"First: This newspaper must not contain a notice of my own death or of any other disaster that would frustrate what I can do with it."

"But shucks," Snulbug protested. "I can't guarantee that. If you're slated to die between now and tomorrow, what can

I do about it? Not that I guess you're important enough to crash the paper."

"Courtesy, Snulbug. Courtesy to your master. But I tell you what: When you go into the future, you'll know then if I'm going to die? Right. Well, if I am, come back and tell me and we'll work out other plans. This errand will be off."

"People," Snulbug observed, "make such an effort to make trouble for themselves. Go on."

"Second: The newspaper must be of this city and in English. I can just imagine you and your little friends presenting some dope with the Omsk and Tomsk *Daily Vuskutsukt*."

"We should take that much trouble," said Snulbug.

"And third: The newspaper must belong to this space-time continuum, to this spiral of the serial universe, to this Wheel of If. However you want to put it. It must be a newspaper of the tomorrow which I myself shall experience, not of some other, to me hypothetical tomorrow."

"Throw me another match," said Snulbug.

"Those three condition should cover it, I think. There's not a loophole there, and the Hitchens Laboratory is guaranteed."

Snulbug grunted. "You'll find out."

Bill took a sharp blade and duly cut a line of the pentacle with cold steel. But Snulbug simply dived in and out of the flame of his second match, twitching his tail happily, and seemed not to give a rap that the way to freedom was now open.

"Come on!" Bill snapped impatiently. "Or I'll take the match away."

Snulbug got as far as the opening and hesitated. "Twenty-four hours is a long way."

"You can make it."

"I don't know. Look." He shook his head, and a microscopic dead snake fell to the floor. "I'm not at my best. I'm shot to pieces lately, I am. Tap my tail."

"Do what?"

"Go on. Tap it with your fingernail right there where it joins on."

Bill grinned and obeyed. "Nothing happens."

"Sure nothing happens. My reflexes are all haywire. I don't know as I can make twenty-four hours." He brooded, and his snakes curled up into a concentrated clump. "Look. All you want is tomorrow's newspaper, huh? Just tomorrow's, not the edition that'll be out exactly twenty-four hours from now?"

"It's noon now—" Bill reflected. "Sure, I guess tomorrow morning's paper'll do."

"O. K. What's the date today?"

"August 21st."

"Fine. I'll bring you a paper for August 22nd. Only I'm warning you: It won't do any good. But here goes nothing. Good-by now. Hello again. Here you are." There was a string in Snulbug's horny hand, and on the end of the string was a newspaper.

"But hey!" Bill protested. "You haven't been gone."

"People," said Snulbug feelingly, "are dopes. Why should it take any time out of the present to go into the future? I leave this point, I come back to this point. I spent two hours hunting for this damned paper, but that doesn't mean two hours out of your time here. People—" he snorted.

Bill scratched his head. "I guess it's all right. Let's see the paper. And I know: You're warning me." He turned quickly to the obituaries to check. No Hitchens. "And I wasn't dead in the time you were in?"

"No," Snulbug admitted. "Not *dead*," he added, with the most pessimistic implications possible.

"What was I then? Was I—"

"I had Salamander blood," Snulbug complained. "They thought I was an undine like my mother and they put me in the cold-water incubator when any dope knows salamandry is a dominant. So I'm a runt and good for nothing but to run errands, and now I should make prophecies! You read your paper and see how much good it does you."

Bill laid down his pipe and folded the paper back from the obituaries to the front page. He had not expected to find anything useful there—what advantage could he gain from knowing who won the next naval engagement or which cities were bombed?—but he was scientifically methodical. And this time method was rewarded. There it was, streaming across the front page in vast black blocks:

MAYOR ASSASSINATED
FIFTH COLUMN KILLS CRUSADER

Bill snapped his fingers. This was it. This was his chance. He jammed his pipe in his mouth, hastily pulled a coat on his shoulders, crammed the priceless paper into a pocket, and started out of the attic. Then he paused and looked around. He'd forgotten Snulbug. Shouldn't there be some sort of formal discharge?

The dismal demon was nowhere in sight. Not in the pentacle nor out of it. Not a sign or a trace of him. Bill frowned. This was definitely not methodical. He struck a match and held it over the bowl of his pipe.

A warm sigh of pleasure came from inside the corncob.

Bill took the pipe from his mouth and stared at it. "So that's where you are?"

"I told you salamandry was a dominant," said Snulbug, peering out of the bowl. "I want to go along. I want to see just what kind of a fool you make of yourself." He withdrew his head into the glowing tobacco, muttering something about newspapers, spells, and, with a wealth of unhappy scorn, people.

The crusading mayor of Granton was a national figure of splendid proportions. Without hysteria, red-baiting, or strike-breaking, he had launched a quietly purposeful and well-directed program against subversive elements which had rapidly converted Granton into the safest and most American city in the country. He was also a persistent advocate of national, State, and municipal subsidy of the arts and sciences—the ideal man to wangle an endowment for the Hitchens Laboratory, if he were not so surrounded by overly skeptical assistants that Bill had never been able to lay the program before him.

This would do it. Rescue him from assassination in the very nick of time—in itself an act worth calling up demons to perform—and then when he asks, "And how, Mr. Hitchens, can I possibly repay you?" come forth with the whole great plan of research. It couldn't miss.

No sound came from the pipe bowl, but Bill clearly heard the words, "Couldn't it just?" ringing in his mind.

He braked his car to a fast stop in the red zone before the city hall, jumped out without even slamming the door, and dashed up the marble steps so rapidly, so purposefully, that pure momentum carried him up three flights and through four suites of offices before anybody had the courage to stop him and say, "What goes?"

The man with the courage was a huge bull-necked plainclothes man, whose bulk made Bill feel relatively about the size of Snulbug. "All right. Where's the fire?"

"In an assassin's gun," said Bill. "And it had better stay there."

Bullneck had not expected a literal answer. He hesitated long enough for Bill to push him to the door marked "Mayor —Private." But though the husky's brain might move slowly, his muscles made up for the lag. Just as Bill started to shove the door open, a five-pronged mound of flesh lit on his neck and jerked.

Bill crawled from under a desk, ducked Bullneck's left, reached the door, executed a second backward flip, climbed down from the table, ducked a right, reached the door, sailed in reverse, and lowered himself nimbly from the chandelier.

Bullneck took up a stand in front of the door, spread his legs in ready balance, and drew a service automatic from its holster. "You ain't going in there," he said, to make the situation perfectly clear.

Bill spat out a tooth, wiped the blood from his eyes, picked up the shattered remains of his pipe, and said, "Look. It's now twelve thirty. At twelve thirty-two a red-headed hunchback is going to come out on that balcony across the street and aim through the open window into the mayor's office. At twelve thirty-three His Honor is going to be slumped over his desk, dead. Unless you help me get him out of range."

"Yeah?" said Bullneck. "And who says so?"

"It says so here. Look. In the paper."

Bullneck guffawed. "How can a paper say what ain't even happened yet? You're nuts, brother, if you ain't something worse. Now go on, Scram. Go peddle your paper."

Bill's glance darted out the window. There was the balcony facing the mayor's office. And there coming out on it—

"Look!" he cried. "If you won't believe me, look out the window. See on that balcony? The red-headed hunchback? Just like I told you. Quick! We've got to—"

Bullneck stared despite himself. He saw the hunchback peer across into the office. He saw the sudden glint of metal in the hunchback's hand. "Brother," he said to Bill, "I'll tend to you later."

The hunchback had his rifle halfway to his shoulder when Bullneck's automatic spat and Bill braked his car in the red zone, jumped out, and dashed through four suites of offices before anybody had the courage to stop him.

The man with the courage was a huge bull-necked plainclothes man, who rumbled, "Where's the fire?"

"In an assassin's gun," said Bill, and took advantage of Bullneck's confusion to reach the door marked "Mayor—Private." But just as he started to push it open, a vast hand lit on his neck and jerked.

As Bill descended from the chandelier after his third try, Bullneck took up a stand in front of the door, with straddled legs and drawn gun. "You ain't going in," he said clarifyingly.

Bill spat out a tooth and outlined the situation. "—at twelve thirty-three," he ended, "His Honor is going to be slumped over his desk dead. Unless you help me get him out of range. See. It says so here. In the paper."

"How can I? Gwan. Go peddle your paper."

Bill's glance darted to the balcony. "Look, if you won't believe me. See the red-headed hunchback? Just like I told you. Quick! We've got to—"

Bullneck stared. He saw the sudden glint of metal in the hunchback's hand. "Brother," he said, "I'll tend to you later."

The hunchback had his rifle halfway to his shoulder when Bullneck's automatic spat and Bill braked his car in the red zone, jumped out, and dashed through four suites before anybody stopped him.

The man who did was a bull-necked plain-clothes man, who rumbled—

"Don't you think," said Snulbug, "you've had about enough of this?"

Bill agreed mentally, and there he was sitting in his roadster in front of the city hall. His clothes were unrumpled, his eyes were bloodless, his teeth were all there, and his corncob was still intact. "And just what," he demanded of his pipe bowl, "has been going on?"

Snulbug popped his snaky head out. "Light this again, will you? It's getting cold. Thanks."

"What happened?" Bill insisted.

"People!" Snulbug moaned. "No sense. Don't you see? So long as that newspaper was in the future, it was only a possibility. If you'd had, say, a hunch that the mayor was in danger, maybe you could have saved him. But when I brought it into now, it became a fact. You can't possibly make it untrue."

"But how about man's free will? Can't I do whatever I want to do?"

"Sure. It was your precious free will that brought the paper into now. You can't undo your own will. And, anyway, your will's still free. You're free to go getting thrown around chandeliers as often as you want. You probably like it. You can do anything up to the point where it would change what's in that paper. Then you have to start in again and again until you make up your mind to be sensible."

"But that—" Bill fumbled for words, "that's just as bad as . . . as fate or predestination. If my soul wills to—"

"Newspapers aren't enough. Time theory isn't enough. So I should tell him about his soul! People—" And Snulbug withdrew into the bowl.

Bill looked up at the city hall regretfully and shrugged his resignation. Then he folded his paper to the sports page and studied it carefully.

Snulbug thrust his head out again as they stopped in the many-acred parking lot. "Where is it this time?" he wanted to know. "Not that it matters."

"The racetrack."

"Oh—" Snulbug groaned. "I might have known it. You're all alike. No sense in the whole caboodle. I suppose you found a long shot?"

"Darned tooting I did. Alhazred at twenty to one in the fourth. I've got five hundred dollars, the only money I've got left on earth. Plunk on Alhazred's nose it goes, and there's our ten thousand."

Snulbug grunted. "I hear his lousy spell, I watch him get caught on a merry-go-round, it isn't enough, I should see him lay a bet on a long shot."

"But there isn't a loophole in this. I'm not interfering with the future; I'm just taking advantage of it. Alhazred'll win this race whether I bet on him or not. Five pretty hundred-dollar pari-mutuel tickets, and behold: The Hitchens Laboratory!" Bill jumped spryly out of his car and strutted along joyously. Suddenly he paused and addressed his pipe: "Hey! Why do I feel so good?"

Snulbug sighed dismally. "Why should anybody?"

"No, but I mean: I took a hell of a shellacking from that plug-ugly in the office. And I haven't got a pain or an ache."

"Of course not. It never happened."

"But I felt it then."

"Sure. In a future that never was. You changed your mind, didn't you? You decided not to go up there?"

"O. K., but that was after I'd already been beaten up twice."

"Huh-huh," said Snulbug firmly. "It was before you hadn't been." And he withdrew again into the pipe.

There was a band somewhere in the distance and the raucous burble of an announcer's voice. Crowds clustered around the two-dollar windows, and the five weren't doing bad business. But the hundred-dollar window, where the five beautiful pasteboards lived that were to create an embolism laboratory, was almost deserted.

Bill buttonholed a stranger with a purple nose. "What's the next race?"

"Second, Mac."

Swell, Bill thought. Lots of time. And from now on— He hastened to the hundred-dollar window and shoved across the five bills which he had drawn from the bank that morning. "Alhazred, on the nose," he said.

The clerk frowned with surprise, but took the money and turned to get the tickets.

Bill buttonholed a stranger with a purple nose. "What's the next race?"

"Second, Mac."

Swell, Bill thought. And then he yelled, "Hey!"

A stranger with a purple nose paused and said, " 'Smatter, Mac?"

"Nothing," Bill groaned. "Just everything."

The stranger hesitated. "Ain't I seen you some place before?"

"No," said Bill hurriedly. "You were going to, but you haven't. I changed my mind."

The stranger walked away shaking his head and muttering how the ponies could get a guy.

Not till Bill was back in his roadster did he take the corncob from his mouth and glare at it. "All right!" he barked. "What was wrong this time? Why did I get on a merry-go-round again? I didn't try to change the future."

Snulbug popped his head out and yawned a tuskful yawn. "I warn him, I explain it, I warn him again, now I should explain it all over."

"But what did I do?"

"What did he do? You changed the odds, you dope. That much folding money on a long shot at a pari mutuel track, and the odds change. It wouldn't have paid off at twenty to one the way it said in the paper."

"Nuts," Bill muttered. "And I suppose that applies to anything? If I study the stock market in this paper and try to invest my five hundred according to tomorrow's market—"

"Same thing. The quotations wouldn't be quite the same if you started in playing. I warned you. You're stuck," said Snulbug. "You're stymied. It's no use." He sounded almost cheerful.

"Isn't it?" Bill mused. "Now look, Snulbug. Me, I'm a great believer in Man. This universe doesn't hold a problem that Man can't eventually solve. And I'm no dumber than the average."

"That's saying a lot, that is," Snulbug sneered. "People—"

"I've got a responsibility now. It's more than just my ten thousand. I've got to redeem the honor of Man. You say this is the insoluble problem. I say there is no insoluble problem."

"I say you talk a lot."

Bill's mind was racing furiously. How can a man take advantage of the future without in any smallest way altering that future? There must be an answer somewhere, and a man who devised the Hitchens Embolus Diagnosis could certainly crack a little nut like this. Man cannot refuse a challenge.

Unthinking, he reached for his tobacco pouch and tapped out his pipe on the sole of his foot. There was a microscopic thud as Snulbug crashed onto the floor of the car.

Bill looked down half-smiling. The tiny demon's tail was lashing madly, and every separate snake stood on end. "This is too much!" Snulbug screamed. "Dumb gags aren't enough, insults aren't enough, I should get thrown around like a damned soul. This is the last straw. Give me my dismissal!"

Bill snapped his fingers gleefully. "Dismissal!" he cried. "I've got it, Snully. We're all set."

Snulbug looked up puzzled and slowly let his snakes droop more amicably. "It won't work," he said, with an omnisciently sad shake of his serpentine head.

It was the dashing act again that carried Bill through the Choatsby Laboratories, where he had been employed so recently, and on up to the very anteroom of old R. C.'s office.

But where you can do battle with a bull-necked guard, there is not a thing you can oppose against the brisk competence of a young lady who says, "I shall find out if Mr. Choatsby will see you." There was nothing to do but wait.

"And what's the brilliant idea this time?" Snulbug obviously feared the worst.

"R. C.'s nuts," said Bill. "He's an astrologer and a pyramidologist and a British Israelite—American Branch Reformed—and Heaven knows what else. He . . . why, he'll even believe in you."

"That's more than I do," said Snulbug. "It's a waste of energy."

"He'll buy this paper. He'll pay anything for it. There's nothing he loves more than futzing around with the occult. He'll never be able to resist a good solid slice of the future, with illusions of a fortune thrown in."

"You better hurry then."

"Why such a rush? It's only two thirty now. Lots of time. And while that girl's gone there's nothing for us to do but cool our heels."

"You might at least," said Snulbug, "warm the heel of your pipe."

The girl returned at last. "Mr. Choatsby will see you."

Reuben Choatsby overflowed the outsize chair behind his desk. His little face, like a baby's head balanced on a giant suet pudding, beamed as Bill entered. "Changed your mind, eh?" His words came in sudden soft blobs, like the abrupt glugs of pouring sirup. "Good. Need you in K-39. Lab's not the same since you left."

Bill groped for the exactly right words. "That's not it, R. C. I'm on my own now and I'm doing all right."

The baby-face soured. "Damned cheek. Competitor of mine, eh? What you want now? Waste my time?"

"Not at all." With a pretty shaky assumption of confidence, Bill perched on the edge of the desk. "R. C.," he said, slowly and impressively, "what would you give for a glimpse into the future?"

Mr. Choattsby glugged vigorously. "Ribbing me? Get out of here! Have you thrown out— Hold on! You're the one— Used to read queer books. Had a grimoire here once." The baby-face grew earnest. "What you mean?"

"Just what I said, R. C. What would you give for a glimpse into the future?"

Mr. Choatsby hesitated. "How? Time travel? Pyramid? You figured out the King's Chamber?"

"Much simpler than that. I have here"—he took it out of his pocket and folded it so that only the name and the date line were visible—"tomorrow's newspaper."

Mr. Choatsby grabbed. "Let me see."

"Uh-huh. Naughty, naughty. You'll see after we discuss terms. But there it is."

"Trick. Had some printer fake it. Don't believe it."

"All right. I never expected you, R. C., to descend to such unenlightened skepticism. But if that's all the faith you have—" Bill stuffed the paper back in his pocket and started for the door.

"Wait!" Mr. Choatsby lowered his voice. "How'd you do it? Sell your soul?"

"That wasn't necessary."

"How? Spells? Cantrips? Incantations? Prove it to me. Show me it's real. Then we'll talk terms."

Bill walked casually to the desk and emptied his pipe into the ash tray.

"I'm underdeveloped. I run errands. I'm named Snulbug. It isn't enough—now I should be a testimonial!"

Mr. Choatsby stared rapt at the furious little demon raging in his ash tray. He watched reverently as Bill held out the pipe for its inmate, filled it with tobacco, and lit it. He listened awestruck as Snulbug moaned with delight at the flame.

"No more questions," he said. "What terms?"

"Fifteen thousand dollars." Bill was ready for bargaining.

"Don't put it too high," Snulbug warned. "You better hurry."

But Mr. Choatsby had pulled out his check book and was scribbling hastily. He blotted the check and handed it over. "It's a deal." He grabbed up the paper. "You're a fool, young man. Fifteen thousand! *Hmf!*" He had it open already at the financial page. "With what I make on the market tomorrow, never notice fifteen thousand. Pennies."

"Hurry up," Snulbug urged.

"Good-by, sir," Bill began politely, "and thank you for—" But Reuben Choatsby wasn't even listening.

"What's all this hurry?" Bill demanded as he reached the elevator.

"People!" Snulbug sighed. "Never you mind what's the hurry. You get to your bank and deposit that check."

So Bill, with Snulbug's incessant prodding, made a dash

to the bank worthy of his descents on the city hall and on the Choatsby Laboratories. He just made it, by stop-watch fractions of a second. The door was already closing as he shoved his way through at three o'clock sharp.

He made his deposit, watched the teller's eyes bug out at the size of the check, and delayed long enough to enjoy the incomparable thrill of changing the account from William Hitchens to The Hitchen Research Laboratory.

Then he climbed once more into his car, where he could talk with his pipe in peace. "Now," he asked as he drove home, "what was the rush?"

"He'd stop payment."

"You mean when he found out about the merry-go-round. But I didn't promise anything. I just sold him tomorrow's paper. I didn't guarantee he'd make a fortune off it."

"That's all right. But—"

"Sure, you warned me. But where's the hitch? R. C.'s a bandit, but he's honest. He wouldn't stop payment."

"Wouldn't he?"

The car was waiting for a stop signal. The newsboy in the intersection was yelling "Uxtruh!" Bill glanced casually at the headline, did a double take, and instantly thrust out a nickel and seized a paper.

He turned into a side street, stopped the car, and went through this paper. Front page: MAYOR ASSASSINATED. Sports page: Alhazred at twenty to one. Obituaries: The same list he'd read at noon. He turned back to the date line. August 22nd. Tomorrow.

"I warned you," Snulbug was explaining. "I told you I wasn't strong enough to go far into the future. I'm not a well demon, I'm not. And an itch in the memory is something fierce. I just went far enough ahead to get a paper with tomorrow's date on it. And any dope knows that a Tuesday paper comes out Monday afternoon."

For a moment Bill was dazed. His magic paper, his fifteen-thousand-dollar paper, was being hawked by newsies on every corner. Small wonder R. C. might have stopped payment! And then he saw the other side. He started to laugh. He couldn't stop.

"Look out!" Snulbug shrilled. "You'll drop my pipe. And what's so funny?"

Bill wiped tears from his eyes. "I was right. Don't you see, Snulbug? Man can't be licked. My magic was lousy. All it could call up was you. You brought me what was practically a fake, and I got caught on the merry-go-round of time trying to use it. You were right enough there; no good could come of that magic.

"But without the magic, just using human psychology, knowing a man's weaknesses, playing on them, I made a sirup-voiced old bandit endow the very research he'd tabooed and do more good for humanity than he's done in all the rest of his life. I was right, Snulbug. You can't lick Man."

Snulbug's snakes writhed into knots of scorn. "People!" he snorted. "You'll find out." And he shook his head with dismal satisfaction.

Elsewhere in this book we encounter representatives from the ranks of ghosts, vampires, demons, elementals and witches. It's really time that their presumed Manager be presented; and the prolific and ingenious Fredric Brown, master of brief horror, does so herewith.

Armageddon

Fredric Brown

It happened—of all places—in Cincinnati. Not that there is anything wrong with Cincinnati, save that it is not the center of the Universe, nor even of the State of Ohio. It's a nice old town and, in its way, second to none. But even its Chamber of Commerce would admit that it lacks cosmic significance. It must have been mere coincidence that Gerber the Great— what a name!—was playing Cincinnati when things slipped elsewhere.

Of course, if the episode had become known, Cincinnati would be the most famous city of the world, and little Herbie would be hailed as a modern St. George and get more acclaim, even, than a quiz kid. But no member of that audience in the Bijou Theater remembers a thing about it. Not even little Herbie Westerman, although he had the water pistol to show for it.

He wasn't thinking about the water pistol in his pocket as he sat looking up at the prestidigitator on the other side of the footlights. It was a new water pistol, bought en route to the theater when he'd inveigled his parents into a side trip into the five-and-dime on Vine Street, but at the moment, Herbie was much more interested in what went on upon the stage.

His expression registered qualified approval. The front-and-back palm was no mystery to Herbie. He could do it himself. True, he had to use pony-sized cards that came with his magic set and were just the right size for his nine-year-old hands. And true, anyone watching could see the card flutter from the front-palm position to the back as he turned his hands. But that was a detail.

He knew, though, that front-and-back palming seven cards at a time required great finger strength as well as dexterity, and that was what Gerber the Great was doing. There wasn't a telltale click in the shift, either, and Herbie nodded approbation. Then he remembered what was coming next.

He nudged his mother and said, "Ma, ask Pop if he's gotta extra handkerchief."

Out of the corner of his eye, Herbie saw his mother turn her head and in less time than it would take to say "Presto" Herbie was out of his seat and skinning down the aisle. It had been, he felt, a beautiful piece of misdirection and his timing had been perfect.

It was at this stage of the performance—which Herbie had seen before, alone—that Gerber the Great asked if some little boy from the audience would step to the stage. He was asking it now.

Herbie Westerman had jumped the gun. He was well in motion before the magician had asked the question. At the previous performance, he'd been a bad tenth in reaching the steps from aisle to stage. This time he'd been ready, and he hadn't taken any chances with parental restraint. Perhaps his mother would have let him go and perhaps not; it had seemed wiser to see that she was looking the other way. You couldn't trust parents on things like that. They had funny ideas sometimes.

"—will please step up on the stage?" And Herbie's foot touched the first of the steps upward right smack on the interrogation point of that sentence. He heard the disappointed scuffle of other feet behind him, and grinned smugly as he went on up across the footlights.

It was the three-pigeon trick, Herbie knew from the previous performance, that required an assistant from the audience. It was almost the only trick he hadn't been able to figure out. There *must*, he knew, have been a concealed compartment somewhere in that box, but where it could be he couldn't even guess. By this time he'd be holding the box himself. If from that range, he couldn't spot the gimmick, he'd better go back to stamp collecting.

He grinned confidently up at the magician. Not that he, Herbie, would give him away. He was a magician, too, and he understood that there was a freemasonry among magicians and that one never gave away the tricks of another.

He felt a little chilled, though, and the grin faded as he caught the magician's eyes. Gerber the Great, at close range, seemed much older than he had seemed from the other side of the footlights. And somehow different. Much taller, for one thing.

Anyway, here came the box for the pigeon trick. Gerber's regular assistant was bringing it in on a tray. Herbie looked away from the magician's eyes and he felt better. He remembered, even, his reason for being on the stage. The servant limped. Herbie ducked his head to catch a glimpse of the under side of the tray, just in case. Nothing there.

Gerber took the box. The servant limped away and Herbie's eyes followed him suspiciously. Was the limp genuine or was it a piece of misdirection?

The box folded out flat as the proverbial pancake. All four sides hinged to the bottom, the top hinged to one of the sides. There were little brass catches.

Herbie took a quick step back so he could see behind it while the front was displayed to the audience. Yes he saw it now. A triangular compartment built against one side of the lid, mirror-covered, angles calculated to achieve invisibility. Old stuff. Herbie felt a little disappointed.

The prestidigitator folded the box, mirror-concealed compartment inside. He turned slightly. "Now, my fine young man—"

What happened in Tibet wasn't the only factor; it was merely the final link of a chain.

The Tibetian weather had been unusual that week, highly unusual. It had been warm. More snow succumbed to the gentle warmth than had melted in more years than man could count. The streams ran high, they ran wide and fast.

Along the streams some prayer wheels whirled faster than they had ever whirled. Others, submerged, stopped altogether. The priests, knee-deep in the cold water, worked frantically, moving the wheels nearer to shore where again the rushing torrent would turn them.

There was one small wheel, a very old one that had revolved without cease for longer than any man knew. So long had it been there that no living lama recalled what had been inscribed upon its prayer plate, nor what had been the purpose of that prayer.

The rushing water had neared its axle when the lama Klarath reached for it to move it to safety. Just too late. His foot slid in the slippery mud and the back of his hand touched the wheel as he fell. Knocked loose from its moorings, it swirled down with the flood, rolling along the bottom of the stream, into deeper and deeper waters.

While it rolled, all was well.

The lama rose, shivering from his momentary immersion, and went after other of the spinning wheels. What, he thought, could one small wheel matter? He didn't know that—now that other links had broken—only that tiny thing stood between Earth and Armageddon.

The prayer wheel of Wangur Ul rolled on, and on, until— a mile farther down—it struck a ledge and stopped. That was the moment.

"And now, my fine young man—"

Herbie Westerman—we're back in Cincinnati now—looked up, wondering why the prestidigitator had stopped in midsentence. He saw the face of Gerber the Great contorted as though by a great shock. Without moving, without changing, his face began to change. Without appearing different, it became different.

Quietly, then, the magician began to chuckle. In the overtones of that soft laughter was all of evil. No one who heard it could have doubted who he was. No one did doubt. The audience, every member of it, knew in that awful moment who stood before them, knew it—even the most skeptical among them—beyond shadow of doubt.

No one moved, no one spoke, none drew a shuddering breath. There are things beyond fear. Only uncertainty causes fear, and the Bijou Theater was filled, then, with a dreadful certainty.

The laughter grew. Crescendo, it reverberated into the far dusty corners of the gallery. Nothing—not a fly on the ceiling —moved.

Satan spoke.

"I thank you for your kind attention to a poor magician." He bowed, ironically low. "The performance is ended."

He smiled. "All performances are ended."

Somehow the theater seemed to darken, although the electric lights still burned. In dead silence, there seemed to be

the sound of wings, leathery wings, as though invisible Things were gathering.

On the stage was a dim red radiance. From the head and from each shoulder of the tall figure of the magician there sprang a tiny flame. A naked flame.

There were other flames. They flickered along the proscenium of the stage, along the footlights. One sprang from the lid of the folded box little Herbie Westerman still held in his hands.

Herbie dropped the box.

Did I mention that Herbie Westerman was a Safety Cadet? It was purely a reflex action. A boy of nine doesn't know much about things like Armageddon, but Herbie Westerman should have known that water would never have put out that fire.

But, as I said, it was purely a reflex action. He yanked out his new water pistol and squirted it at the box of the pigeon trick. And the fire *did* vanish, even as a spray from the stream of water ricocheted and dampened the trouser leg of Gerber the Great, who had been facing the other way.

There was a sudden, brief, hissing sound. The lights were growing bright again, and all the other flames were dying, and the sound of wings faded, blended into another sound—the rustling of the audience.

The eyes of the prestidigitator were closed. His voice sounded strangely strained as he said: "This much power I retain. None of you will remember this."

Then, slowly, he turned and picked up the fallen box. He held it out to Herbie Westerman. "You must be more careful, boy," he said. "Now hold it so."

He tapped the top lightly with his wand. The door fell open. Three white pigeons flew out of the box. The rustle of their wings was not leathery.

Herbie Westerman's father came down the stairs and, with a purposeful air, took his razor strop off the hook on the kitchen wall.

Mrs. Westerman looked up from stirring the soup on the stove. "Why, Henry," she asked, "are you really going to punish him with that—just for squirting a little water out of the window of the car on the way home?"

Her husband shook his head grimly. "Not for that, Marge. But don't you remember we bought him that water gun on the way downtown, and that he wasn't near a water faucet after that? Where do you think he filled it?"

He didn't wait for an answer. "When we stopped in at the cathedral to talk to Father Ryan about his confirmation, that's when the little brat filled it. Out of the baptismal font! Holy water he uses in his water pistol!"

He clumped heavily up the stairs, strop in hand.

Rhythmic thwacks and wails of pain floated down the staircase. Herbie—who had saved the world—was having his reward.